LAIR RECKONING

LAIR
— • 3 • —

D.V. SULLIVAN

TP

TRANSMARINIA PRESS

ISBN for ebook: 979-8-9866781-3-9
ISBN for paperback: 979-8-9866781-7-7

For readers 18+. Contains brief descriptions of domestic violence.

Cover design by Trif Book Design.

Transmarinia Press
2709 N Hayden Island Dr
STE 330550
Portland, OR 97217

*To the person
you never thought you could become,
but have*

ONE

We see the polar bear an hour before dawn.

The other sights came thick and fast as we kayaked in the freezing sea off Svalbard. First were the seals and penguins hunting for fish, sleek shapes diving under the rippling blur of the water. Then walruses bathing on icebergs like tusked curmudgeons, their garrulous barks making us laugh. At one point the marbled vastness of a whale breached high in the air, so close its crashing splash rocked our sea kayaks and soaked us with its spray, making me gape with awe. But there's something different about the bear, something noble and rare. It stands on an ice shelf, watching us with its beady black eyes as we float past. It must weigh over a thousand pounds, its fur as white and fluffy as the snow around it, its forepaws as big as my head. It lifts its snout to scent the air (it's probably never smelled the undead before), then turns and shambles off into the freezing gloom.

I can't help but take its sighting as a sign. An omen.

Everything will turn out all right.

I rest my paddle across the kayak and look up at the Northern Lights.

It's impossible to get used to them. They hang in the gloaming sky in a shimmering, dancing aura of many colors, so close I feel I can reach out and touch them, pull their magic inside me. The north glows with it, reflecting it in the smooth glass of the sea, on the slopes of the snow-capped mountains—a mysterious half-light that makes it seem as if day never truly leaves this place. The land of the midnight sun.

This is what I'd needed. After everything that had happened in the past week, I'd needed a breather. A moment to decompress before plunging into the next terrifying step before me. And Adrian, of course, had known this. He'd arranged this date without fuss or letting me know what was up, and I'd only grasped it when he'd led me down to the stern of the *Lair* in the gloom of the predawn hours, and I'd seen the two kayaks waiting for us in the water.

I hear the almost noiseless stroke of a paddle, and another kayak noses up beside me. "It's hard to get used to them, isn't it?"

"Yes," I grin, my breath puffing fog in the cold.

There's no answering fog of breath beside me. "Now you know how I feel."

I roll my eyes. "Oh *God*."

He laughs, an achingly gorgeous sound in that untouched wilderness.

"Jesus, you've gotten *so* corny," I groan.

I don't mind, though. I don't mind at all.

I finally turn to look at Adrian Voper. In the enchanting half-light, I can make out the gleam of his creamy linen shirt (why bother dressing warmly when you're undead?), the sleeves of which are rolled to the elbows to expose forearms corded thick with muscle. The look in his vivid blue eyes makes my heart stumble, and his dark, brambly hair makes me want to run my hands through it. I settle for reaching out and taking his hand.

"My Northern Light," he whispers through crooked lips, his face glowing white as the polar bear, and now it's hard to breathe for the tightening in my throat.

His bare thumb brushes my engagement ring under my warm mitten. It was only days ago that he'd knelt under these same lights and revealed that ring to me. It still doesn't feel real. How is all this not a dream?

It takes me a moment to realize that the shivering of my body is not solely from my feelings for Adrian Voper. I'd bundled myself up like a cartoon character—thermal underwear under a wetsuit, fleece jacket, kayak vest and life jacket, neck warmer, thick wool socks and hat—and somehow I'm still freezing. I'd long ago accepted I was cursed with a poor circulatory system, but seriously? *Right now, Arie?*

Adrian has a solution for this too, though. "Hang on," he says and rummages through the cockpit of his kayak. In a flash, he's produced a silver thermos, and prying off its lid he holds it out to me with the shyness of a boy presenting a school paper. Steam coils out of it into the frigid air. "I thought you'd appreciate some hot chocolate."

My mouth does something between a pout and a sob. *How has he become so adorable?*

But there's more. "Wait!" he says, lifting a pale finger, and rummages into his cockpit again before he drops a few puffy white cubes into the thermos. "Can't have cocoa without marshmallows," he says simply.

I'm officially in a state of shock as I cradle the warm thermos in my mittens. It's hard to even recognize this Adrian beside me. How could this be the same Adrian who once fired staff for the slightest infraction, who couldn't see beyond himself other than to demand perfection from everyone around him?

I'd changed that. I'd done that.

He'd done it for me.

But it's more than that. No guy has ever treated me like this. No guy has ever made me feel this special and taken care of.

No guy has ever made me feel safe.

Adrian sees it coming. He tilts his head and purses his lips. "Oh baby," he soothes, checking the hot prickling behind my eyes. "Careful now, your tears will freeze."

I hiccup a laugh and shake my head, wipe clumsily under my eyes with a mitten. Then I take a sip of scalding sweetness from the thermos to distract myself, letting its warmth spread through me.

Adrian, mouth crooking gently, pulls my kayak close and rubs my back. "I can't wait to be human so I can warm you up."

"I'm looking forward to that, too," I quip, teeth chattering. "In more ways than one."

He shoots me a sidelong look, and we both burst into laughter. I laugh so hard, so freely, I have to gasp to get enough air into my lungs. By the time I'm done they feel rimed over with frost and I have to take another sugary mouthful of cocoa to thaw them out.

Then we're bobbing on the sea in silence, listening to the warbling of vast colonies of birds nesting on the cliffs.

I know without asking that we're both thinking the same thing. The next step. What I'd told him.

Me. Going after the Commodore. Alone.

It's been an unspoken tension between us ever since I first announced it, and I've been amazed he hasn't pursued it further. But I know it's coming now.

He doesn't try to talk me out of it, though. At least, not in the way I'd expected.

"You don't have to do this, you know." His voice is so low I can barely hear him. He's staring at his paddle athwart his kayak before him. "You could find someone human and not have to risk your life for me—"

"Don't say that," I blurt, voice edged with anger. "Don't ever say that."

He nods, takes a breath and looks up at the miles of white mountains ranged about us, the hyperborean spell above them. "I'm just worried. How could I not be? You going off, alone, to kill the head of my coven to free me—" He cuts himself short, checking a rising anger, the muscles in his jaws pulsing. "But I know it's your choice."

His knuckles show as he grips his paddle. "And I want you to have that."

I turn to look at him, that gratitude burning behind my eyes again. How hard it must be for him, going from controlling everything in his world to letting me go off on my own, beyond his reach, into the lair of his enemy.

"Thank you," I whisper.

He rolls his paddle slightly, watching the light catch on its carbon blades. "Just—promise me this won't change you, okay?"

"What?"

He still doesn't look up. "Please?"

Something about the stiffness in his voice, the vulnerability in his hunched shoulders, makes the hairs on the back of my neck prick. *What is going on here?*

"Hey," I say, tugging his kayak close. "Hey." I pull his face to mine, and our lips touch. He grips my jacket and breathes in, as if taking in as much of me as he can, leaving me dizzy. When I lean my forehead on his, he's shuddering as if—impossibly—he's been taken with a chill.

I don't know what this means. What *he* means. But it fucking scares me.

"You won't lose me, okay?" I whisper. "*Ever.*"

He nods, eyes shut. "Okay." And he smiles, that dazzling curve of teeth still able to make my heart soar.

We're still like that, kayaks bumping, holding each other brow to brow under the dancing lights of the aurora, when our crew radios crackle.

"You two aren't having sex on an iceberg or something, are you?" The unmistakable baritone of Captain Redfearn, resonant as aged oak.

I smirk and fetch the VHF marine walkie-talkie out of my cockpit. "You and your timing, Arnold." He's been grumpy as all hell since Mrs. Colding was medically evacuated a few days ago, and I've been doing my best to lift his spirits with the odd joke. But still. His reply is far more dour than I expect.

"Let's hope we have time for apologies later," it hisses over the radio.

The blood slows in my veins. Adrian and I share a look.

"Come again?" I tap the walkie-talkie.

"I'd get your asses back to the *Lair. Now*," the captain urges. "I've picked up two incoming signals on sonar, only a few miles off. They're closing fast."

Adrian's eyes are wide. My breath coils in shivery veils of fog in the cold.

"I think it's them. The Nosferyachtu Club," Captain Redfearn continues, the dread thick in his voice. "They've found us."

TWO

The pink haze of the coming dawn is peeking above the mountains as Adrian and I race back to the *Lair*.

We'd left her around a bend in the ice sheet towering above us, somewhere in the maze of icebergs floating everywhere. Five minutes away? Ten? I can't remember. My thoughts keep fraying. Large shelves of ice choke the waters, and smaller clumps slurve past our kayaks, scraping against the fiberglass hulls and slowing us down. *We could die out here*, I think. *We're going to die.*

"Where are you?" Captain Redfearn's voice crackles over the radio.

"Getting there," Adrian grunts between paddle strokes.

"They're getting closer. Only a mile out. They should be right behind you."

My back prickles with a chill. Adrian and I share a look, then glance behind—a stretch of mist-hung water, the towering shapes of icebergs . . .

Nothing.

I'm clammy with sweat under my layers of clothing. My muscles ache. The breath rattles searing and subzero in my lungs; I can practically hear the icicles forming on them. I don't know how much longer I can do this. And Adrian, so much more powerfully built than I am, is pulling ahead of me. Of course we had to take single-seat kayaks.

We race against the current, all but flying over the water. Ice clumps carom off our kayaks with soft *thumps*. My breath streams in a white vapor behind me. I wonder, through the spitting static of fear in my head, how they found us. We'd lost that ship following us from the Nosferyachtu Club. Was Evangeline in contact with other boats? Had they decided to close in after they hadn't heard from her?

"They should be right on top of you," the radio crackles. "You don't see them?"

We dart looks into ice alleys flanking us, looking for the flickering of an unfamiliar hull. Still nothing.

"Hurry," Captain Redfearn breathes. "My God, hurry."

I wheeze, shoulders trembling with exhaustion. Adrian has, unwittingly, far outstripped me at this point. I try to call after him. "Adrian," I rasp.

He glances behind and stiffens, stops paddling. "Come on," he gestures. "You can make it."

"I don't," I gasp, a giddy, hysterical terror seeping into my brain like a cancer. "I don't know if—"

But coming abreast of Adrian, I see the *Lair* waiting only a hundred meters away.

I all but sob with relief. Adrian and I share a joyous, beaming look.

That's when we hear the low *thwop, thwop, thwop* of a helicopter.

Adrian's face slackens as he looks at me. We wrench around—and see the sleek body of a chopper bank around a monumental ice shelf, homing in on us. It's less than a half mile behind.

And it's accompanied by the flash of two yacht hulls in the distance.

Adrian whips back to me, his expression screaming fear.

Then Captain Redfearn's voice snaps us out of it. "MOVE. *NOW.*"

We dip our paddles in deep and power ahead, heads straining forward. Fog whiffles around us. The splash of water fills our ears, almost loud enough to drown out the approaching roar of the helicopter.

I train my eyes on the *Lair*, its gleaming fiberglass hull looming closer, higher, filling my world with the hyperreal intensity of a dream. Figures appear like mirages on the swim platform, parkas with the *Lair* logo gleaming white in the gathering light—deckhands, ready to help us aboard. And at a wing station flybridge Captain Redfearn watches, his silver hair and the brass buttons of his captain's coat shining. Waiting on us to depart.

The chatter of the helicopter echoes in the arctic wilderness. It must be right on top of us.

Then our kayaks are sliding alongside the swim platform, and burly deckhands are lifting us out as if we were children. One of them lifts a walkie-talkie. "We got 'em."

In answer, the whole length of the *Lair* thrums to life. Thrusters and generators hum. The water roils into a froth at the stern, spinning the kayaks away. My stomach lurches as we take off at speed. I'm coughing and wheezing in air, my throat raw with cold. Adrian ushers me up one of the grand staircases onto the aft main deck, and that's when we turn to look.

The helicopter's not thirty meters away from the *Lair*, hovering before the rising sun like some hallucinatory vision of destruction. Spikes of light bounce off its smooth, polished exterior, and it's because of this glare that it takes me a moment to comprehend what's hanging out the side of the chopper.

A helmeted door gunner, clipped into a harness and leaning outward with one boot on the helicopter skid, hefting the long-barreled monstrosity of a machine gun.

"Fuck," I whisper.

It all unravels like a bad dream. Time seems to slow as that barrel spouts fire, a corona of light, and I get a glimpse of orange tracers arcing through the air like angry hornets. *Oh God*, I think, *Oh no*, and before I can do anything Adrian wraps me in his arms, lifts me up, and swings me around to block the shots with his body.

I've never before heard the ragged sound that comes out of me as Adrian's body jerks from the impacts, my gut hunched and knees drawn up in howling despair. It almost drowns out the sickening noise of bullet rounds thwapping into flesh, one after another, too many for any single body to take. But Adrian only grunts and raises his arms to cradle my head. Blazing metal zips past my ear. Splinters of teak puff up from the deck as it's raked with fire. Then it's over. Time speeds up again. The helicopter swoops overhead like a passing hurricane, blowing my hair in my eyes, and Adrian's fierce grip around me relaxes. He slumps to the deck and onto his side, all the strength gone out of him. Mission complete.

And the world breathes once more, engulfed in hell.

I blink in place like a bomb victim, unable to process it, a high tinnitus sound ringing in my ears. Then I snap out of it and kneel. "Adrian?" I screech, shaking him. "*Adrian?*"

His linen shirt is torn to shreds. Blood is everywhere, pooling on the deck, glistening on my trembling palms with surreal brightness. I can't see. Tears scorch my eyes. I'm making gasping, gobbling noises of horror.

Then Adrian groans, eyes rolling beneath their lids.

He's alive.

The world quivers. That wave of nausea rises in my throat again, then passes.

Swallowing, I look up.

The helicopter is cutting a large arc through the air, circling back for another pass. We have maybe seconds.

Pull yourself together, Arie.

I turn to the deckhands quailing in the lee of the deck lounges, faces white in shock. "Help me get him inside," I snap. "*Now!*"

The fierceness of my tone breaks them out of it. They grab Adrian under the arms and drag him toward the doors of the lounge, leaving a long smear of red on the teak decking. My belly gives a warning flop at the sight. I think I'm about to throw up.

The doors are thrown open, and we've barely hustled Adrian inside when it hits me in a slow crawling of gooseflesh—the lounge is lined with floor-to-ceiling windows.

When I swivel my head to look, the helicopter is hovering outside like death itself, its gunner training his barrel straight at us.

"Get down!" I scream, and we all drop to the teak decking continuing into the lounge as the long, expansive windows explode inward, letting in a stammering of tracers that rip up the furniture and pock up the wood with huge round holes. That chopper is doing one helluva job of redecorating.

But Adrian.

We drag him behind the cover of a white leather couch. He's spasming, flailing out and gripping fistfuls of shirts and limbs. I brush a twinkling of glass out of my hair and cup his lolling face in my wet hands. "Adrian. *Adrian.* Do you hear me?"

"'S okay," he slurs, lifting a weak hand. "It'll heal."

I stare. This? *Heal?* I roll him over, lift up his rag of a shirt, and have to clamp a hand over my mouth to keep from screaming.

His deliciously muscled back is a desecration, puckered with a dozen bullet holes punched into his corpse-white body with the neatness of post-mortem puncture wounds. They gleam shiny and wet. As I watch they ooze blood, or what must be blood. It looks like runnels of black jelly, like an endless ooze of fetid slime.

This can't be happening, I think to myself. *This isn't real.*

But it is real. And there's more. Bullets begin to push themselves out of his body, slowly unscrewing out of cratered flesh and plinking onto the teak floor.

Adrian cries out and clenches his teeth, jaws seized, hunching into a fetal position as if in the throes of some unnatural childbirth. I reach out trembling hands. "Oh baby," I whisper, my eyes glassing up. A deep ache, a fierce and heavy love, brims up in me. "What did they do to you?"

Above, the chopper roars.

A cold, vibrating rage hoods my eyes. My skin buzzes. Something inside me has taken over, an instinct passed down over millennia that all women carry, all mothers know, all lovers understand. It does not have time for the sobs that want to come out of me, has no use for grief that does not serve a purpose. I know now what's to happen. I know what I'm going to do.

A line has been crossed, and I'm ready to burn down the whole fucking world.

I rise, hands balled at my sides, and stride off. One of the deckhands notices. "Hey, where are you going?" he calls after me. "What—what do we do with him?"

"I'll be right back," I grit through clenched teeth.

And I am. When I return from below with the grenade launcher in my hands, the eyes of the deckhands go round as dinner plates.

"What—what are you—"

"Just stay here with him," I order, marching past, glass crunching under my feet. One of my eyelids twitches in a spasm of pure, mainlined wrath as I set my jaw. I am giddy with madness. "I'll be right back."

The *Lair* is well underway when I step out onto the ravaged aft deck. Our wake froths behind us as we skirt the ice shelf—Captain Redfearn must be pushing fifteen knots, as fast as he can in this minefield of ice—and the sun is a hot white point in the brightening sky.

Far behind, in the billowing mist, a hull flashes.

A yacht pursuing us.

But I don't have time for that; that is secondary. Vengeance is the matter at hand. I make sure the grenade launcher is loaded with all six shots and stalk out onto the deck, eyes searching the sky. "Gonna go after my man, huh?" I mutter under my breath, panting like a madwoman. "You think you can take my Adrian from me?" An anger I have never known has been unleashed in me. Blinding red fury spikes my brain. I am quivering from head to foot, feeling a new measure of myself. I am a rising phoenix, an avenging Valkyrie shedding her old self to reveal a blinding inner core of teeth and mail and claws. It's magnificent and terrifying.

The helicopter is hovering abeam of the *Lair* at amidships, waiting for me.

I don't hesitate. I step out into full view and lift the grenade launcher to my shoulder. "Well fuck you," I breathe, and fire.

The recoil is bruisingly strong, almost knocking me off-balance. There's a pneumatic-sounding *thump*, and a shell glints in the sun as it arcs past the helicopter. The sleek aircraft swerves to the side, unperturbed, and responds with a cannonade of fire.

I duck down behind the *Lair*'s gunwale, eyes squinted against the racketing of bullets all around me. Blooms of wood pop out from teak planks. Deck pillows shred open in disembowellings of foam. Sparks leap off the chrome rails with an angry spang. When bits of fiberglass ricochet, batting my eyelashes and cutting my cheek, I bury my face in my shoulder. It's like being on a boat full of invisible and vengeful spirits.

Then it stops, and rising from my crouch I fire again—*thump*—and the helicopter explodes into a giant ball of flame and crashes into the sea.

The ensuing silence is shocking. I'm panting hard, shoulders heaving, my lungs filled with burned air. *Yeah,* I think. *Damn fucking right.* I turn to find a deckhand standing in the doorway to the lounge, mouth hanging and walkie-talkie held limply at his side.

"Arie?" it crackles. "You okay?"

I grab the walkie-talkie from the deckhand's nerveless fingers and press down on it with my thumb. "Ask me again later."

The captain's response is prefaced with an admiring snort. "How about our new friend? Can you do anything about that?"

I turn to look. That flash of hull is much, much bigger now. It's speeding up behind us, going at least twenty knots. Some kind of cutting-edge trimaran. It looks more like a spacecraft than a seacraft, a lean and mean raider ship with curved wings and a long, narrow nose, skimming across the waves like a mosquito out for blood. And rippling from its bow staff in fangsome grandeur—the jolly roger of the Nosferyachtu Club.

I lift the crew radio to my lips. "I'll see what I can do."

THREE

The wind whips at my hair as I take my position at the top of the staircase leading down to the swim deck. This still gives me a slight height advantage on the gleaming, 140-foot trimaran closing in on our stern, which is preferable.

Because I've decided to start with the most obvious solution.

I fit the grenade launcher to my shoulder, stare down whoever's inside that vessel worthy of a supervillain, and double-tap the trigger.

The grenades whiss through the air and detonate directly on the trimaran's sweeping bridge windows in a wrathful boiling of flame. I shield my eyes against the wave of heat, breath held. Then the wind whips the flames away—leaving the trimaran unscathed.

Bombproof. Of course.

Did you really expect it to be that easy?

I pace the aft deck, fuming. Two rounds left. What now?

Then I look toward the bow. A canyon looms ahead, a strait of water running between two rugged walls of icepack soaring up for hundreds of feet, overawing in its scale.

I unclip the walkie-talkie on my hip. "Arnold."

"Yes, ma'am."

"Take us into that alley."

A moment's silence. Then I hear the smile in Captain Redfearn's voice. "Roger that."

As I hustle up the gangway stairs to the bridge deck, the bow of the *Lair* swings starboard, taking us into the canyon. A shadow falls on the *Lair* like a giant hand. The light turns blue, as if I've become trapped in the heart of a glacier. And looking back, I note that the trimaran has taken the bait and followed us in.

Maybe this'll work.

I take a moment on the aft bridge deck, gauging our rate of speed, the distance between the trimaran and the *Lair*. A last flicker of doubt grips me *(Are you fucking INSANE?!)* and I shove it aside. Aiming my grenade launcher high up and a boat-length ahead of the *Lair*, I fire the last two rounds in quick succession.

They thump into the ice sheet with puny-sounding muteness. Snow piffs out from the wall, and I hold my arms over my head as icy fragments rattle down upon the deck, dancing about my feet like shattered crystal. I lower my arms again, lips parted and hair dusted white, as we pass beneath. *Did it not work?*

Then a crack streaks across that fissured surface like lightning, and with an unholy, crunching grinding, a three-hundred-ton shelf of icepack formed over centuries calves away and plunges into the sea.

The trimaran has nowhere to go. With a rumbling impact that's felt as deep as bone, the shelf buries the vessel, wiping it out in a brilliant crash of ice and waves. It is annihilated.

I grip the handrail as the *Lair* rides the resulting swells, staggering relief washing through me. *Did I just do that?*

Sunlight hits my face—we've just shot out of the canyon. I tilt up my chin to soak it in. I suddenly feel drained, spent of all adrenaline. There's also a piercing ringing in my ears, high and unreal. Then I remember, speaking it aloud, "Adrian."

I need to get back to Adrian.

I stiffen all over, thinking of his bullet-pocked back, his blood on my hands, and feel a sick twinge of nausea. I let the empty grenade launcher drop to the deck and whirl aft. He has to be okay. He has to be.

Captain Redfearn's voice bursting over the radio makes me jump. "You okay?"

My hand is shaking so much the crew radio flies out of my fingers onto the deck. "Fuck," I hiss, and when I stoop to pick it up the blood leaves my head and I hold out my arms, black spots dancing before my eyes. "Whoo." I clutch the rail and press my brow to its coolness, feeling a cold sweat break out on my skin, and breathe carefully through puckered lips as my stomach heaves and I reassure myself, over and over, *He was healing. He can't be that hurt.*

He can't be dying.

"Arie?" the radio crackles. "I need you up here."

I have a hard time pressing the button to speak. "Just give me a sec," I manage and hold to the rail like a drunk.

You can do this. Adrian will be okay. Check in with the captain first. Then you can go to him.

When I'm certain the nausea's passed, I straighten and lift the radio again. "Coming your way." I stumble back along the gangway, one hand on the rail, not bothering with trying to stow the radio anymore. The flybridge is unattended, and so I dip into the wheelhouse. Captain Redfearn must have ducked inside to the main helm when the ice shelf came down.

He elevates a grizzled brow when he sees me. "Remind me to never make you angry."

"Yeah, well," I shrug, slapping the crew radio on the nav console. "It's been a rough day."

"And it's not over." He points. "Remember, we had two friends following us."

I turn to look. Emerging out of the labyrinth of icebergs is our second pursuer: a bulky-looking superyacht that looks more like a glorified warship than a pleasure boat. My heart sinks. A petulant urge to cry fills me. Jesus, *another* one?

I scan our new surroundings. We're near Svalbard's coast again. Craggy mountains dusted in a heavy sugaring of snow curve around a bay jampacked with drift ice; everything is so white it's blinding. I have to squint against the glare a moment to finally put it together: a channel snaking through the ice floes, too narrow for the other yacht to follow us.

I tap Captain Redfearn's shoulder with the backs of my knuckles and point. "If you put us through that, can we get out to open sea and escape?"

The captain looks between the other yacht and the channel, scowling. "It's worth a try."

He ramps down the propulsion and guides us in. The entry is hardly seamless—something strikes the hull with a hollow bong, and the *Lair* judders all the way down to the bronze blades of her azimuth propellers. But then she's in, slipping dainty as a lady through the closely packed floes, the odd debris bumping off her.

Captain Redfearn and I beam at each other—until we see what the other yacht is doing.

It's not bothering to follow us, or go around the ice floes at all—it's turning *straight into them.*

My mouth goes dry. "Why is it . . .?"

All color leaves the captain's face. "Damn."

"*What?*"

"It's an exploration yacht."

The little hairs on my arms stand on end. "What does that mean?"

Captain Redfearn throttles the propulsion, eyes filled with that yacht's reinforced hull. "It's an icebreaker."

The blood slows in my veins, and when I turn to look again the exploration yacht crashes into the ice floes with a low, booming crack that fills that pristine bay with echoing thunder. Snow explodes in a white blast, and then immense floes are breaking up before that axe of a hull, shelving up around it in a grinding, ravening roar of plaintive ice.

Captain Redfearn grasps it only too late: It's gonna cut us off.

He curses and cuts all propulsion, blasting the bow thrusters to reverse. The *Lair* shudders and we stagger forward as she lurches to a sudden, bubbling stop just as that monster of a boat glides in front of us. Then silence falls, appalling in its clarity in that unspoiled wilderness, and the two superyachts face each other on the far side of the world.

A standoff.

The captain and I huff white vapor, scanning the boat. No crew are to be seen. But that luxurious icebreaker has gadgets galore sparkling on its helipad or in exposed lockers: a helicopter, two expedition RHIBs, one dive support boat, various submersibles. How will they attack?

Then a cool, male voice blares out into that silence with enough force to cause an avalanche. Some kind of deck horn or loudspeaker. "Motor yacht *Lair*. Hand over Adrian Voper and your crew will be spared."

Goose bumps spread up my arms—I don't need to see the speaker to know he's not among the living.

Death is in that voice.

"You should let them take me," Adrian says behind me.

I whirl, my gut plummeting. He leans in the doorway leading back into the *Lair*, haggard and face tight with pain, still in his bullet-shredded shirt. He looks as if he's about to keel over.

And he starts to before I rush forward and catch him. "You shouldn't be standing," I scold, my throat lumping up in emotion. "Are you—are you okay?"

But he brushes off my concern with a wave of his hand. "I won't have anyone dying for me." He glances behind him, and I see the two deckhands who'd brought Adrian inside, still covered in his blood. Behind them, filling the hallway, are the pale and terrified faces of what looks like the entire crew of the *Lair*.

I swallow and dart a look at Captain Redfearn. His gray eyes are hooded with resignation.

The blood sizzles in my veins.

"No," I splutter, shaking my head. "No, they'll kill all of us anyway—"

Adrian's face softens. "Aurora—"

But I can't look at him. I can't accept it. "There has to be another way—"

The icebreaker hails again, making me jump. "We repeat. Hand over Adrian Voper or we will board you."

I fly my gaze up into Adrian's, caught. The universe tilts.

And I hear the low, almost subsonic boom that makes the walls rattle and the floor hum beneath my feet, causing the spinning disc of the *Lair*'s gyrocompass to go haywire.

We all jerk to see a warbling sphere of golden light pop into being under the waves and collapse in on itself, like a dying sun going nova. Then it blinks out and a concussive geyser erupts into the air as the exploration yacht buckles upward in the middle, almost lifting out of the water as it breaks its back in a shockwave that turns the whole sea around it white. My eardrums throb. My insides turn to jelly. I shrink back, clutching at Adrian. And then the exploration yacht explodes. For a moment, I'm blinded by a great red flash. Steel screams. The world fills with the shriek of tortured metal. It's as if the very air were cooking. And we watch with mouths ajar as that monument of engineering capsizes in a rising mushroom cloud of flame and rank black smoke.

We stand there gaping at each other, almost too shocked to be elated, half-formed smiles twitching our mouths. *What the . . . ?*

Our answer introduces itself like a mirage. In the stretch of water between the *Lair* and the flaming wreck, waves begin to froth and bubble. Then they part as a shadow the size of a whale rises out of the sea in a great displacing of water. Navigation towers climb toward the sky. Water drips from guardrails and antennae, cascades off a curved metallic gray hull that's equal parts luxury vessel and Navy destroyer. It's a superyacht—but it can't be. It's a *submarine yacht.*

Before I can pick my jaw up off the floor, a portion of the hull folds down with a hydraulic whir and Ilsa Knackenkusser, the Shipwright of Transmarinia, steps forward in a gray skirt suit and cocks her hip, her pale blonde hair blowing in the spark-filled wind.

"Looked like you could use some help," she says into a walkie-talkie, her smoothly accented voice crackling through our comm, and allows herself an icy smile.

FOUR

"I call her the *Lady Revenge*," the Shipwright declares with a wave of her hand. "Not bad, no?"

Adrian and Captain Redfearn stare at each other, dumbfounded. I open my mouth, trying to form a sentence with the seared air of that battlefield.

But Ilsa goes on.

"You'll forgive me if I placed a tracking device on the *Lair* when it was in my yard last. I suspected you would need assistance soon."

A shaking Adrian picks up the walkie-talkie resting on the nav console, his voice thick with emotion. "Ilsa—"

"No time to dawdle, Herr Voper," she cuts him off. "We can't stay here. Follow me back to Transmarinia. We'll speak when we get there." She swivels on her heel and struts back into the interior of her gleaming invention, the hull side-hatch folding in after her.

Adrian and I glance at each other, beaming—before Adrian sags.

I catch him before he collapses, throwing Captain Redfearn a look. "I'll take him back down. You good up here?"

He nods, his expression grave, and juts his chin. *Go.*

When I turn, Adrian's arm around my shoulders, the hallway of faces watches us. My throat dips in a swallow. Captain Redfearn has a lot of explaining to do.

I hold my head high, gaze straight ahead, and shuffle forward. One by one, they part before us. They do not speak, do not even whisper to themselves. They stare unblinking at Adrian, at his wounds that would be fatal for any man. It is like a reception for a martyred saint returned from death. A miraculous reappearance. Adrian will be paying quite the bonus this year for them to forget everything they've seen today.

It takes a while to get him back to the master suite. In the bathroom I give him a look, and he nods. I unbutton his shirt and peel it off him, gingerly pulling the clinging cloth from his skin. He hisses in a sharp breath, eyes squeezed shut, but does not say a word. Then I turn him and look.

It's no easier seeing it the second time. The bullet wounds have mostly stopped bleeding, ungaping themselves in a slow, uncanny crawling of reknitting flesh; his whole back writhes. But it's still gore-slimed and desecrated, like an experiment gone wrong. He looks, for once, like exactly what he is—a walking corpse.

"It'll be better in a few days," he promises me. "We can heal from almost anything."

I can't take this in fully, not when I'm staring at what's been done to him. I hush him and draw him into the glass-walled shower, turn on a blasting spray of water and gently wash the wounds with a soft sponge. The blood thins and runs down his body in vivid braiding streams, swirling away toward the drain. He does not speak. His head turns slightly as my sponge lingers on the wounds, the evidence of his love for me. My throat closes shut. Everything is suddenly blurry; I am suffused with a tenderness I've never known before. He turns about in the clouds of steam and we are eye to eye, brows touching as the water channels down our faces. My heart swells and aches in my chest. I press myself against him. "Adrian," I whisper, and my voice breaks. He cups my chin, brushes back a lock of hair plastered to my face. "I know," he says.

He knows it's coming before I do. I begin to shiver. My pulse bangs in my temples. And then my breath sucks in and I bend forward, gasping and knees wobbling as if I've just finished a long and furious run. The relief is blinding, the shakes as purgative as vomiting. What is happening to me?

"It's okay," he soothes, drawing me into his arms. "It's over. You did it." And then, the admiration hushing his voice as he ghosts a thumb across my cut cheek, "You were amazing today."

That's what it is. It's the adrenaline. The adrenaline and terror of the morning finally wearing off.

And him acknowledging what I've done. How I am changing.

I don't think. I grab his neck and pull him down, give him a bruising kiss that communicates all my gratitude for him in this moment, all my brutal hunger for him.

And he meets it.

He sweeps me to him, one powerful arm wrapping around my lower back to press the full length of my body against his. It crushes the air out of me, but I'm too distracted to care. Because his other hand has hooked around my jaw to cradle my neck as he returns my kiss, breathing a low rumble of need into my mouth. Goose bumps pop up all over me. I shiver and go soft in his arms, a helpless desire gathering in my gut. I can feel how hard he is, pressing into my stomach. It makes me tingle.

When he finally breaks off our kiss, I'm gasping, my nipples going hard as they brush against his chest. I bite the flexing plane of muscle beneath his collarbone with furious need, my hands slipping around him, digging into his back, and he flinches.

I freeze.

"I'm sorry", I gasp, flying my eyes up into his face. "Maybe we shouldn't—"

"Fuck that," he growls.

In one thrilling movement he picks me up and slams me against the steamed-up glass of the shower wall, the whole pane shuddering under the impact. My stomach goes funny. Burning desire flames through me. My legs wrap around him, my heels digging into his flesh and reopening some of his wounds, smearing red in his blood.

And then he's pushing up into me, pinning me against the glass.

The pleasure is torturous. I arch my head back, moaning deep in my throat, wanton and unrestrained. I curl my fingers in his hair and claw them in luxurious lust down the brawny mountains of his shoulders, feeling those bullet wounds he took for me, tracing and investigating them as if they were delicious erogenous zones. He grunts hard against my neck, but it's mixed with pleasure now, a shivering, covetous, pain-loving need, and I feel him grow harder inside me. He grinds up into me, bouncing me up against the shower wall with every thrust, my flesh slick and squeaking along the condensation on the glass, and it's driving me crazy. I rake my wet hair out of my eyes and look down with parted lips as I hold his head to my breasts, his mouth finding my nipples, his tongue doing naughty, swirling, flicking things to them. "*Fuck*," I groan.

He begins to move faster now, and I'm grinding my hips on him, that depraved pleasure deepening as I see his blood streaming down his back in a red sheen under the needling force of the showerhead. I shouldn't be so turned on by this, I know. This is twisted. This is deviant. This is perversion.

But I am. I am turned on by it. A nasty, greedy part of me exults in itself, in his selfless, courageous, unthinking love for me. I think of him shielding me from that machine gun, wrapping me in his arms as he took those bullets without a moment's hesitation, and it pushes me over the edge.

I buck and cry out, hanging onto his neck as the waves of pleasure roll through me, the shuddering spasms as intense as the adrenaline earlier. "*Fuck*, baby," I gasp into his ear, my legs quivering, my mouth round and hanging. "Oh, fuck."

But he's not done. He sets me down on unsteady feet and spins me around, pushing me hard against the shower wall. My breasts pillow against the glass, nipples rubbing hard and tingling as he begins to pound me from behind. I can feel my ass cheeks bouncing, feel a joyous, decadent thrill already making me tight around him. And as I look at my hands braced on the fogged-up glass, I see that they've left red smears there, are dripping with Adrian's blood.

As he comes inside me, crying out with harsh abandon, I look down to see my lover's blood swirling about my feet, jumping under the rain of the shower, and smile in those clouds of rising steam.

This is my lover. This is our love.

This is his love for me.

We both sleep like the dead that night, bone-tired and holding each other like children in the master suite's enormous bed. I don't just fall asleep; I *plunge*, tumbling into lovely darkness, leaving behind all my worries and the wretched achiness of my body. In that dark, I dream.

I dream of boiling flame and bullets whapping into flesh. I dream of Adrian holding me as the world comes part.

Whap, whap, whap.

I startle upright, putting out a hand as if to protect Adrian—but he's not there. What woke me?

The *Lair*. It *thrums*, and I catch the tail-end of a series of *thumps* along its hull, as if it were getting battered by the tentacles of some legendary kraken. I grip the bed, wide-eyed and breath held. *What the hell?*

Then the whole world judders in a brief moment of suspension, and my insides turn elastic and strange.

What now?

I hop out of bed, pulling a sweater over my head as I stumble out of the darkness of the master suite and out onto the deck. Cool air roses my cheeks, and I have to blink and brush the hair out of my eyes to make sense of what is happening.

It's not yet dawn, the world hushed and dark, and across from me in a gentle and trembling fog irradiated by floodlights are the shapes of a superyacht, the iron girders of a crane, a covered building hall. And they're sinking.

The *Lair* is being lifted into the air.

I dart to the rail and peer down. From bow to stern, hydraulically operated arms press against the hull of the *Lair*. The boat is clamped in some kind of cradle consisting of a series of metal beams welded together to form a backbone of keel blocks. This in turn rests on a timbered platform, which is being raised by winches in a slow reeling in of wire rope, lifting a dripping *Lair* out of the water in a ponderous groaning of eight thousand tons.

It's only now that I can fully appreciate the size of the *Lair*, and how much of her is usually hidden beneath the waterline. Hull furred green with algae emerges. Fiberglass gleams. The sheer immensity of the ship, with its dizzying deep V of a hull, telescopes in a jaw-dropping swoop of awe.

Vertigo takes me.

Holy shit.

I pad down the gangway to the bow where I find Adrian in white chinos and a chunky cable-knit sweater. Captain Redfearn stands beside him, wrapped in his black captain's coat with its rows of brass buttons. They're both watching the proceedings.

When they see me, Adrian's mouth curves. "You're up."

"Yeah, only took a heart attack," I grumble, giving him a light push. "You could have woken me."

Adrian's eyes are gentle. "You looked like you needed the sleep."

I shake my head and look at Captain Redfearn, who smirks. Seems they both know me all too well. I always push myself until I drop.

"Glad you're still among the living, Arie," a smoothly accented voice crackles.

I jump and press a hand to my chest, and Captain Redfearn holds out the culprit: a walkie-talkie.

I look out across the bow.

The dark is ringed by the soaring hulks of dry docks stenciled with TRANSMARINIA in ten-foot-high letters. And not fifty feet from us, at almost our height, a control tower looms in the fog, its top little more than a glass-walled box. The monitor inside it glows on the pale, porcelain face of Ilsa Knackenkusser.

I lift the handheld radio to my lips. "Thanks."

"I admire your handiwork back there. Even if you were destroying *my* work."

I raise a droll eyebrow. "You're very understanding."

The Shipwright fights back a smirk. "The floating dock is occupied," she explains after a pause, "so we're berthing the *Lair* on land today. Hope you don't mind."

"Not at all," I quip. "I hope you're up for the repair job. The Nosferyachtu Club got it into their heads that she needed some redecorating."

Captain Redfearn snorts. The corner of Adrian's mouth quirks.

But the Shipwright doesn't answer.

I frown, turning to study her in the control room. "Ilsa?"

She's looking down at her phone. Even from here, I can see the tension in her body as she lifts her radio. "A client is arriving sooner than expected."

We all stiffen, glancing at each other.

A client. Meaning another vampire.

"Much sooner, actually." The Shipwright looks up at us, the dread thick in her voice. "We have five minutes to hide you and the *Lair*."

The three of us on the bow all look at each other. At the *Lair* sitting as helpless and obvious as a beached whale on the shiplift.

Fuck.

FIVE

There's a scurrying of movement on Transmarinia's outfitting quay. I peer down and catch a glint of steel lines, a delicate tracery of silver—it's laid out with a grid of rails like a trainyard. As I watch, a transport guides a long chassis of wheelsets mounted with hydraulic cylinders under the horns of the trestles cradling the *Lair*. There's a hiss, and the *Lair* shudders as she's jacked ever so slightly off the ground. It seems the plan is to tow the whole kit and kaboodle via rail into one of the waiting building halls.

And it seems it might work. The transport starts forward, slowly, slowly creeping the *Lair* into motion along the rails and onto shore, a gleaming, multimillion-dollar mountain on the move.

But then she stops. The hydraulic cylinders depress. Workers in hardhats scurry like ants around the *Lair* to turn the many wheels of her transfer trolley ninety degrees to the right. She's going to have to switch tracks to get into the empty building hall ahead.

And the Shipwright in her tower has turned to watch something. I follow her gaze and the blood knocks in my ears.

It's glimpsed only for a moment. The drifts of fog part, revealing—like an apparition—the unmistakable shape of a megayacht approaching the shipyard, the burgee of the Nosferyachtu Club snapping from its bow staff. She's perhaps a mile out.

Then the fog rolls on and it's gone again.

"Jesus, Mary, and Joseph," Captain Redfearn breathes.

A high whine builds in my ears. A furious powerlessness grips me. Adrian meets my eyes, face tight with fear. "There's not enough time."

"We don't know that."

"We need to get you off—"

"*No.*"

Adrian grits his teeth. "I don't want you here when they find me—"

"Just *wait.*"

The *Lair* moves beneath us, rumbling laterally onto the next track over. Then another hydraulic hiss. They're turning the wheels again.

Come on, come on.

I look back into the bay. The navigation lights of the Nosferyachtu boat pulse in the fog like corpse lights, growing closer.

Hydraulic jacks hiss. The *Lair* creeps forward again with agonizing slowness, rumbling along the rails. I look ahead to the looming maw of a building hall and its concealing darkness—so close, and yet an eternity away. Then I look back to the fog.

The navigation lights are larger now, blazing with uncanny color.

In less than a minute that boat will be out of the fog, and the *Lair* will be sitting here on the quay as plain as day, a Thanksgiving turkey waiting to be carved. How long would it take for the rest of the Nosferyachtu Club to descend upon Transmarinia?

As we crawl past the control tower, the Shipwright steps out onto its metal stairway, sleeking her hair to the side with a trembling hand. "I'm going out there to distract them," she calls, voice breathy with urgency, a low amp of panic. "Hang tight. And don't come out until my say-so." And she fast-pedals down the winding stairway onto the quay.

We look out to sea again. The navigation lights are a sinister constellation giving shape to that boat. Any moment now.

Captain Redfearn paces, hands in his hair. Adrian finds my hand and grips it tight.

And I think, *I love you, Adrian.*

And as the *Lair* rumbles into the shadows of the building hall, the Nosferyachtu boat hoves into full view, shredding the fog like a knife, and I think, *Does it see us? Does it see?* and the last thing I see is the Shipwright striding across the quay to head it off as a huge, fold-up fabric door is whirred down, shuttering us into darkness.

SIX

The *Lair* shudders to a halt, and I fight to steady my breathing and get my bearings. We're in some kind of painting shed with the steel looms of scaffolding glinting along the walls. A suffocating claustrophobia presses up against me, and I think of that cave in Sanguisuga; of vast, arched ceilings carpeted in a rustling of bats.

There's movement below. Scaffolding is being rolled forward by the shipyard workers in here with us.

"Come on," Adrian whispers, tugging my hand.

We feel our way through the dimness to the stern, a grumbling and bad-tempered Captain Redfearn trailing in our wake. "Get back inside. And stay quiet," he growls to a gaggle of crew members whispering to each other on the aft main deck. When we descend to the swim deck, we find that a working platform has been pushed right up to it, a collection of towering scaffolding structures linked by wooden planks. They creak and groan under our feet, rickety and risky, seemingly ready to collapse at any moment. I find my heart is thudding in my chest. I grope in the dark and find the head of the ladder that takes us down to the building hall floor. Adrian insists on going first, and I hear the clicking of his heels on the rungs. I follow him with sweating hands, my stomach swooping as I sense the airy nothingness around me. Then Adrian's arms are lowering me to the ground, and I turn and see the figures in hardhats waiting in the shadows.

My heart knocks in my ribs. My flesh creeps. But those figures only nod, and I leave the question of whether or not they're among the living behind. We creep past across the floor, tripping over construction debris from countless refits: welding slag, rust, flakes of paint and clogged tracks. Captain Redfearn kicks a corroded pipe across the concrete in a wild, ringing clatter of metal and curses under his breath. But I'm concentrating, my nostrils filled with the heady reek of waste chemicals, oils, grease. I have to hear. I have to know what's going on.

When we're at the fabric hangar door, we press our ears close and listen.

I hear nothing but the wind at first. And then, gradually nearing, two voices. One light and with a German accent, the other low, male, and chilling in its flatness. The Shipwright and her client.

"I expected a little more time to fine-tune the repairs," the Shipwright remarks. "Any reason for the early pickup?"

The response is stiff and grudging, dripping with contempt. "Some lost soul decided to defy the

Commodore. We need every vessel we can get to search the northern seas."

Adrian and I glance at each other in the darkness. Captain Redfearn slides a hand down his face.

"But you know the futility of such defiance," the client continues. "Don't you, Miss Knackenkusser?"

There's a long silence in which the wind blows. The fabric door rustles, gusting against us.

"Yes," the Shipwright says at last.

"You learned your lesson."

"Yes," the Shipwright repeats with careful neutrality, knowing what's required here.

"We were gracious, after all. To give you all this after what you did. You're very lucky, Shipwright. And you're so—very—*grateful*." Footsteps punctuate these words, as if one body were pressing up close to another. "Aren't you? Because you know how easily that could be taken away again. You know we don't do third chances."

Nothing but the wind.

"So if you saw motor yacht *Lair* pass this way, or received any word of Adrian Voper, you wouldn't hesitate to tell us, would you?"

My nostrils flare, inhaling dusty, corrosive air as anger and fear vie in me.

"Do you have anything to share, Shipwright?" the client persists with venomous quiet.

My breath slows. Adrian, Captain Redfearn and I look at each other. The silence on the other side of that fabric is far too long.

Then Captain Redfearn's eyes water as another gust of dust tickles his throat, and he can't help it—he coughs.

We all freeze, petrified.

The captain's face turns red as he suppresses another fit, and I clap a hand over his mouth with the firmness of an assassin and stare him down. I glance at Adrian. We all look at each other, adrenaline spiking, ears straining. Did they hear? They must have heard. They *had* to have heard. Why don't we hear anything?

Then the electric motor that runs the door roars to life, the cables overhead pulling it up with a grinding whir.

We all stumble back, startled and off-balance. My heart feels like it's pounding out of my chest. It occurs to me that I should run, but I can't move. The big hangar door rises and rises, revealing six-inch heels, long bare legs, a silver-gray skirt and suit, and I think, *It's over, it's all over, we've been betrayed.*

Then the fabric door glides up and the Shipwright stands there, alone, in the blinding glare of the shipyard floodlights, the quay behind her empty but for the thinning fog. She cocks her head. "Well," she sighs. "I guess using the *Lair* for your little scheme is definitely out of the question."

Captain Redfearn lets out a gush of air. I almost stagger with relief, grabbing Adrian's arm and resting my forehead on his shoulder. Adrian shakes his head with a grin.

Ilsa Knackenkusser watches all this for a moment, a slight smile on her lips, before she adds, "I may have a solution. Arie?" She lifts a brow. "Shall we get some sun?"

SEVEN

She packs lightly. Big black sunglasses, a white-and-blue striped umbrella twirling on her shoulder. Her heels dangle from her hand as she leads me onto a path meandering through a lush beechwood forest, sunlight dappling prettily through the branches. I don't even know what to think. I barely know this woman. How can I be comfortable being alone with a vampire who isn't Adrian? Am I being stupid?

And her? Getting *sun?* What does *that* mean?

It's nice out here though, the Baltic Sea air mild against my skin. It makes me think of convalescing soldiers, sanatoriums full of the wounded and melancholic. Or the exiled.

It's enough to lull me into the thought: *Just wait and see.*

The sun is getting high in the sky by the time we walk out of the woods, and I see the beach.

I blink. The sight is surreal. Dozens of tall wicker chairs line the strip of sand, facing away from the sun. They're colorfully striped and hooded, the kind you'd find along the beachfront resorts of the German Riviera.

Strandkorb: The name comes to me from some travel magazine. Ilsa Knackenkusser weaves through them with her umbrella carefully angled, her feet sinking as neat as a doe's hooves into the sand. I slip off my shoes and discover the sand is warm, already beginning to bake in the sun. You could almost mistake the temperature for summer. My face is dewy as we pass the rows of traditional German beach chairs, and when I turn my head to look inside them, the hairs on my arms stand up.

They're not empty. Many shadowed figures sit inside, shining eyes watching me.

Ilsa stops at the row closest to the water and claims a strandkorb, folding herself inside with a sigh. It's cozy, upholstered in striped canvas, and once I'm seated beside her Ilsa tucks her parasol away and pulls the strandkorb's colorful hood out to ensure no trace of sunlight finds her.

For a moment, you could almost believe we were two girlfriends on holiday, enjoying the sunlight twinkling off the Baltic Sea.

"It's nice, no?" Ilsa remarks after a while. Her voice is tight with something I cannot place.

"Yes," I reply, hesitantly.

"This is what we're given," she says, almost laughs, though there is no humor in it. "Some recompense for eternal servitude, wouldn't you say?"

I eye her in silence. I don't know what to say. I don't know what she is getting at.

She edges her eyes behind us, and I lean forward and follow her gaze.

Looking back at them, I can see it now. Those shadows tucked away in the sheltering alcoves of wicker and canvas—dozens, fifty of them—are all women, staring out to sea like the bereft widows of sailors, waiting for a husband who will never return. A life that will never return.

The dawning comprehension: It's not just the Shipwright who was banished here.

A chill prickles all the way down to the base of my spine.

"This is what they do with us," the Shipwright confirms. "With women of our race."

All those shadows in hardhats in the building hall . . .

"Stranded here, with our strandkorbs and welding tools." She turns to me, legs crossed and hands folded in her lap. All that fury held rigidly in place. "I wanted you to see before I asked you. I have been waiting a very long time for someone like you to come along and challenge them. I built the *Lady Revenge*, in secret and over many years, for that very purpose. To fight back." She takes in a quivering breath, as if almost afraid to say what's next. As if it were too close to her heart to speak it aloud. "I tried and failed, long ago. And I have betrayed the coven for you and risked my death—"

I open my mouth to speak, but she lifts a pale hand.

"It was my choice. I am done with hiding. You need a ship, and I have one that is unknown to the Nosferyachtu

Club. So here is my condition: You can take the *Lady Revenge* to find the Commodore and kill him . . . as long as I come with you as its captain."

It takes a moment for her words to register. Then a confusion of fear and leaping joy fills my throat, which is swiftly tempered with doubt. I shouldn't trust her, should I? Even after what she's put on the line? How can I trust anyone after what I've been through?

But I realize—with not a little astonishment—that I *do* trust her.

Perhaps it's to do with seeing how the Nosferyachtu Club treats her. Another woman understands, after all.

Or somehow, like with Mrs. Colding, there's a connection you simply can't ignore.

When I hold out a hand, I'm unable to suppress the grin that stretches my mouth from ear to ear. "That's a deal, Captain Knackenkusser."

The change in her face is remarkable—as if my reply had been too important to dare hope for. She lets out a gush of air that's halfway between a laugh and a sob, eyes bright and glistening, and takes my hand and pumps it once. "Thank you," she whispers.

We settle back into the coolness of the beach chair and watch the bright green waves crest and pearl toward shore, listening to the raucous cries of gulls. Before long we're chatting. She's asking about me. My past. Amazingly, I feel safe enough to tell her. My abusive ex, his gaslighting and violence achieving the monotony of a long, bad dream that changes you forever. My escape.

Meeting Adrian. She nods, her blue eyes steely with understanding. A woman knows.

"You will come to the heart of it, then," she muses. "Facing Volok." She looks at me. "You will have to face your abuse. You know that, don't you?"

My hide prickles. My ears fill with a distant roar. I nod, shakily, and clear my throat. "Yes."

"There is no getting around it. You will face it, or you will fall. Are you ready?"

It is hard—it is very hard—to meet her eyes. "Yes," I say again.

She holds me in her gaze a long moment, as if seeing in me much more than what is before her. Then she spares me and asks, with wry amusement, what Adrian's like in a relationship. The relief is almost blinding; she also knows the importance of a subject change, then.

And to my disbelief I tell her.

"*No*," she says when I'm done, admiring my ring. "He proposed under the Northern Lights?" She tuts. "Hello Herr Voper, dewy-eyed romantic."

I can't help it—I throw my head back and cackle.

How surprising, how welcome, to feel safe here.

Here. In this land of the undead.

I should be afraid. I should be terrified. I look about at this beach that's like some bizarre, picturesque vacation spot for vampires and watch the damned walk by in the liquid waves of heat, umbrellas angled just so, laughing and enjoying themselves. They look at me with curious, wondering eyes as they pass, heads bent to whisper to each other—as if, perhaps, they know who I am. Some of them even smile. How do they feel so safe, out in this annihilating sun, with nothing but a flimsy umbrella or hooded beach chair to protect them? I can't help but feel a surge of admiration at the bravery, the determination to find happiness—to lead as normal a life as can be had—in this prison. They have found a way to manage their fear.

There's something to be learned from that.

"It is too bad you are not a vampire," the Shipwright says, startling me.

She is watching me very closely.

My heart rate rackets. Disgust fills me, and something else that's harder to place. Very slowly, I look over at her.

She only shrugs. "By our laws, whoever kills the Commodore becomes the Commodore. But you must be one of our kind. If you were one of us and you killed him, you'd become—what is the word?—the *Mammadore*."

I snort. "I doubt all those good old boys would take kindly to that." We eye each other sidelong, the corners of our mouths trembling, and burst out in laughter as the shadows of the strandkorbs lengthen across the sand. I almost forget that one of the shadows in those beach chairs watching me looked distinctly male.

We find Adrian and Captain Redfearn back at the shipyard in the building hall, craning their heads to look up at the *Lair*. In the unforgiving blast of the hall lights, the full extent of the damage done to her by that helicopter is shocking. The windows of the main deck are shattered and jagged with shards of glass, the polished perfection of the hull stippled and chipped silver with a stigmata of bullet holes. Chrome handrails lean dented and askew. Even the awnings and courtesy flag at the stern hang limp and shredded. Seeing her like this brings a sudden sting of tears to my eyes.

"Your workers are gonna take good care of her, right?" I ask the Shipwright. "I still intend to get married on her."

Ilsa gives me a solemn nod. "She'll be as good as new when we get back."

I nod in return, and taking a deep breath I approach the two men in my life.

"I've decided—" I begin.

But I stop, for I see that Captain Redfearn is pulling out of an embrace with Adrian, a slight mistiness to his eyes. He sniffs and nods at me. "I know."

That's when I see the roller bag at his feet.

I blink. "What—"

"I spoke with Miss Knackenkusser last night. I think it's a smart decision."

I throw a look at Adrian. Judging by his expression, he was just told this, too. "What do you mean—"

Captain Redfearn steps forward and takes my hands in his big rough ones. "I think my part in this is over, Miss Strand."

An unforeseen hurt, startling in its intensity, tightens my chest. "No—"

His voice is calm, steady, as methodical as everything else about him. "I wouldn't know the first thing about piloting whatever that contraption is the Shipwright invented, and I need to be with Mrs. Colding right now." He brushes my chin with a thumb. "You have no more use for me, sweetheart."

I find I'm blinking back tears. I laugh and dash a wrist across my cheek. "That's not true."

Captain Redfearn's face is very gentle as he looks at me. "You're going to be fine. You've done more for me than you will ever know. I stayed on as captain of the *Lair* to help this one"—he jerks his head at Adrian—"through his fucked-up grieving process."

I hiccup a laugh. Adrian shakes his head, grinning.

"Because I wanted to believe that I could do the same. Or rather, I was afraid he was what I could become." Adrian blinks and drops his eyes. Captain Redfearn glances at him almost ruefully before continuing. "But you helped him out of that. And because of you—because of your *tenaciousness*—I know what I have to do. I know I need to track down my daughter and ask for her forgiveness." His throat bobs in a swallow. "I can't thank you enough, Arie. I am so proud of you."

I can't speak for a moment. I feel winded and light-headed, and I have to fight through the thicket of sobs in my throat. "You have more than one daughter, you know," I finally manage. "So, you better come back when all this is over. Because my dad died when I was young, and I want you to walk me down the aisle when I marry Adrian."

For a moment, I think Captain Redfearn hasn't heard me. His face slackens, the skin around his eyes unwrinkles. Then he shocks me by bursting into tears. It's a noisy, astonished, unpretty sob of gratitude that shakes his broad shoulders, the tears streaming down his cheeks. He doesn't let me see it for long. He crushes me to him, hiding his face in my hair, his bristly stubble tickling my skin. "You get that bastard for me," he chokes into my ear.

"And you get your daughter back."

He nods, and sniffing hard he turns away before he can't anymore, grabs his roller bag and strides off with the perfect posture of a Navy captain. The building hall door rattles up, turning the outside day into a blinding glare of light. And then Captain Redfearn has stepped into it and is gone.

EIGHT

"Welcome aboard the *Lady Revenge*," the Shipwright says.

It's dusk off Transmarinia as we begin our tour. Ilsa Knackenkusser sweeps across the strip of deck running along the topside of the submarine yacht, her bare heels thudding with the authority of stilettos. She gestures airily. "Sun deck and sail deck. When above water, I wanted her to be mistaken for any other superyacht."

And she could. She may have some dead giveaways—her topside terminating in a tail with propellers and stabilizing fins, for one. But the outside of the *Lady Revenge* is as glamorous as her creator. The sun deck is complete with sunbeds and a pool, and below us enormous side-hatches are open to reveal a gleaming beach club with bar and lounges and minisub bays.

Passing beneath the *Lady Revenge*'s tower with her periscope, radar and communication masts, the Shipwright undogs a door. "Now inside."

The contrast is stunning. Above water, the *Lady Revenge* is indeed a thing of luxury, destroyer-like styling notwithstanding. Inside, however, all of that ostentation is stripped away in favor of pure function and spareness, her hull smooth and white and arched—the subaquatic lair of a warrior.

In the bright and humming engine room with its profusion of piping, the Shipwright slaps a long and bulky engine that looks like some vast mechanical heart. "Stirling engines for silent propulsion. She'll go fifteen knots at a maximum depth of a hundred and fifty meters. Ideal for stealth. We'll be running below water for the most part to avoid unwanted attention." In the lower sub deck, she opens a door to a room racked with torpedoes, a small smile on her lips. "And, as you witnessed, she's well-armed." She shuts and locks the door. "She should be up to the task."

Returning to the beach deck, she gestures. "And this is our crew."

A group of perhaps twenty stands at stiff attention before an immense viewing gallery looking out upon Transmarinia—skirts neatly pressed, hair pulled back into ponytails, soft skin deathly pale.

They're all women.

"They all know the risks," the Shipwright assures Adrian and me. "And they came anyway."

A lump rises in my throat. "Thank you," I say to them.

They nod.

After a moment, one of them steps forward, hands twisting together, her dark brown hair shining sleek and lovely in the dimness. "Is it true you took out two of their boats?"

There's a taut silence, and I sense a wonder here, the realization that the impossible can be made possible. I swallow. "Yeah."

Shocked looks, whispers among the crew. Another woman steps forward, the words jerking out of her before she can stop herself. "And you killed Anatoly Anatolovich?"

Cold touches my spine. I nod.

The woman's face changes. "He murdered my sister," she blurts. "I never . . ." Tears fill her eyes. "I've always wondered what justice would look like for that, but I never thought . . ."

You never thought you'd get it, I think.

The woman's voice grows soft to steady itself. "Thank you," she whispers, her face twitching with a trembling passion. "I hope you get the Commodore. I hope you take that fucker down."

I feel a buzzing in my chest, the impact of what I'm doing slamming into me like a delivery truck, and realize that Transmarinia is not just a gulag; it's a survivor's club. A sisterhood. One I've been a part of all my life without realizing it. Because every woman like us, every woman who has gone through what we've gone through, wants to see justice as more than getting away, more than simply living. They want a retrieval of what's been lost. They want suffering. They want a return paid in blood. Even if that will never bring back what's been taken from them.

I fight that lump back down my throat.

"You're welcome," I whisper back.

The Shipwright looks between us all, waits a tactful moment. "Shall we, then?" She unclips a crew radio from her hip. "Rig for dive."

A series of responses crackle back: "Control room, rigged for dive," "Forward room, rigged for dive," "Battery forward, rigged for dive." When they've all trickled in, the Shipwright nods.

"Take her down."

There's a *thunk*, a hissing of ventilation and thrumming pulse of generators, and the water outside the viewing window froths and dances up the glass. The world outside rises, pushed out of sight by a bubbling flood. The crew of the *Lady Revenge* watch with solemn eyes as their home and prison of centuries disappears. That island with its beaches and strandkorbs. Its shipyard of cranes and building halls where the *Lair* now sits empty and abandoned, its crew ferried off to mainland Germany and back to normal life. The responsibility settles on me now. Mrs. Colding and now Captain Redfearn gone. And all these people depending on me. Because if I mess this up, it comes back on them, too. Their lives are in my hands.

Me. A farmgirl from Oregon who has to move on to that next step on her own, without the help of others.

Am I ready for it?

Adrian's hand slips into mine, and we turn and look into each other's eyes as the *Lady Revenge* sinks below the waves, casting our faces into shadow.

In that sudden envelope of quiet, one of the crew members turns to me. A redhead with a spattering of freckles across her nose and bold, fierce eyes. "You better know what you're doing," she says and strides away, leaving my stomach in knots.

The rest of the crew drift off, giving me furtive looks. When they're gone, the Shipwright turns to me with an apologetic gaze. "They're just scared."

I nod. "I get it. I would be, too."

Adrian gives me a meaningful look. "Especially if you didn't know the plan."

Agreed. Time to share.

I face the Shipwright. "The Commodore and his blood son share boat crews. So, I'm going to get hired on Radomir's boat, then get transferred to the Commodore's." I lift my chin. "Where I'll take him out."

The Shipwright narrows her eyes, mulling this over. "Then the first step is to locate Radomir's boat." She cuts a look at Adrian. "Any ideas, Herr Voper?"

My nerves sing in stupid hope as I turn to Adrian. He slides his hands into his trouser pockets, pale face drawn—then surprises me by smiling. "I know a lot of harbormasters. I'll let them know they'll be handsomely rewarded if they tip me off when Radomir puts into port." He shrugs, almost irresistibly cocky. "Should be simple enough."

The Shipwright leads us to our suite and bids us good

night. The room is a glowing white cocoon tucked inside a sleek submarine shell. There are hardly any features to it other than a porthole giving a sense of movement through dark, unexplored regions. I don't care for the view right now, though. I flop on the bed and huff a sigh, feeling drained, vulnerable, and slightly attacked. Leadership is overrated.

"Fuck, I'm starving," I say to the ceiling.

Adrian perches on the edge of the bed and watches me, cheeks dimpled in a faint smile. "I suppose the Shipwright didn't anticipate provisioning for the living. I'll let her know." He doesn't go, though. He keeps watching me, a strange mixture of pride and uncertainty in his eyes, and I think of that worry I saw in him back in Svalbard. *(Promise me you won't change.)*

I touch his hand. "What is it?"

He draws back and looks away, as if caught in a shameful thought, and presses his lips together in what's not quite a smile. "Nothing."

I sit up, one hand on his arm. "Adrian—"

But his phone chirps—he's received a text. He seizes on the distraction and checks it. After a breath, his eyebrows rise in appreciation. "That was quick."

"What?"

He holds up the glowing screen. "Radomir's in Croatia."

In a little over a week, we're off the Dalmatian Coast.

At nightfall we surface, and the Shipwright, Adrian and I climb up to the observation platform of the sail, the *Lady Revenge*'s tower-like structure, and look out at the glittering port of Hvar Town.

It's ancient, a clustering of red-roofed stone buildings atop a hill of lush cypress and palm trees. And its harbor is filled with boats. Rows of tenders and local fishing boats, the bigger superyachts anchored off on their own in the bay. I'm beginning to wonder if Radomir has moved on to another port when I see the nameplate, illuminated in deep red: *Neck Romancer*.

"She's here," I whisper.

"Indeed," the Shipwright concedes, turning to me. "And now?"

I have to take a moment to ride out the black tumble of fear in my gut. "And now," I say, taking a breath, "I ensure the *Neck Romancer* is in need of a new stewardess."

NINE

My leg jumps up and down with nerves as I wait. It's nearly noon, and the sun flashes off the bay with dazzling intensity. I'd left the *Lady Revenge* out at sea and motored into port in a rigid inflatable boat or RIB, then claimed a table under an umbrella at a quayside taverna. A colorful crush of tourists blurs past, laughing and gabbling, pointing at the yellow Venetian stone buildings and the day's catch lined up along the quay in their troughs of ice. I hide behind a big pair of sunglasses and an uninviting demeanor, legs crossed and hand poised on my sweating cocktail glass. My nostrils fill with the briny stink of fish, the tobacco from the old men smoking on the harbor wall. It's nice here. Quaint. Too bad all I have eyes for is the superyacht bobbing like a herald of death in the harbor.

I've been watching her for hours. Her doors and hatches, the swooping lines of her silver hull and her floating aft stairs painted a vibrant red. The vessel of a diva. I'm considering ordering my third mojito when what I've been waiting for happens—a gaggle of *Neck*

Romancer stewardesses hop into a tender for a day ashore.

Jackpot.

When they jump onto the wide, stone-paved promenade lining the waterfront, they don't head up into the old town. Instead, they follow a concrete path skirting the water, passing in and out of the shade of olive trees. Even from here I recognize one of them: Riley, the mousy stewardess I'd spoken with during the Monaco Yacht Show.

I pay my bill and follow.

Away from the bustling noise of the harbor, the furious shrilling of cicadas fills the air. The shade is hot and warped. The path winds, and occasionally I glimpse Riley and her crewmates up ahead—Riley silent and brooding, her friends chatting away—before they disappear around the next turn. The boat moorings and tourists and gleaming white yachts melt away, and I find myself on a wild, rocky coastline. Black stones shimmer with heat.

Then it opens up, like a dream, and across a private cove shines an oceanside palace with white stone colonnades. A beach club. The *Neck Romancer* stews are approaching it.

I hang back and watch as they speak to a woman in an all-white uniform. Within moments they're led out along the club's stone dock lined with almost a mile of sunbeds and colonnades. If I served a bloodsucking fiend, I'd have to unwind, too.

"And hold the cinnamon," Riley calls as she orders a cocktail. "I'm, like, deathly allergic."

Uh-huh, I think, and pay for a sunbed and cocktail of my own. I toss the bartender a winning smile. "Extra cinnamon, please."

Cocktail in hand and towel draped over my shoulder, I let my hips sway in my denim cutoffs as I stroll down the dock, high sexy sandals clicking on stone. Women lazing on sunbeds look up at me with faces scrunched in ugly resentment. One even slaps her ogling boyfriend. I sweep past them, wondering when I found this new, head-turning confidence. Somewhere along the way, my pain has been transformed. It has become something else. But I cannot think of that now. If I look at it directly, it will transfigure my world.

I rivet my attention on what's ahead. A few baldachin-style beds draped with dreamy white curtains stand on decks jutting out over the gorgeous water. Riley lies face-down on one in a black bikini bottom and no top as a masseuse works lotion into her skin.

Her cocktail is set on a table by the bed.

My focus tightens, the world narrowing in around that glass.

I glance about. The nearest guest is a supermodel glistening with oil, eyes shut and hard at work on her tan, and Riley's crewmates have jumped shrieking into the water for a swim. I could switch the cocktails without anyone noticing.

But that doesn't mean I feel comfortable about it.

So I do the stupid thing and openly stride out to the baldachin.

I hear a huge sigh as I approach—Riley letting out tension. "No scalp massage, okay?" she says in a nervous voice, eyes shut, and the masseuse murmurs a response. When my shadow falls across her, she squints up at me. Then she goes rigid and pops up onto her elbows, eyes wide. "What are *you* doing here?" she breathes. "You—you got me in a lot of trouble—"

"I'm sorry about that," I reply, sincere but calm, and glance at the masseuse. "May I speak with you? Alone?"

She stares at me for a long moment, and I meet her gaze. Whatever she sees there must be sufficient. She nods—wary, hesitant—and the masseuse slips away.

"Thank you." I sit on the edge of the baldachin and cross my legs, setting my cocktail on the table. Riley glances at the water and pushes herself up, facing away from me as she tugs on her bikini top. When she's done, she sighs, holding her trembling hands in her lap. The baldachin curtains flutter in the breeze.

"What do you want?"

"I have a proposition for you." I eye the stews splashing in the water, the long blur of sunbeds flashing in the sun. We're facing away from each other like two secret intelligence contacts in a movie. "What if I told you I could set you free? From your job aboard the *Neck Romancer?*"

She stiffens, shoulders tight with feigned bewilderment. "What makes you think I want to leave?"

I give her a look. "Trust me. I know."

She half-turns, brows drawn and wondering. "Why would you do that for me? So you could take my place?" Her eyes narrow, and she unconsciously pulls at her dark hair. "Do you know . . ."

"I do."

"Then . . . are you *crazy*? Why would . . ." She stills, wrenching all the way around to look at me now. She sees everything she needs to see in my face. "My God, you *are* crazy, aren't you?"

I do not answer.

She shakes her head. Her friends are coming in from their swim, climbing up a ladder to rinse themselves off under outdoor showers. One of them glances at us curiously.

Riley swallows and quickly averts her eyes, her fingers twisting in her hair, pulling away from her scalp. Dark strands cling to her fingernails. "It's not that easy. They won't just let you quit. They'll . . . they'll go after you . . ."

"And if you were too sick to work?" I pose in a soft voice. "Would they hire a replacement then?"

Her fingers still. She edges a look at me. "What do you mean?"

I lean forward, pick up both of our cocktails. "It's hard when you have a severe allergy, isn't it?" The cocktails switch places in mid-air. "All it takes is sipping from the wrong drink to send you to the hospital." And I set the cocktails back down, the surface of her new one dancing with thick swirls of cinnamon garnish.

Riley's eyes widen. She looks at me, at the outdoor showers, mouth working. "I—I could *die*—"

"And you have an EpiPen, right?"

Her fingers pull obsessively at her patchy hair. "This is so messed up—"

"Don't you want to be free of that fear?"

Riley's hand freezes. She slowly lowers it into her lap. Her lip trembles and she bites it, tears welling in her eyes.

I glance over at the stews from the *Neck Romancer*. One of them has her head arched back under her outdoor shower, water droplets sparkling off her brow. The other is watching us closely.

Not much time.

I reach out and take Riley's hand. "Hey." I wait for her to look at me. "You want them to pay?"

The showers turn off. Footsteps approach. "Riley?"

My heart rabbits. My eyelid tics. A sweet and almost rapturous rage surges through me as I promise it. "I am going to make them pay. Believe it."

And I offer Riley her cocktail glass.

Her gaze drops to it. She swallows, tears sheening her eyes. The soft fluttering of the baldachin curtains fills the world as her gaze lifts to my face again.

"And?" the Shipwright prompts, a brow arched on her pale, doll-like face. "Did she take it?"

I'm back on the *Lady Revenge*. Adrian and the Shipwright wait on my answer as schools of silvery fish glide past the viewing gallery. I bite my lip and incline my head in a shaky nod. "She was red all over by the time the ambulance got there." I look up quickly. "But she's okay. I gave her an EpiPen injection. She stabilized."

"Jesus," Adrian whispers and drags a hand down his face. "So now what?"

I shrug. "You created that fake identity for me?"

He nods.

"And sent my résumé in to Lair Yachting Incorporated?"

Another nod.

"Then we wait, and hope I catch their—"

RRR. RRR. RRR.

My phone vibrates in my pocket, startling me so badly I jump. When I pull it out and check the incoming call, the screen says what I knew it would say: *Unknown.*

We all look at each other, faces tight. I accept the call. "Hello?"

The voice that answers makes me prickle with chill. "Jamie Harris?"

"... Yes?"

The accent is Eastern European—Ukrainian?—and stiff with formality. "This is Dragica Bartosh, Chief Stewardess of motor yacht *Neck Romancer*."

Another chill, bumping up the skin along my arms, my scalp, tingling all over. Adrian and the Shipwright trade an apprehensive look.

"We found your résumé through Lair Yachting Incorporated."

"Hi, yeah—"

"It is acceptable. Can you be in the port of Hvar Town, Croatia by sundown tomorrow to sign the paperwork?"

The words are so unexpected the room spins for a moment. I place a hand to my brow. "Oh. Uh, yeah. I'll be there."

"Don't be late."

Click.

When I stare down at my phone, my hand is trembling.

"Well?" Adrian asks, his voice hollow.

I lift my eyes, bewildered, shaking, overcome with a dizzying rush of elation and terror. "I'm in."

TEN

I go lie down in the guest suite reserved for Adrian and me. My chest is almost too heavy to breathe; it's as if something is crouching atop it, squeezing all the air out of my lungs. It's the pressure. The reality of what's coming.

It's all about to begin.

Tonight will be my last night with Adrian for who knows how long. And what if I don't come back? What if this is it, and I'll never see him again?

It's enough to almost take me out of myself, smash me down into a purging darkness. I barely remember Adrian stroking my hair, whispering assurances into my ear.

I wake to find the sun sliding down the sky, leaking its light into the sea. And I think, *Adrian*. I turn over—but he's not beside me. Where he'd been, there's a cute summer dress laid out, a note tented atop it: *When you're ready.*

When I open the door to the guest suite, the Shipwright is waiting in the hallway. A small, gentle smile frays at her iciness when she sees me, taking in my dress. "You look beautiful," she says simply, and gestures. "This way."

A tender boat is waiting for us at an open side-hatch, bobbing in the water. The Shipwright claims the helm and I seat myself in the stern, brooding on the moonlight etching the dark waves as the wind whips at my hair. What is going on?

We cut an easy arc away from the *Lady Revenge*, skipping across the waves with the spray misting our skin. We're rounding an island, its black bulk blotting out the stars. Hvar? Another uncharted isle in the Lairverse? I can't tell. Ilsa's pale blonde hair is a ghostly banner in the dark, lustrous and quicksilver. She looks back at me only once, and I cannot read her expression.

Then a private bay appears before us, a strip of beach accessible only by boat. The sand glows, flames lick the dark. I grope forward, grip the steel strut by the tender's helm for balance, and squint. It's a bonfire, a heap of flaming driftwood sending up chains of sparks into the night. Tiki torches surround a table set for two, and fairy lights twine about an enormous canopied bed. It looks like some surreal safari set-up in a story.

And a silhouette waits by the candle-lit table in a billowy white Ralph Lauren shirt, barefoot with tan trousers rolled up above the ankles. Even in the dark I can see the flash of Adrian's smile.

I turn to the Shipwright, open-mouthed. She's grinning at me. "*What . . .?*"

"Go," she says and laughs. It's a beautiful sound. "Enjoy yourself."

Two other silhouettes are approaching. One of them grabs a line and pulls the tender onto the gleaming shore. Another reaches out, helps me hop down into the surging foam of the surf. It's one of the crew members. The freckled redhead who'd been none too happy with me and my plan. When she looks into my face, there's such sisterly warmth there it takes me aback. Something has transpired. A threshold has been crossed. I've proven something to them.

She squeezes my shoulder, and she and her compatriot share a smirk as they head past me for the tender. I'm too distracted to track this. My heart is throbbing in my chest in painful joy. Adrian glows as he crosses the beach to meet me, grinning as I look at him with a wary you-shouldn't-have look. "Baby . . ."

He shrugs. "I thought you'd appreciate some alone time before you leave tomorrow."

I shake my head, taking it all in again. There's a music player somewhere on the beach. Some old summer love song floats on the air, and Adrian and I smile at each other as we step into each other's arms, shy as new lovers. I lay my head on his chest and we sway in place, bare feet shuffling in the sand, heavy with a wild and unruly hope. There will be more of this. There has to be.

We revolve slowly on the beach and I eye the canopied bed with its twinkling lights, speak into Adrian's chest. "Are you just trying to get some?"

"Is it working?"

"Yes."

I can feel his smile above me: tender, sad. I tilt my head back to look up at him and he searches my eyes, hooks a strand of hair behind my ear. I swallow back a stinging of tears.

"What if—" I begin, but he places a finger to my lips.

"Shh," he says. "Don't. This is *not* goodbye. As hard as this is for me . . ." He shakes his head, lets out a wondering laugh. "Jesus, I wish I could do this for you." The muscles in his jaw pulse, and he looks at me. "But I know this is the right decision. Because I trust you. I know you can do this. I believe in you, Aurora."

I bite my lip, a furious ache swelling my chest. *Don't cry*, I tell myself.

"I want you to listen to me." He cradles my face in his hands. "I'm here for you, whatever it is. Do you understand? Even if you want to call it quits." He pulls something out of his pocket. "This is a burner phone. It doesn't look like much, but you'll be able to get through to me wherever you are. Never text. Never use my name. Only call when you need to. But when you do, I'll be there. We'll be following you in the *Lady Revenge* the whole way." When I accept it, his throat dips in a swallow and he draws in a shivery breath. "You can do this. You *will* do this. And when you come home—because you *will* come home—I'll be waiting for you. No matter what happens. Do you hear me, Aurora Strand?"

I nod, blind with tears, unable to speak. I'm trembling, I'm shaking all over. I tug off my engagement ring—my hands are barely working—and press it into his palm, fold his fingers over it. "I'll be coming back for this," I promise.

He doesn't reply. His mouth trembles and he pulls me to him, burying my face in his chest. His stifled sob is lost in my hair.

My heart is pounding. I cannot breathe. When I look up, I cup my hand behind his neck and draw him down to me, seal his lips with a long, deep, trembling kiss. When I pull away, he understands.

I take his hand and lead him to the bed. Little glowing lanterns have been set into the beach around it, warming the sand in circlets of flickering gold, and its four posts are hung with gauzy mosquito nets and cascades of twinkly lights; it's something out of a fairy tale. Adrian pulls one of the curtains aside, crawls in after me onto the soft white bedding, and I pull him on top of me.

For a moment, we merely look at each other. We don't need words right now. We wouldn't know what to do with them.

He bends to kiss me, and then his hands are on my body, roving over me.

He begins to unclothe me.

Our lovemaking is different tonight, achingly tender, infused with the knowledge that this may be our last night together. That this is goodbye. I lock my legs around his hips and move against him with a new, desperate strength, clutching him to me until my nails score his back. His rumble of need vibrates in my chest, making me tingle. His teeth tug at my ear, his mouth blazing down my neck, along my collarbone, finding the quivering pulse at the base of my throat. He grips my ass, sweeps one arm around me to hold me close with breathtaking power, his pants frantic against my skin. A gasp slips out of me, my cheeks flushed with passion. A hard, hungry want moves within me, and I act on it. I brace my hands on his chest and push him up, roll us over so I can ride him, feel myself claiming him, taking him deep inside me, making him mine. Adrian's eyes widen, bright with surprise and intense arousal. He looks up at me, hands cupping the sweet drooping of my breasts, his face full of love and wonder and dazzling heartache. I almost can't bear to look at that nakedness; it hurts too much. But I do. I don't look away. Everything else blurs and dims—the fairy lights, the ring of lanterns in the sand, the sigh of the sea—until the world is just us, and that tension builds and builds as we stare at each other, lips parted, his eyes raking over me, drinking in my body as I dance above him, for him, showing him what's his. He does not hide his appreciation. He bites his lip, his blue eyes hazing black, and his hands land on my hips, gripping hard into flesh, guiding me. My breath catches in my throat. That tingling pleasure between my legs deepens and intensifies until I'm all but writhing on him, thighs clamping and shivering, drawing out low, encouraging moans from Adrian. Then we've arrived at that place where there's no turning back from, and it's happening, I'm grinding hard and fast on him to take us over the edge, and we're coming together in a rush of curses and I bend down to take his moans into my mouth, feel the salt of his tears on my cheeks. Whatever happens tonight, I will take this moment with me. I have consigned it to memory. It lives within me now.

Afterward, we lie there for a long time in each other's arms, listening to the wild thudding of my heart.

ELEVEN

I don't wait for sundown to leave the next day; to wait till then would be torture. I change into yachtie clothes and pack a light bag, the burner phone tucked in my pocket, Adrian watching me and looking as faded and helpless as a ghost. We do not speak. I feel as if I might burst into tears, into a conflagration of anguish, at any moment. When I'm ready I turn to him, and he nods.

The disembarking side-hatch is open, a rigid inflatable boat bobbing in the water in the shaded lee of the *Lady Revenge*. The whole crew waits at the hatch, Ilsa at the fore. One by one they hug me, cold flesh trembling with gratitude. "Thank you," they whisper. "Thank you." Then the Shipwright of Transmarinia is before me. She tilts her head and studies me with a small smile, her enamel skin shining with kindness. I draw her into a tight hug. "Take care of Adrian while I'm gone," I tell her.

"I will," she vows. "See you soon."

I nod and pull away; now for what cannot be borne. Adrian waits for me, looking insubstantial and amazed, as if outside of his body. His mouth trembles as if he's struggling not to cry. The trembling reaches his chin, quivering helplessly, and he opens his mouth as if to say something, thinks better of it and locks up his jaw. Then he swallows hard and steps forward. I lift my face to him, but he does not kiss me. He presses his lips to my brow as if in blessing, leaving them there until I shut my eyes and let out a slow and wavering exhalation to keep from sobbing. I understand. He's doing it for us. A self-preserving refusal, a kind and dreadful caution. A warning.

No.

We cannot kiss, cannot speak. If we did, it would all crumble around us. I'd never be able to leave.

So I do. I find it's not beyond me. I wrench away and hop down into the RIB, wiping at my eyes. Crew members throw the lines into the boat, and with shaky hands I throttle the engine and point the bow toward Hvar Town. The boat galumphs across the crests of the waves. Spume flies up against my cheeks. I can barely see. And somewhere in my mind, a disbelieving part of me keeps thinking, *Adrian, my Adrian.*

And also: *Don't look back. Don't look back.*

I look back once and catch a devastating glimpse of him. He's broken down. He is hunched over, hands fisted in Ilsa's suit jacket, heaving out sobs. That's when it crushes me. The wail of grief comes out, a single, choked cry of astounding purity, like a wounded bird, and I have to clap a hand over my mouth. And somehow, I am still pointing the RIB toward Hvar Town. I am keeping my course. I am rushing across the waves and away from my love.

I'm a walking wreck the rest of the day. I order dinner at a taverna and chew with numb vacuity, tasting nothing. There's a buzzing in my ears, a tingling all over my skin. *How am I enduring this?* I wonder. *How do I go on? How does any of this go on?*

Before long, dusk is falling.

I roll my bag out to the dockside and wait, still shivering with vulnerability. To hell with it. As long as I'm making the farewell rounds, I may as well go all the way.

I call Cailee.

When I hear her familiar "What's up, buttercup?" on the other end, it's enough to almost make me lose it again. I let out a choked laugh and cover my eyes with a forearm.

"It's good to hear your voice, babe."

"You better be calling to tell me you kicked that ex-wife off the boat."

Jesus, she can always make me smile.

"Yeah. Yeah, Cailee. That's why I'm calling."

"Good girl." There's a pause on the line. "You okay?"

I swallow. "Uh-huh." There's a sleekly-designed tender heading straight for me, leaving a frothing V in its wake. It's manned by a burly deckhand in a black yachtie polo.

My ride.

I get it out in a rush. "You know you mean everything to me, right?"

Another pause. This one longer. "Of course."

"I never thanked you for . . . for everything. I want you to know it meant the world to me."

"Arie, what's—"

The deckhand's killed the engine and is coasting toward me now. Seconds away.

"I gotta go," I blurt breathlessly. "The boat's leaving. Take care of yourself, Cailee."

I end the call before her voice can stop me, or my own comes apart. My hands are trembling, my heart thumping away in my chest. But I don't have time to dwell—the tender boat is here. It swings nicely alongside the dock and the deckhand peers up at me, black polo clinging to heavy musculature, his face lean and clean-shaven and scarily blank behind a pair of black sunglasses. "Miss Harris?"

I straighten my spine and put on a bright smile. "That's me."

The deckhand doesn't say another word as he motors me out into the bay. I stand beside him at the helm, scanning the sea in the wine-colored dusk. But I can't find any sign of the *Lady Revenge*. I am on my own.

A shiver passes over my body.

I feel my finger recently naked of its engagement ring, as if I could find strength there, as we approach the *Neck Romancer*.

Her nameplate glows red in the gathering dark, her exterior lighting system making the water about her pulse a bloody crimson. It hits me now, with sudden, breathtaking force, that there's no turning back. This is it. I'm here. I'm finally doing this. And I can't help but think it. The question poses itself, too frightened to even want an answer, a plea to the night: *Will I come out of this alive?*

As we near, the *Neck Romancer*'s stern *moves*. Those striking scarlet stairs leading down to the swim deck split, spreading out over the water in two curving fans of floating steps like wings, like a deployable red carpet, glamorous and sparkling. It has the feel of an unfolding opera house, a sort of sexual beckoning. And as the tender boat drifts up to the foot of one, a woman in a black stewardess uniform descends like a debutante at a ball. Stout and matronly, hard-faced, with a ham-colored birthmark on one cheek, her platinum blonde hair pinned severely back in an updo. She holds her arms rigid at her sides and tucks her chin back into her bullish neck.

"Miss Harris," she says, stiff and harshly polite. "Madam Bartosh. We spoke on the phone." She steps aside and gestures up the curving stairs behind her. "Welcome aboard the *Neck Romancer*."

TWELVE

So, I think as I follow Madam Bartosh up those sweeping stairs, *this is the Mrs. Colding on this boat.*

The same imperiousness, the same brisk efficiency. Her platinum blonde hair gleams, a color that to me communicates a hard heart, a certain willingness to deal in the sordid and immoral. We ascend to the aft main deck and I blink. It's laminated in a red mirrorlike finish that gleams like a dance floor, a pooled dollop of blood.

Without a word, Madam Bartosh pulls a chair out from a table that looks like a slab of black glass, pointedly waits until I sit. Then she's gone, vanishing inside the yacht. I barely have time to notice the aft stairs have furled back into their normal arrangement—where did the deckhand go?—before an inch-thick pamphlet lands with a whump on the table, making me jump. A non-disclosure agreement.

I stare. It must be fifty pages long. I glance up at Madam Bartosh—she hasn't seated herself, choosing instead to hover at my shoulder—and flip through it. I'd signed an NDA when I was hired aboard the *Lair*, and I see some familiar phrases: . . . *no posting to social media without approval from the owner . . . no disclosing the location or destination of the yacht . . . no divulging any information whatsoever concerning the owner or associates, including entities known as Nosferyachtu Club, Transmarinia, Palace of the Fang, Bloodtown and Lair Yachting, Inc.* But there are some stipulations here I have never seen before: *. . . any questionable behavior witnessed must be reported first to employee's superior . . . any mysterious "injuries" or "wounds" cannot be revealed to crewmates or the public . . . any physical violence cannot be revealed . . . any battery . . . sexual assault . . . molestation . . . rape . . .*

Not revealed.

Not revealed.

Not revealed.

My mouth has gone dry. My skin, I find, is crawling.

Madam Bartosh seems to feed on this. She leans down, implacable behind her birthmark, and offers a pen. "Is there a problem?"

No. Not like Mrs. Colding at all.

When I sign, she sweeps the NDA shut and tucks it to her bosom, a Russian madam with the bookkeeping, and slides open a glass door, glances back at me. "Don't tell me you're having second thoughts."

No. No room for that, is there?

I lift my chin and walk past her into the yacht.

It's as flashy as the outside—gleaming mirrorlike ceilings, alligator hide chairs and tables made of fine Baccarat crystal. Madam Bartosh leads me down a spiral staircase paneled with scalloped silver-leaf walls to a lower hallway. A stewardess passes us, a pretty black girl with a smooth, dark, brooding face, her hair spun into an edgy bob of Senegalese rows. The whites of her eyes flash at me before a glance from Madam Bartosh makes her lower her head and hurry on.

Then Madam Bartosh is waving me ahead of her into the crew quarters.

It's windowless, tiny, the bunkbed leaving barely enough room for two people to squeeze past each other. Madam Bartosh lifts a clothes hanger out of a closet and turns to me. "Here is where you change into your new uniform."

I wait for her to offer the hanger and leave, but she looks straight at me until I understand. She's not going anywhere.

Heat rises up my neck. So this is how they let us know what we're in for. A preliminary humiliation, leading to darker, final revelations.

Or simply how they groom us for obedience.

"I hope you're not a baby," Madam Bartosh says.

I strip in silence, letting my skirt and polo drop to the floor. The entire time, I do not break eye contact with Madam Bartosh. I'm determined not to give her that satisfaction.

When I'm standing there sweating in my underwear, my chin held at a stubborn angle, she smirks and hands me the hanger.

Once I'm in my *Neck Romancer* uniform with a crew radio clipped to my hip, I'm led back up the spiral stairs, down another hall into a more intimate recess of the yacht. Madam Bartosh seems to have treated this whole episode as an icebreaker. Her briskness is almost cheerful now. She grows chatty and confiding. "I hope you're better than the last girl. Worthless thing got herself sick. Drank something that didn't agree with her." She opens a large sable door and steps aside. "The owner's suite."

My heart tics in my throat. My eyes suddenly feel strained. I hadn't expected to see Radomir already. This is too soon.

Madam Bartosh sighs, as if she can't be bothered to tell me to hurry up, and I step through the door.

It's a lavish space, with the bed—unsurprisingly—as its focal point. It's raised and stepped to provide a band of integrated mood lighting around its frame, and the covers glisten in luxurious troughs of silvery silk. Tinted sliding glass doors open up onto a private balcony overlooking the sea, and three stewardesses in yellow latex gloves kneel on the floor, scrubbing something wet and red off strips of ash gray hardwood. Radomir is nowhere to be seen.

There's a click behind me—the door shutting—and the stewardesses sit back on their heels and watch me with walled eyes.

"Hi," I say, uncertain. "My name's—"

"Shh!" one says, holding up a finger. They weren't looking at me at all. Their gaze is up near the ceiling, as if caught in thought, and it hits me—they're listening to make sure Madam Bartosh is gone.

What they hear must satisfy them, for their bodies relax. The air moves again.

"Grab some gloves," one says, as if grudgingly remembering me, and gestures to a cleaning caddy.

It's the stew I passed in the hall earlier. When I'm gloved up and scrubbing, I offer in a whisper, "Name's Jamie."

"Nicole," she replies, in a way that says she's busy.

At least she responded, though. The other two—baggy-eyed, with the look of girls who have recently lost a lot of weight—are too busy for even that. They work in silence, with a grim, vigorous rhythm, and I get the sense of an inviolable circle, a bond of suffering.

I won't get far with that.

"Someone spill some wine?" I venture, studying the sudsy red mess of the floor.

Tense exchanged looks.

"What?" I ask.

Nicole eyes me. "You'll find out soon enough," she says at last.

Despite myself, I feel a chill.

They all know, then.

Time for a subject change. "Where's the owner?" I offer, trying for a lighter tone.

Nicole sits back on her heels, arming a sweaty brow. "On the *Shadow*."

"The what?"

A chin juts toward the balcony. "See for yourself."

Frowning, I strip a glove off one hand and slide the glass door back, slip outside into a buffeting wind. The *Neck Romancer* is underway, slicing through the Adriatic with menacing ease. Alone.

Leaning over the rail, I cast my gaze back toward the distant radiance of Hvar and see another superyacht trailing the *Neck Romancer*, yellow deck lights glowing like miniature suns. But it's no normal yacht. The front third looks the same as any other luxury vessel, with its bow and bridge and puffy white radomes, but the final two-thirds are one long open aft deck on which are stored a collection of sports vehicles, tenders, submersibles, jet skis, even a seaplane.

"Must be nice to have a whole other boat for all your toys," Nicole deadpans behind me. "I'd spend most of my time there, too."

Eyeing the monstrous bulk of that support vessel, I can't help but shiver.

So. That's where I need to get to.

THIRTEEN

I wait for my chance as I get used to life on the *Neck Romancer*.

Madam Bartosh is ever-present, hard-faced and self-satisfied, her admonishments as crisp and damaging as a ball-peen hammer to the shin. "You think that will do?" she incants in a gloating whisper, preening in her role. "You think that's good enough if the owner comes aboard?"

She keeps the *Neck Romancer* running on pure fear, all the stews flitting about like hummingbirds. Polishing metalwork, tableware, mirrors. Hoovering and cleaning the cabins. Doing laundry. I have barely a moment to myself. Even so, I chance it. I can't help standing at the stern at times, hoping to catch a glimpse of the *Lady Revenge*. I never do.

(Don't look back. Don't look back.)

Here and there I'm able to steal a moment and slip abovedeck to survey my objective. During the day, that shadow vessel is decidedly unexciting, trailing its mothership in silent deference. Other details can also be seen. Its high-powered deck crane situated amidships, the somewhat industrial bulwarks and superstructure, the exterior styling that matches the *Neck Romancer* via a subtle gray colorway accented by pops of scarlet. There is also a noticeable lack of windows under the bridge—some kind of lounge? But no one stirs aboard that boat. I don't see a soul upon it for days.

As evening falls on the seventh day, though, that all changes.

The sky fills with a chopping roar, rattling the glassware in the galley of the *Neck Romancer*. I glance at the other stews, but they don't look up from the crystal tumblers they've been polishing. Their faces have gone hard as stone.

So I peer out a porthole and see the helicopter alighting on the *Shadow*.

Long, toned legs descend, a parade of models and escorts in shimmering dresses whipping in the wind. A muscly deckhand in a tight-fitting polo leads them through the maze of man-toys on the open deck into the lounge.

I look back at the stews, but none of them have moved.

Soon, deafening club music is blasting from the *Shadow*. It lasts for hours. I lie awake in my bunk, eardrums throbbing, and hold my burner phone against my heart, thinking of Adrian's lips on my brow.

In the surreal calm of morning, there's a shuffling of feet in the hallway. It's an exodus of stewardesses. Heads hung, eyes down, carrying cleaning caddies. I follow them out onto that pop of color of an aft deck and see the *Neck Romancer*'s red-carpet stairs have winged out. A tender is bobbing at the bottom on the starboard side, engine idling. The stews are getting shuttled over to the *Shadow*.

The blood pounds in my ears.

I've started down the floating steps after them when a hard voice stops me.

"Not you."

Heads jerk up. Madam Bartosh stands behind me, arms at her sides, her birthmark splotchy and livid on her face. "You haven't proved yourself yet."

My insides turn. I glance at the stews. Their eyes are lowered.

The fenders are brought in and the tender glides out in a rippling of froth to the *Shadow*.

I don't see the stews again until mid-afternoon. When Nicole slips into our shared cabin, the look on her face makes me swing my legs out of my bunk. "What's wrong?" I ask, standing. "What happened?"

She won't look at me. Her chest is heaving, nostrils flared. I reach out to touch her arm. "Nicole—"

She shrinks away and worms past me, climbs up into her bunk and rolls to the wall in a ball. She doesn't say a word for the rest of the day.

This pattern repeats itself every few days. The drop-offs, the nighttime music, the stews ferried over the following morning. I can feel Madam Bartosh watching me, gauging my reaction, and I keep myself still and dead inside.

After a week on the *Neck Romancer*, my opportunity presents itself.

It's after another night of partying on the *Shadow*. I pass a clump of stews carrying cleaning caddies in the hall, dip into my cabin to fix my hair and freeze, the hairs on the back of my neck standing up.

The cabin isn't empty.

I can hear voices. Madam Bartosh stands in the doorway to the ensuite head, leaning over and speaking in a low, seething tone.

"And what am I supposed to do now? You've left me high and dry, haven't you?"

"I'm sorry."

"That doesn't do me much good, does it?"

Someone is there. Someone else is there, hunched over the toilet. Shivering and weeping.

"I can't. I can't do it."

"You will. I gave you a job when nobody else would have you, and this is how you repay me?" Madam Bartosh leans lower. "I wouldn't believe your weakness," she breathes, "if it was anybody but you." She straightens, plumped up with satisfaction. A matter has been settled. "You'll be on that boat in two minutes. See what happens if you aren't."

She turns and catches herself when she sees me, as if caught in a lie. Then she lifts her nose and pushes past me, knocking me aside, her birthmark pulsing like a wound.

No sound at all for a few moments but the choked sobs in the head.

I ease the cabin door shut and leave a hand there, as if afraid it'll fall off its hinges otherwise. Then I drift toward the head. Nicole slouches before the toilet, brow on forearm, sucking in loud, dragging breaths. I kneel beside her and touch her shoulder. "Hey."

She whirls at me, quailing, eyes wide and puffy. When she sees it's only me her face scrunches up and she buries it in her arms again.

"It's all right," I soothe, rubbing her back. "It's okay."

She raises her face to the ceiling and exhales, eyes shut, as though imploring God. Then she snorts. "Girl, you don't even know. You don't know." She wipes angrily at a cheek and adds, in a smaller voice, "I was so grateful to get this job. No one in this industry hires people like me." She gives a weak laugh. "Now I know that's exactly why they hired me."

I swallow and look down into my lap, my voice almost a whisper.

"I could go in your place."

Nicole jerks at me, appalled, eyes shining out of her Senegalese twists. "You're not cleared. And you won't be for a season at least."

Which is why this is my chance to get to Radomir.

I shrug off her comment. "They need another stew, don't they? That's what the tender pilot will be waiting on."

"But Madam Bartosh—"

"I'll deal with her when I get back," I say firmly, not adding, *Which means I'll have to charm Radomir before she can kick me off the boat.*

No pressure.

I lift my chin. "And you can say by the time you went up the tender was gone. Unless you want to go?"

Nicole's eyes skitter away and back to me. Wary. Appraising. "You're crazy."

I grimace a smile. "So I've been told."

Nicole's lip trembles, and the words thin as they come out, so that she almost mouths it. "Thank you."

She's curled her hand into mine. I give it a squeeze, feeling the leathery roughness of skin callused from the tedious, thankless labor of a yachtie. My pulse knocks strangely. "What she said about you?" I say, and swallow the lump in my throat, forcing away an old, familiar voice in my head. "Don't believe it. People will claim to see in others what they loathe in themselves; it's how they bear living. The only way to beat them is to live a happy life, okay?"

I can see it fly into her eyes. The shock. Then her face screws up, the tears slipping down her cheeks, and she nods.

I lurch for the door before the terror throbbing through my flesh can stop me.

Peeking my head out of the spiral staircase, I scan the main deck. Madam Bartosh is in the lounge, chatting with the captain with her back to me. Luckily, the sliding glass door leading onto the aft deck is open, so that's one less thing to worry about.

Now or never.

I march out with head held high, never once looking back, the boom of my heart narrowing my throat. *Please,* I think. *Please, please, please.* The slice of open door looms. I wait for sharp voices to sting my back. But then I'm through, past that dining table like a slab of polished obsidian, away. All the stews stare as I fast-pedal down the deployed aft stairs and hop into the tender. "Sorry I'm late," I gush out. "Ready to go."

The deckhand turns to me, and my nerves fizz.

But a flicker of impatience is all I get before he thrums the tender away in a flume of spray.

I'm in.

Breathe, Arie. Just breathe.

And I sit there in the stern of the tender, heedless of the stares burning into my flesh, as I watch the approaching hull of Radomir's lair fill the world.

FOURTEEN

We climb onto the *Shadow* at the stern.

Deckhands are waiting for us, hands offered to help us onto the strip of swim deck before the tender garage door. Then we're following them up a short set of stairs and before us stretches that wide open aft deck with its array of toys lashed in place or mounted on chocks, as crowded as an aircraft carrier. I have to blink to take it all in. Sunlight flares off bulky-looking off-road vehicles, sleek tenders that look like speedboats, submersibles and quad bikes and even a Triumph motorcycle with a naked woman emblazoned on its engine block. We're on a floating toybox that costs millions.

So, I think. *Radomir's a thrill seeker.*

We pass beneath a boom crane that looks like the neck of a dinosaur and line up. Bottles of glass cleaner and Formula 409 rattle in a cleaning caddy—the stew ahead of me is shaking uncontrollably, the flesh of her arms pricked into distinct goose bumps. Behind me a stew looks like she's trying not to cry, glassy eyes staring unseeingly ahead. The terror in the air is so visceral I can practically smell it.

Why are we waiting?

I crane my neck. Up ahead there's a beefy, buzzcut deckhand who looks like a Marine. He's patting down the stews before they pass through into a yawning black hole in the *Shadow*'s superstructure, and it hits me: *They're checking for phones. Whatever's in there, they don't want it recorded.*

My stomach plunges. I pat at my skort and feel my soul exit my body.

My phone. My burner phone.

I have it on me.

My knees go weak. Distance compresses, goes strange and queasy with a shimmer of claustrophobia—there's only one stew ahead of me in line.

What am I going to do? What will happen when they find the phone on me?

I have to get rid of it. Now.

I glance about. On either side, nothing. No lounges with scatter cushions, no storage compartments. Just bare deck and a snazzy-looking luxury tender that's nowhere close enough for me to get to without being seen.

No options. No chance. I'm fucked.

Unless.

My eyes latch onto a skort pocket of the stew ahead of me, and I have the sudden, shameful thought of dropping the burner phone into it.

My cheeks grow hot, and I push this thought away. No. I couldn't. I couldn't do that to her.

The stew ahead of me steps into darkness, and the deckhand waves me forward.

My turn.

Sweat beads my hairline. The deckhand's face, rugged as a boulder, wavers before me. I am on a high precipice at the edge of a straight drop. What am I to do? Think on that fear. How can I use that? How can I play into what they expect of a petrified little stewardess?

I step forward, let a shiver overcome me, and drop my cleaning caddy to the deck.

Scrub brushes and leather chamois and bottles of cleaner spill out and bounce across teak planking. I hiss in a breath and wince, feigning mortification. "I'm *so* sorry."

The deckhand rolls his eyes and kneels to pick up a bottle of Murphy's Oil Soap rolling past. The stew behind me has also crouched down to help, and I don't see any other deckhands about. This is it.

I dart to the side, toss the burner phone lightly into the leather-upholstered cockpit of the luxury tender, and dart back in time to grab the Murphy's Oil Soap from the deckhand. "Thank you," I beam at him.

He scowls, and my hands are shaking as I restock the caddy. *Holy shit, that actually worked.* I could almost laugh from the relief. Then the deckhand is gesturing and I'm lifting my arms so he can pat me down. I'm almost too stunned to brace myself for a leering lingering of the hands, but that never comes—it is all executed with admirable efficiency and propriety, if not boredom. He must do this all the time.

Then I'm waved through.

Oh. Right. This is all happening so quickly, I've had no time to worry about what's next. Going inside. To where the other stews fear to tread. The lap of waves against the *Shadow*'s hull becomes a crashing roar, and I think, *I don't know if I'm ready for this.*

But I have to be.

Taking in a big gulp of air, I step into darkness.

It takes a moment for my eyes to adjust to the change in light. Then a blinding flash from a sphere of hundreds of silver mirror tiles: a disco ball. It dominates a ceiling whose edges are lined with glitzy mood lighting. Another dazzling spin of the ball, and I catch glimpses of plush leather, stainless steel poles, backlit liquor bottles. The fact slowly comes to me: It's a sex club. A floating nookie room tricked out with striptease poles and lounges and a glowing bar, the walls paneled in dark wood and mirrors.

Then another, revelatory flash from the disco ball, and the smell hits me as I see it.

"Jesus, Mary, Mother of God," I whisper.

It's an abattoir. Blood is everywhere, painting the club red. The floor, the lounges, even splashed up onto the sparkling tiles of the disco ball. There is blood on the bar's countertop and stools, bloody handprints on the mirrors and stripper poles. Here and there on the floor, great pools and smeared tracks, as if bodies had been dragged away and disposed of.

So this is what Radomir does in here.

A sudden wave of nausea rises up my throat. I feel an eyelid tic. I shut my eyes.

Behind them, I can see Josh. I can see my blood on his knuckles. I can see his mouth forming the words, *See what you made me do?*

The world catches and holds in place for one lush, trembling moment.

And I open my eyes.

The other stews have already started; they have their routine down. Mops and scrub brushes for the floors, saddle soap and microfiber cloths for the leather lounges. One of them catches my eye and juts a chin at the walls and disco ball. "Start from the top."

But my eyes are not on the walls. They're on bloody footprints leading down a hallway off the club. The footprints belong to a man.

Understanding sends cold sweat dripping down my back. I have no illusions about what waits for me down that hallway. *Who* waits for me. But do I, though? Do I really know what I'll find?

Does it matter?

I'm here now. I have to go all the way to come out of this.

So I face that shadowy entrance and grip the cleaning caddy tightly in my hand, steeling myself. I march forward.

There's a startled voice behind me. "Hey! Not in there. He doesn't like to be disturbed after he—"

But the words fade away as I'm swallowed by the maw of that hallway.

The tracks gleam like puddles of melted popsicles in the dark. It's a long hallway, longer than it should be. My breathing sounds much too loud in my ears. I feel like an astronaut clambering through the sticky, gothic corridors of an alien spaceship.

Then everything is light.

It's a spa. All bright, white tiles, glass-walled saunas and beauty salons and open baths. No mirrors to be found, but still—a place of vanity. The footprints terminate before a showerhead; blood flows toward a drain. Someone has just taken a shower.

Not a soul anywhere.

I feel slightly light-headed as I look about, kneel down and begin scrubbing at footprints in a messy smearing of red. Is he still here? Has he retired to some master suite below? How am I going to—

A sudden hiss makes me jump. There's a glass booth in here. Amid the spa's clean-lined maze of glass walls, I hadn't noticed it. It stands in an alcove with some of its sections obscured, so it takes me a moment to comprehend there's a blurry form inside it. I glimpse a long, shredded back, muscular buttocks—a man. His skin is so white he's almost albino; he looks like an experimental subject awaiting some dreadful transformation. He holds his arms slightly away from his body, fingers spread. A nozzle moves longitudinally down a track, spraying a fine mist back and forth. *What?*

Then the nozzle whirs around the booth so it can spray the man's backside. When that jet of mist works its way down that pale skin, leaving it a buffed and beaming gold, it finally clicks.

It's a tanning booth.

This vampire's getting a *fucking spray-on tan.*

The spray gun shuts off and I hurriedly drop my eyes and scrub. My flesh has gone cold. My ears are blocked up with a deafening pressure. I repeat to myself over and over, *Stay calm.*

"What you think?" asks a lithe, Slavic-inflected voice above me. "Is good?"

The blood son of the Commodore stands over me, hands spread in invitation of appraisal. He is completely naked. Though not tall, he still looms, lean and slithery as a swimmer. His abundance of bare flesh is overwhelming—as is the startling presence of what's being thrust in my face.

Clearly intentional on his part.

"Well?" Amusement tinges his voice. "I have hard time getting tan. I have what you call skin condition." He all but titters. "Flesh. It look better with color, no?"

My neck turns pink, but I know I cannot falter here. This is a test.

I look him over—all of him—before forcing myself to meet his eyes. They are startlingly blue and clear, his blonde hair slicked back in a gleaming wave, cheekbones sharp as razors, his mouth a thing of cruel charm. He is a beautiful Satan.

"Is good," I assure him.

His mouth slowly curls in a smirk. He is both an insufferable frat boy who has won a joke and a little boy put at ease. He unhooks a fluffy white robe off a wall, studies me as he ties the sash around his waist. "You do not have fear," he says. It is not a question.

I respond with one, though, intent on the blood-smeared tiles again. "Should I?"

I feel his attention bend and focus on me, like light around a black hole. Then suddenly his hand cups my chin—I force myself not to recoil—and lifts it so his eyes can search mine. I can't hear anything for the drumming of my heart. Then, after a long moment, "My lifestyle," he breathes, and juts his chin toward the hall. "It not bother you?"

I edge my eyes to the side. In the club, one of the stews is puking onto the shiny black floor. Another grips the rim of her mop bucket, beaded in sweat and looking green around the gills.

I look up into his face again. Shake my head.

His eyes narrow. He is looking upon a new phenomenon. "And you are not curious what happen here?"

I take a breath; I have to remember to keep breathing or I'll lose myself here. "It's not my place to ask questions."

It's there and gone almost before I can see it—a flash of hot pleasure. Somewhere deep inside a voice reminds me, *He likes a woman who takes charge.*

It's very clear then what needs to happen next.

I drop my rag and stand, face lifted to his. We are inches apart. "But that doesn't mean I'm not curious."

He stills as he stares down at me, blue eyes gleaming with avid fascination. "Is so?"

The air thickens as if growing with an electric charge. As if we were both infused with the same aura of danger. And—

"Miss Harris!"

It's Madam Bartosh. Hands balled at her sides, eyes blazing, quivering with rage. She drags her gaze away from me and puts on a horrid smile. "I apologize. She is not cleared to be here. As she well knows." She shoots me a withering look. "I hope she hasn't been a disappointment—"

"On contrary," Radomir purrs and his lips seam back, for the first time, to show a mouthful of unending teeth. "Could be fun to see how much more *Miss Harris* can take."

There's a singing in my ears. A sudden light-headedness grips me. Nonetheless, I turn to Madam Bartosh. I give her a small, defiant grin of triumph. *Nice try*. And there, in the eerie brightness of that shadow vessel reeking of death, her birthmark throbs like a bruise as she glares at me, as if trying to puzzle out a riddle in need of squashing.

"Go change now," Radomir is saying. "We leave soon."

FIFTEEN

The burner phone, miraculously, is still in the luxury tender when I emerge onto the aft deck. I casually scoop it up and drop it into a skort pocket as I follow the deckhand leading me to the tender boat at the stern. He looks back at me once, frowning, but continues on.

I call Adrian when I get back to my cabin on the *Neck Romancer*.

There's no sign of Nicole anywhere. I change into short-shorts and a bikini top, my hands shaking with nerves, the burner phone pinned between ear and shoulder. I listen to it ring and ring, feeling my insides twist. What if he doesn't pick up? What if the *Lady Revenge* is out of range? What if—

"Hey you," his voice says into my ear, and I have to choke back a sob.

"Hey you," I whisper.

Tears are starting in my eyes. I guess I didn't know until now what heaven sounded like.

"I missed you," he says. "God, I missed you."

I put a hand over my eyes. If he keeps talking like that, I don't know what's going to happen.

"You okay?" he asks. His voice is low and tight with worry.

I nod, trying to get my breath back, and comb a hand through my hair. I have to change the subject. Now. "Mmhmm. I just—I need to give you an update."

"Okay." His voice is still worried, but more formal now. Professional. "You're on speakerphone. Ilsa's here."

"Hi, Arie. What's going on?"

I crack the cabin door and check the hallway, just in case. Shut the door again. It's not easy to keep the low-grade panic out of my voice. "I've spoken with Radomir."

There's a silence on the other end of the line. "Oh?"

"I—made an impression. I think he's going to take me out to see something soon. Possibly on another boat. I—I'd like you to follow. Just in case."

"Of course." There's a careful pause. "How—"

"I showed him I wasn't afraid of him," I fill in quickly. Guilt roses my cheeks, stopping me from adding, *After he showed me everything.*

But Adrian can guess all that just the same. "So what's your plan?" he asks unhappily.

I swallow. He's not going to like this.

"I'm going to pretend I want to be turned into one of them. Which should get me to Volok. He's the only one allowed to turn a woman, isn't he?"

Here it comes.

There's a long sigh, loud and staticky. "Yes," he admits. "But that doesn't mean anyone won't try to feed on you before then—"

"That won't happen," I say firmly.

"But how do you know—"

"I don't," I snap, and pinch the bridge of my nose. That came out harsher than expected. "I'm sorry. But I might have to do some things you won't like to pull this off."

I can feel his astonishment from here. And his anger, black and sullen. He must have his hands in his pockets. I can all but see his jaw muscles flashing.

The seconds stretch out, and finally the Shipwright answers for him.

"We understand, Arie. You should do what you think is best." There's a pause, and I know the Shipwright has given Adrian a glare. "We'll follow you. And if you ever feel like you're in danger, just call us and we'll surface. Okay?"

"Okay." I wait, my chest tight, and bite my lip. "I love you, Adrian," I whisper in a small, hopeful voice.

His voice, when it comes, is grudging yet tender. "I love you, too."

It's not enough for me. Not nearly enough.

But there are footsteps in the hallway. I gotta go.

"Bye," I whisper and end the call. I have to stare up at the ceiling to stop the tears from spilling down my face.

By the time I go abovedeck, the burner phone burning

a hole in the pocket of my denim shorts, we've docked. I don't know what port we're in, or even what country. Still in Croatia, by the looks of it. More palm trees, more houses roofed with terracotta tiles.

Madam Bartosh is waiting for me on the aft deck.

She turns to me with arms held at her sides. She's smirking, I don't know what for. Her face is crawling with hatred.

"He's waiting for you on the *Shadow*," she says in a tone of scornful pity, as if I have committed a crime beyond all hope of redemption.

Perhaps I have.

"Thank you," I reply.

The *Shadow* is docked beside the *Neck Romancer*, side-to. When I ascend her passerelle, Radomir is waiting in the shaded overhang of the main deck gangway, dressed in deck shoes, white chinos, a blue-striped poplin shirt with the sleeves rolled up to the elbows, a Rolex flashing on his wrist. He's not alone. Perhaps fifteen men are on the gangway with him, all in preppy yachting attire, black shades gleaming. My blood slows.

As I step past them for Radomir they turn and watch me, sunglasses reflecting all my bare skin. "Look at this little sucket," one of them drawls.

My flesh is crawling by the time I get to Radomir.

He stills when he sees me, eyes filling with pleasure. His white teeth grin. "Ah. Just in time."

I remember to smile back. I've let my hair down and have to drag flying black threads out of my eyes. "For what?"

Radomir nods at the dock. "The choosing."

I follow his gaze. A fleet of Mercedes has rolled up to the dock. Doors click open, and a horde of women in tight dresses slip out, hair flashing in the wind. They are all nipped, tucked and plumped. All gorgeous. I swallow down a growing dread and look over at Radomir—he is watching me with a shrewd expression. And I can feel it happening. I feel myself enter into new, thrillingly heightened territory.

There are jeers, whoops, laughter. The women line up on the dock and pout their pillowy lips or flash sunny smiles, hands on cocked hips, batting their lash extensions. The men on the *Shadow* begin to point and shout, going down the line. "No. No. You. No. You come aboard . . ." Eventually, they've all picked their companions. The ratio is three women to a man. It's all casual, brisk, cruel, shading into vulgarity. "Where they finding these?" they grouse. "Polack hags. Pfaw!" "But that one!" They guffaw and elbow each other. The women preen. They giggle and push their boobs together. The chosen saunter out of the line-up—radiant, contemptuous with privilege, their victory undercut by crude promises shared among the men. It all crowds against my ears in raucous cacophony, hammering me down to nothing. I have to grip the side rail to keep from falling. I have to bite the spongy tissue of my cheek to keep my scream of rage in check.

This is how. This is how you are elevated in this world. This is how they destroy you.

There's a sleek sportfish yacht waiting in the garage of the *Shadow*: the *Neck Romancer II*. It's long, towered, with hull side-vents for the bilge. I follow Radomir onboard, and once we're at sea she's launched out of a side-bay and lowered into the water, a deckhand at the helm. I stand on the rolling aft deck and stare out across the waves, my hair whipping behind me. We're in the midst of fifteen other sportfish yachts all heading out to open sea, all emblazoned with outrageously suggestive monikers on their transoms: *Bloodsucker*, *Fangdango*, *Vampussy*.

I've come across the frat boys of the vampire world.

But what are we doing out here?

I glance back inside the *Neck Romancer II*. Radomir has unfolded himself on a rear-facing lounge in the shuttered gloom of the salon, the cores of his eyes glowing out at me, his slicked-back hair curling at the ears like horns. Satan indeed.

I do not ask him why I don't see any of the fighting chairs, rod holders or livewells you normally see on a fishing boat. I fear the catch has already been caught.

Staring out at our frothing wake I whisper, "You better be following me, Adrian."

SIXTEEN

We sail for hours.

I wait at the stern at first, watching the other boats and avoiding joining Radomir. It's already turned into a booze cruise. Girls cavort on the aft decks and hoist vodka bottles the size of parking bollards, shrieking and laughing. Others sunbathe on foredeck lounge areas in skimpy bikinis, flipping back their hair and striking seductive poses for unseen male gazes. A prickling of unease creeps through me.

After a while, though, the threat of seasickness is too great. I have to go inside.

I needn't have worried—Radomir doesn't pay me much attention, seemingly put into a drowsy state by the daytime heat. He dozes on and off, stretched out on his side on the lounge, one arm folded under his head. That kind of carefree attitude must be nice—to never have to worry about a predator.

But I surprise myself. I prop myself up on one of the lounges, and before long my chin is nodding on my chest and I've drifted off, dreaming of submarine yachts cruising through the depths.

A shriek of jittery fright and pleasure startles me awake again.

I jolt upright, whipping my head over at Radomir—his eyes are faint slits of amusement in the dark, watching me. Chills bump up my skin.

I pad outside to see what's happening, heart in throat.

It's Sodom and Gomorrah at sea. All the yachts have been rounded up in a circle in the middle of the ocean to create a boat-formed pool. Inside that pool, it's pure Spring Break Cancun madness. Women in brightly-colored bikinis are everywhere: chugging vodka bottles, diving and cannonballing off yachts, soaking each other with super soakers, whacking each other with foam penises on inflatable floaties. Conspicuously, none of the men are to be seen. At least, not at first glance. Here and there I can make out male forms in the doorways of boats watching the events, teeth and eyes shining. Women make out or dance for their enjoyment to the beat of the music booming from the stereo systems, teasing them to come out. Some call from the water. One girl grinds on an inflatable flamingo to whoops and cheers. "*Fuck*, I'm horny!" she screams. "Is no one gonna take care of this for me?" The men only smile their sharp smiles. They flutter hundred-dollar bills off the mezzanine decks of the yachts into the water, sending women splashing and swimming after them. Dark laughter follows.

Uneasy relief drops through me. *It's okay. Nothing's wrong. Nothing is going to happen here.*

When I swallow and look over my shoulder at Radomir he's standing behind me, a dark shape in the gloom with a knowing smile on his face. He juts his chin, and I look.

The sun is going down.

A freezing cold seeps into my gut, turning my blood frigid.

The hard-partying girls carry on, oblivious. Bottle corks pop like gunshots and champagne sprays through the air, expensively drenching the mass of bikini-clad bodies on their flotilla of floaties. An orgy of excess and oblivion.

Meanwhile, the last flare of sun dips below the waves.

A cool blue twilight descends on that dome of sea.

And all around the circle, the vampires glide out onto the aft decks of their boats, mouths wide and dentate.

A cold hand folds its fingers over my shoulder, keeping me in place. "Good time to look away," Radomir breathes into my ear.

But I know that's not what is wanted here. That's not what he wants to see.

So I fight every survival instinct inside me and wait for it to happen.

The first scream comes a few boats down from me. A tall and stooped vampire in a preppy blazer has buried his face into the neck of a blonde in a sexy black one-piece swimsuit. The blonde's scream soon turns to a gurgle and she hangs limp in his long, taloned hands. Nobody notices. The screams of revelry, despite the fading light, are still too rampant, too similar. It's the second victim that gets their attention. A young girl in a frilly hot pink bikini shrieks on the skylounge of the *Fangdango* before a fanged mouth finds her. She's still spasming when the vampire rips his head back in a ferocious debriding of her throat and exhales, speckling the air with blood in a deep sigh of release, and pitches her body disdainfully off the deck. It makes a hollow *thump* as it strikes the side of the boat and pinwheels into the water. By the time the sound of the splash has faded and the freckled impact of the girl's head on the fiberglass has begun to run, the orgy in the boat-pool has gone dead quiet. Women drift on ridiculously cheerful unicorn and watermelon and donut floaties, mouths open and faces drained of all color. A ripple of murmurs sweeps through them, a hushed smattering of "Did you see that?" and "What *was* that?" and "Oh my God."

Then another girl screams as she's seized, and all hell breaks loose.

The hysteria is contagious. My body turns to pins and needles as women shriek and yell and paddle furiously for their boats, but what they're fleeing from is happening everywhere. The girls on the yachts go first. Red blood splashes on white fiberglass, white leather lounges. It drips out of bilge vents, leaks from high decks down gleaming hulls. Bodies tumble from above, are tossed over pushpits into the pool. The confused and unwary are snatched out of the water and soon jolly-looking floaties are floating masterless in the plashing crush of bodies, splattered red. Others have pale and drained bodies draped over them, heads dunked and hair trailing in the water in gloomy swirls. It doesn't take long for the water in the center to churn dark with blood. Women are crying now, praying to their god or saying they want their mommy. Tears sting my nostrils. A hopeless, despairing rage congests my head, turning my marrow to fire. But I cannot look away, I cannot turn from this. Because Radomir is watching me.

That dark cloud settling deep into the sea has drawn other lovers of blood. The sinister dorsal fin appears like a mirage, like an absurd slap of unfairness, knifing through the water before one of those lifeless bodies jerks and the water blooms with more blood as a chunk of meat is wrenched free. This, of course, only draws others. Soon it's a feeding frenzy, a fever dream of lashing and rolling bodies, the sharks snapping at each other and tugging at the woman's corpse with pieces of meat spilling white from their forever-swallowing jaws. Girls kick and lunge to get away, screaming hysterically. "Ohmygod. *Oh my fucking God!*" The sharks leave them alone for the moment, but they're excited and that doesn't last for long. A woman paddles straight for me, screaming, hands reaching for me. She looks no older than myself. She might have been my neighbor back home. "Help me!" she shrieks, nearly incomprehensible in her terror. "*Help me oh God help me!*" My heart drops out of my chest. I almost move—I *have* to move—then stiffen, remembering Radomir.

A dangerous furrow has appeared between his brows. I can't. It'd be over. I'd have failed his test.

And wouldn't I be next?

So I hold myself in place and think, *I am not here. I cannot see this. I cannot hear it.*

This is how you manage fear. This is how you survive.

Closer, closer, Radomir watches me with an almost perverted pleasure, as if sensing my conflict. And I can feel it—the tension. His look all but oozes it. I can't tell if he wants to fuck me, or eat me.

Perhaps for him they go together.

The woman's hands slap at the deck at my feet, groping for my ankle. And I do it. I take a quivering step back.

Yes. That's all right.

Forgiveness—self-forgiveness—can come later. Surely there are such miracles.

Radomir, inches from me, smirks in approval.

And it happens. The woman is yanked back, and for a moment I see the roll of a strange, opaque eye, rubbery lips pulled back from rows of inward slanting teeth, and think, *I've seen that look before*. The noise of ripping flesh is unforgettable. The woman goes under in a fount of gore, the sudden violence of it shocking. It's as if those pyramid-shaped teeth have chomped into my own flesh.

The nausea pushes sweat out of me all over my body. I have to blink; my eyes are burning. I somehow remain standing and tell myself, *She would have died anyway. There's nothing you could have done.*

The screams in general rise now, become witless sounds of nerve-splintering terror. Where to go? Stay in the water and be eaten, or flee to the boats and be eaten? The watching vampires are amused by the conundrum. They chuckle and hail their brothers of the sea with lofted glasses. This is their joy.

I find, with gradual awareness, that my hand is clutching the burner phone through my shorts, almost clawed in rage. The realization dizzying: I could put a stop to all of it. I could summon up the Shipwright's submarine yacht waiting beneath the waves and save them all. I could have euphoric vengeance.

But Volok. But Adrian.

All that would be ruined.

And would it change anything, in the long run? Wouldn't Volok keep going on as he has? Wouldn't this cycle of predation continue?

And wouldn't Radomir kill me before the call even went through?

My hand, very slowly, drops away from my shorts. I pry open my warring teeth. I must keep playing this part.

"What are you?" I manage to whisper to Radomir beside me.

He shrugs, a dark mischief in his eyes. "Can guess, no?"

I watch the other vampires feed, some of them coupled to their dying victims. They whisper into their ears like devoted suitors.

I force my eyes to clear, my voice to steady. "What do you get out of it?"

Radomir makes a small moue of his mouth. "Life. Youth eternal."

I nod. That would be enough for most, after all.

Radomir leans and plucks a bobbing arm out of the water, inspects it like, *Hmm, why not?* and bites into it.

I keep my eyes ahead as I listen to him suckle the last ounces of hemoglobin out of that pale limb, trying not to dwell on the fact that it belonged to the woman I chose not to save.

There's a splash—Radomir has discarded his snack and turned to me. Waiting.

I understand, distantly, that I am somehow not paralyzed with fear for my physical safety. Somehow, inside the careening blur of this nightmare, I know that harm—bodily harm—is no longer what I have to worry about. That is not what's at hazard here.

I turn to him with lifted chin. His lips are slimed with blood. Perfect.

Now to sell him on my role.

I do it before I can stop myself. I swipe one finger across his bottom lip—he stills all over—and placing it in my mouth I suck on it with slow, delicious carnality.

He watches me with huge, transfixed eyes.

Yes. I know what he wants. Not submissiveness, but a responding savageness, to be challenged but not outmatched. Just like any other man, then.

The finger exits my pillowed lips with a loud *plop*. "So," I trill, and arch a brow. "How can I become like you?"

With the red waters eddying against our boat and the shrieks of the dying still in our ears, Radomir studies me and smiles.

SEVENTEEN

Nicole finds me in our cabin on the *Neck Romancer* furiously brushing my teeth.

"Hey," she chirps, leaning in the doorway. "Thanks again for what you did."

I gargle mouthwash and spit, rinse my mouth and spit again.

"For real," she continues, undeterred. "You're the best." The best.

"Madam Bartosh punished me with extra work. But I can take it." She smirks. She's all but shining with a new and genuine joviality.

I place my hands on the edges of the sink and shut my eyes, trying to calm the shivers overtaking my body.

Nicole sniffs. "Hey, did you . . . vomit in here?"

"I gotta take a shower," I blurt.

"Oh. Okay." Nicole dislodges herself from the doorframe, concealing a faint hurt. "Sure thing."

When I clatter the shower door shut and fumble the spray of water on, I immediately slide down into a heap by the drain and sob into my hand, waiting for a miracle.

After my shower, I check to see that I'm alone—no Nicole. Easing down on my bunk, I take out my phone and stare at it, feeling spent. Empty.

I'm ready to call Adrian.

He picks up on the first ring. "Thank fucking Christ," he swears when he hears my voice. "We saw the bodies sinking past—the blood—the sharks—"

I shut my eyes.

"I thought—I thought you were—"

"I'm okay."

"I don't know if I could've waited another hour, another minute, of not knowing—" There's a rough, steadying breath cut short, as if hands just scrubbed hard across a face. Then Ilsa's voice comes on the line.

"What happened?"

I shut my eyes against a flash of water frothing red. "I don't wanna talk about it."

Trembling silence.

"Did Radomir touch you—" Adrian begins.

"Adrian—"

"Because if he did—"

"He didn't."

"I swear to fucking—"

"I'm getting transferred to Volok's boat."

It takes a moment for Adrian to gather words. "You are."

I put my face in my hand. "I . . . proved myself to him. He said I'll get transferred to Volok's boat, and that he'll try to forward my case. But he can't promise anything."

I can feel Adrian and Ilsa sharing a look. "When is this happening?" she says.

"Today," I reply. "Now. So you'll have to be ready. I don't know where we're going."

"We'll be ready," Ilsa promises.

"Okay."

The following silence feels more exposed and vulnerable than it has any right to be.

Adrian is the one who breaks it. "Aurora," he says, very gentle. "Are you okay?"

The tenderness in his voice makes my face screw up. "I don't know," I confess, and have to clear my throat. I sit up straight. "Someone's coming, I gotta go. Love you." I let the phone slip out of my hands and grip my hair, taking in big, wavering breaths.

It takes us three days to make the passage to Volok's anchorage.

I don't have time to track our route; Madam Bartosh keeps us too busy to see more than glimpses out of portholes. Now and then I hear exotic names unrolled like a magic carpet: Albania, Carpathian Sea, Karpathos. It's enough to get the sense of countries changing, time blurring, the *Neck Romancer* journeying back to an older world.

I get no chance to call Adrian again.

Maybe it's just as well. Because as the shock of that booze cruise (*blood cruise*) wears off, I feel a kindling ember, a responding change that is as yet unwilling to reveal itself, and which leaves me hushed and breathless, glistening in a sheen of strangeness.

I feel righteous anticipation.

On the third night we're summoned onto the aft deck with its al fresco dining area. As we file out of the sliding glass door, I find we've anchored at sea. A fog is up—the water is a flat black mirror wrapped in hurrying silk, the *Shadow* a menacing shape in the gloom. Far above the wisps of gray, stars ride in the dark.

Madam Bartosh waits at prim attention at the end rail, looking unduly pleased with herself. A prickling of foreboding steals into my bones.

Some act of spite is in the offing.

We line up in a neat row in our skorts and evening shoes, as demure and dutiful as choir girls. Madam Bartosh steps forward and looks us over with pursed lips. She is shrewd and theatrical with her presentation of news. "As I'm sure you've all guessed, we are transferring to Volok's boat tonight."

Whispers and worried looks amongst the stews. Madam Bartosh endures it as if she were a put-upon saint.

"As much as we must be on our toes on this ship," she continues in a soft voice that quiets all, "I think we all know Volok's expectations are of another breed." She draws herself up, an old witch readying her poison. "Therefore, only those stews who have proven themselves to be exceptional this past season will come with us."

The stews eye each other, bewildered. My foreboding sinks deeper.

Madam Bartosh begins at the end of the line. "You." She nods at a blonde. "You." She hesitates before Nicole, eyes glittering—then nods. "You."

She stops before me.

Our eyes meet. A corner of her mouth curls.

And she lifts her brows, looking over the stews. "That's all." She presses a button and the articulated aft stairs deploy over the water like unfurling wings. "Come along."

I feel as if I've been gut-shot. I share a shocked look with Nicole. This must be a mistake.

And as a smug Madam Bartosh descends with the stews to the limo tender idling at the bottom of the stairs—

Radomir glides out of the shadows in a red leather jacket, a small smile on his lips. He offers me a pale, upturned hand. "Miss Harris."

Heads whip. Madam Bartosh freezes on the stairs, the blood draining from her face as she looks up at us. She gathers herself with visible effort. "Unfortunately, Miss Harris will not be joining us—"

"Then you make mistake," Radomir purrs. "And you know how I feel about mistakes."

Madam Bartosh swallows hard. If I didn't know any better, I'd say she was trembling.

But I don't have time to think about that. Radomir leads me forward, and now we are gliding down those floating red-carpet stairs as if we are the couple of honor at a ball. All the stews stare, open-mouthed. A flush creeps up my neck, turning my ears pink. I am pervaded with a mystifying embarrassment.

And as we pass Madam Bartosh, Radomir lifts a hand and pats her blotchy, birthmarked cheek. "Is okay, I forgive you."

The look on Madam Bartosh's face, as I step onto the limo tender, is terrifying. "Thank you," she breathes with the air of an assassin, and rolls her eyes up at me as she bows her head. The impact of the look is almost physical, its meaning clear:

I'm coming for you.

My scalp prickles. I feel myself hovering over this moment. I grope past sets of bare knees and find a spot in the stern, feeling Madam Bartosh's gaze on the back of my neck like a sunburn, promising vengeance.

Something to be dealt with later.

Now, I have to focus. Things are moving quickly. Once Madam Bartosh's matronly mass is settled, there's the rising whine of twin diesel engines and the tender glides away, shredding through the ghost-silk of the fog and dragging wispy tails in its wake. We are voyaging across psychic seas. We are gliding through dense vapor which swallows the side-lights of the boat. The red and green glows are smoking.

When I look back, we have left the *Neck Romancer* and the *Shadow* behind.

The pilot is not worried—he seems utterly confident in where he is going, his hands moving smoothly across the controls of the helm with its pebbled cherry leather. The stews, on the other hand, huddle in their stern seats not looking at each other. Not looking at anything. They have assumed the grave and blank faces of spirits.

Radomir, standing beside the pilot, looks back at me and grins.

When the bank of fog clears, I see the ship.

It's enormous, nearly three hundred meters in length, its carbon masts raking the stars—a sail-assisted motor yacht. I feel my jaw drop in awe. It (I cannot call it a *she*, like any other boat) is as black and gleaming as a hearse, uncanny green lights emanating in the water about it like ectoplasm. It isn't natural. It looks like a phantom ship out of some seafaring legend, a remnant of dark antiquity dreaming away in a substratum of mist. As we round it, the roiling white fog boils away from the nameplate on the transom, backlit, glowing, queerly green: KEEP.

For isn't that what it is? Not a floating coffin, but a floating castle. Dark, and forbidding, and in its own way as fantastical and full of horrors as some old decrepit fortress in Transylvania. I'm suddenly filled with the certainty that I was always going to end up on this boat, sooner or later. That it's been waiting for me all my life.

Nicole's hand creeps into mine and grips tight. I look up at Radomir, and even on his imperishable face there is a look of faint apprehension.

Cold water floods my veins. I lift my eyes to that gleaming black hull. Those soaring masts. Those lights.

This is it. I'm finally here. I've found him.

I've found the Commodore.

EIGHTEEN

We disembark onto the swim deck by the huge light-up nameplate. I half-expect a footman with a lantern, some kind of gypsy servant in sheepskin boots and a strange conical hat. Or perhaps some mysterious figure in a nightgown that flows behind like a fan of blood. But no horror movie clichés present themselves. There is no one waiting for us. Radomir leads the way up one of the huge sweeping staircases flanking the transom, Madam Bartosh a step behind. When I look back to see the *Neck Romancer*'s limo tender droning away, I feel a small pang of loss, a brief flurry of panic: I am stranded here. I am on my own, and I don't even know if the *Lady Revenge* was able to follow.

When I catch up to the others on the main deck, my skin turns cold.

The *Keep* is as alien and barren as a tomb. There are no flower arrangements, no tablescapes, no sunscreen baskets, nothing at all that gives a superyacht its sense of life. Pale teak stretches away like a decking of bone. Green uplights glow at our feet. The boom of the mizzen mast looms overhead like a god-like finger. The only sound is from the pool stretching before us. Ripples spread, water purls and mists. I lift my eyes and gape. A waterfall is flowing into the pool from the aft deck above, sheeting down in an elegant veil that is lent a phantasmic quality by the boat's neon lighting.

A shadow glides behind that blur of water. Someone is coming.

The little hairs on my arms stand on end.

The form flows down the edge of the pool toward us, tall and gaunt and stooped in an obsequious bow. It is a man. His hands, in short white gloves, look as tender as a kitten's paws. The tails of his archaic black coat flap behind him. Beneath that coat he wears a white silk shirt and gray vest, a patterned batwing-shaped bowtie. Before I can breathe he has drawn up before us. He is lifting his head with its few strands of black hair combed back over a large, liver-spotted skull. He is parting his lips to show a mouthful of sharp little brown teeth in a warm and inscrutable smile.

I take a step back.

"Welcome aboard the *Keep*," the man simpers in a dry British accent, spreading his white-gloved hands like a carnival barker. "The master the Commodore bade me take all care of you."

The old-fashioned words send a shiver down my spine.

A butler at sea, I think. *How interesting.*

The butler turns his gracious and frightening smile on Radomir. His tone is mannerly and faintly contemptuous. "Ah, the blood son returns!"

Radomir's eyes are as cold and distant as glaciers. "Fesperman."

No love lost between these two.

The man Fesperman turns away again with a slight smirk. His eyes fall on me and narrow—a wrinkle has appeared in his smoothly-run affairs. "And who is this young lady?"

The air thins.

Fesperman turns and says in a hard, cheerful voice, "My dear Madam Bartosh! We did not forget that all crew coming aboard must be vetted by me first, did we? I know you could not be as careless as that!"

Madam Bartosh seems to wilt under that gaze. She darts a look at Radomir and opens her mouth, but Radomir interrupts. "Decision was mine."

Fesperman tilts his head, brows raised. "Oh?"

Radomir glances at me, then steps forward and whispers in Fesperman's ear. Madam Bartosh's brows draw in. The stews throw me curious looks.

Then Fesperman's eyes widen. Radomir, it would seem, has told him my cover story.

The cadaverous butler looks at me now with new and avid fascination. "Indeed?" he muses. He glides forward—my back stiffens—and clasping his gloved hands behind him he peers at me with eyes so dark they look black. "What is your name, my dear?"

The words are so soft, so compelling, I almost give my real name. "Harris," I manage at last. "Jamie Harris."

"Harris," he breathes as if tasting the word on his tongue.

I have to speak. I feel an uncontrollable urge to end this scrutiny. "A pleasure, Mr. Fesperman."

The little brown teeth make another appearance. "Just Fesperman will do. I am but a humble servant of the Commodore." He straightens, and I feel as if an iron band around my chest has been loosened. "Come. The Commodore does not linger long anywhere."

He marches away in black balmorals buffed to a mirrorlike shine, and I follow in a daze along with everyone else. I feel stares on me, and Nicole is trying to catch my gaze, but I'm too busy catching up to the implications of these latest developments. Of this new, unforeseen obstacle. And there's more to consider. As we head for tall double doors behind the waterfall I see, for the first time, a scattering of silhouettes lurking on the deck of the *Keep*. My skin goes rough and hard with gooseflesh. They're security guards. Solidly built men all in black with assault rifles held across their chests, a pledge to imminent violence. As we pass, one of them looks at me and says some sort of code into his two-way radio clipped to his chest harness. A cold sweat breaks out on my brow.

The Commodore increased security after finding out Adrian was going after him.

And on top of that, not only do I have a chief stewardess out for my blood, but a suspicious butler already sniffing around me.

Fan-fucking-tastic.

The waterfall roars. The double doors loom. And as Radomir looks back to flash a reassuring grin at me, I feel a low hum through my feet. I look up—the gargantuan carbonfiber masts are *rotating*. There's a hydraulic whir and they still. Then miles of ethereal canvas widen across the sky. Mandrels inside U-shaped booms are dragging out the fully battened sails in eerie automation. They fill the night like shrouds, like the glowing sheets of some storm-driven ghost ship. The wind fills them, and I feel the *Keep* almost imperceptibly shudder and lurch forward.

The voyage has begun.

NINETEEN

Inside the double doors soars a lofty atrium I immediately know is the heart of the *Keep*. It's cold, all black onyx marble with white veining, black tufted velvet barrel chairs, fixtures in frosted crystal globes. It feels like a floating necropolis, its dark opulence overwhelming. The stews do not bat an eye—they've seen it all before. They are well-acquainted with what's in store for them. They shuffle along like shackled slaves, mute with terror. I feel that panic rise in my chest again. I try to meet Nicole's eye, but she won't look at me. She hides behind her bob of Senegalese twists, her bottom lip trembling. Even Madam Bartosh's pushy superiority seems diminished here.

It repeats in my head, over and over, like a crazed chant: *I am on Volok's boat. I am on Volok's boat.*

Fesperman, however, is full of smug anticipation. He strides under a showstopper chandelier toward two security guards flanking a bulky shaft running through the center of the atrium. An elevator. It's glass-fronted, its green interior lighting making it glow from within like some unholy tabernacle. Surely the only access to what's below.

I know what's down there.

I'm shaking when Fesperman spins on his heel and extends a white-gloved hand in courtly welcome. "The master waits."

He is speaking to Radomir. But Radomir does not answer, does not move. Only stares at that glowing elevator as if it were the rising sun.

"Come now!" Fesperman cries. His mouth has thinned into a mean little smile. "Are you not excited to see your father? I am sure he is excited to see you." His voice turns sly as he takes in Radomir's leather jacket and spray-on tan. "What father would not be proud to have you as a son?"

Radomir's head whips. His eyes blaze. His hands curve into claws at his sides. Madam Bartosh averts her gaze, while the stews stare at their feet. But I do not look away. Fear is not my response.

That is not what I feel for Radomir in this moment.

He turns to me now. With his tan, and the sudden vulnerability in his face, I can almost believe he is like any other man.

"We will talk soon," he promises.

I nod and offer a smile. It's the first true smile I've given him.

It makes his eyes pulse like coals.

He turns and strides away, leaving me shaken and feeling as if a line has been crossed, a transgression committed. But I cannot let it distract me. I shift to my right to watch him go. A security guard is speaking into his two-way radio. Radomir is pressing a thumb to a glowing red square on the stainless-steel detailing of the elevator. The square turns green, and the glass doors slide open—

And Fesperman blocks my line of sight, a hard, knowing look in his eyes.

I look right back at him, willing all the guilt out of my expression.

After a small eternity, his mouth swells in a fat, amused smile.

"It is late." He lifts his face. "I trust you can escort these ladies to their quarters."

Madam Bartosh, grateful for the opportunity to assert herself, jerks her head in a nod. "Of course." She turns, imperious. "Ladies."

But Fesperman is not done. He tugs at his bowtie, his tone mild. "Oh, and Madam Bartosh?"

The chief stewardess stiffens. "Yes?"

"I will be checking in on Miss Harris from time to time. To ensure she is integrating smoothly into the team. We cannot have a weak link compromising the service aboard the *Keep*, now can we?"

I can feel my cheeks heating up. Madam Bartosh darts a look at me and swallows a retort. It has been made clear—very clear—who runs service aboard this boat. "Of course," she agrees in a voice like cooling iron.

When she leads us deeper into the *Keep*, Fesperman stares after us with his long and harrowed face wearing that mask of a smile. Watching me.

"What was *that* about?" Nicole demands in our dim quarters. "What did Radomir whisper to Fesperman? Why are you *really* here?"

I hesitate, studying the shadowy faces of the stewardesses before me. As much as I want to trust them, I can't. Nor can I afford to have them hating me.

Lies it is, then.

"I don't know," I say, throwing up my hands. "Radomir—he seems to have taken a liking to me—"

Someone snorts. "In this industry, that ain't a good thing, honey."

My flesh prickles with a chill. But I have to keep performing, so I shrug a shoulder in feigned ignorance. "What does that mean?"

Dark looks. "You sure you don't know?" one of the stews scoffs, crossing her arms. "After what you've seen?"

I gulp. "Maybe I do."

Nicole sighs and shares a look with her crewmates, steps forward and lays a hand on my shoulder. "We'll do what we can to look out for you. Just—stay the hell away from Radomir, okay?"

I nod, putting on an uncertain, grateful smile. "Thank you."

When I lie awake in my bunk later, holding the burner phone to my chest, I take stock of things. I've already discovered how to get down to the Commodore's lair, but it's guarded and locked behind a fingerprint sensor. Which means I can't get in there without Radomir. Which means I'll have to take out both Radomir and Volok at the same time.

Yeah. Great. Totally doable.

A heavy regret and self-recrimination begin to set in. What am I doing? I am out of my depth. These things are ancient, and eternal, and have the means to do anything they want in this world. Why did I think I could possibly pull this off?

Because they're too arrogant to think a woman could ever do it.

I hold the burner phone to my ear and mouth the words into it: *I miss you.*

It takes me a long time to fall asleep. When I do, my dreams are a feverish blur of images: a pale fiend's face spotlit as in an opera, a speargun with its barbed tip dripping blood, Radomir kneeling between two bare, spread legs.

This last image is so vivid and sickeningly wrong—Radomir's terrible face glowing with pleasure as it lowers between those trembling thighs—that I want to scream.

And then I am back in the cave again. Back on Sanguisuga, in that cave filled with the reedy murmurings of bats. Its subterranean lake gleams, and Adrian stands chained to a rock on a small island at its center. He turns to me. "You'll always be my Northern Light," he says, and the morning sun streams through a hole in the cavern ceiling and strikes his face.

I scream. I'm wading into the lake, trying to get to him, to free him, but the water is as thick and grasping as tar. High up in the darkness the bats are peeping shrilly and Radomir, on the far shore, is laughing his dark little laugh. And then Adrian's head has caught fire and I trip and fall, plunging into the water . . .

. . . and right back into my bunk bed on the *Keep*.

My stomach lurches with vertigo and I grip the mattress, eyes shut and damp with sweat, and wait for the impossible realness of the dream to recede. *Jesus.* Already this boat is getting to me, working its way into the deepest recesses of my subconscious.

There's a faint peep above me.

I go rigid, my flesh creeping. No. It can't be. But I can hear it—the gentle rustling of furred bodies, leathery wings. And when I inhale deeply, there's that rank animal smell, hot and pestilent. Have I not left the cave?

A dream. It's still only a dream.

I open my eyes.

My body presses itself back down into the mattress. I am not in the cave. I am on my top bunk in the crew quarters, and a mere three feet above me the ceiling is carpeted thickly in a writhing mass of bats. They hiss and dangle and clamber over each other, wrapping themselves up in their wings in sinister elegance. And among them, not noticed at first amid all this jostling diabolic fruit, there's a bigger one. A much bigger one. As long as a grown man, adhering lengthwise to the ceiling by some cunning. Its wings also wrap around itself like some strange entombed being, fine fingerbones hooked like claws. It opens its bright, rabies-red eyes in its wrinkled pug face, eyes that glitter like drops of blood, and I see that it's my own face.

My mouth yawns down to unleash a scream, to unleash all the crawling horror inside me, and the bats take flight in a frantic whirling of bodies, fluttering into me in a rush of felty, smothering impacts, leaving me frozen and staring helplessly at my unholy double with its bare lips crimped in a hideous smile and when I truly wake in my bunk bed on the *Keep*, panting and sobbing and overcome with a furious denial and unclean shame, I swear I can hear that scream echoing in chilling intensity somewhere in the night above.

TWENTY

I don't sleep again that night; every time I close my eyes, I see that vespertilian form smiling down at me. In the gray light before dawn, I give up and slip out of bed, dress in silence and tiptoe abovedeck. The air is cool, the fiberglass of the *Keep* beaded in sparkling dewdrops. Far off beyond the mist coiling off the Carpathian Sea, the austere crags of Greek islands shift in and out of sight.

I take my time searching the *Keep* for security blind spots. The guards seem to be everywhere, strolling the decks with submachine guns casually pointed down. They look me over as I pass, more interested in the hemline of my skort than anything else. They're on the top deck, the bow, the stern. And they're crawling everywhere inside. Fortunately, there seem to be no security cameras onboard; it would appear Volok is still too arrogant for that. His kind, after all, won't show up on them. And why worry about mortals?

One advantage to me, then.

I resort to the only spot I think could be safe: under the aft deck waterfall. With any luck, the sound will mask any conversation.

"Hey."

"Hey." Adrian's voice on the phone is nervy, wired. I can only imagine what the worry is doing to him. "It's just me."

"God, it's terrible being without you," I whisper, feeling an unexpected roil of heartache and guilt. "I dreamt about you last night . . ."

"You did?" He sounds concerned. "What did you dream?"

I shift uncomfortably, thinking of Radomir's face lowering between those legs, and change the subject. "You follow me okay?"

He takes in a long, shivery breath. He must be nodding. "We're a mile behind you. Good thing Volok's boat doesn't have sonar."

I glance about. "Yeah, well, don't expect me to be tucking you in every night over the phone." There's a guard down the gangway. He paces toward me, and I feel my hand grip hard into the phone—but he turns and begins pacing the other way. I let out a whoosh of air. "I gotta be careful—there's security everywhere here. Guess you got Volok spooked."

Adrian blows out a breath. "Shit." Then I hear it. It creeps into his voice like a low radio frequency, wavering and unmistakable: fear. "You haven't . . . *seen him*, have y—"

"No. I found out where he is on the boat, though."

His voice hollows. "Yeah?"

"There's an elevator that takes you down into the hold. I think it's the only way to get to his suite. And it has to be accessed by a fingerprint sensor. So, I'll have to be escorted down."

"It just gets better and better," Adrian grumbles.

I can't help but grin at his grouchy protectiveness. "Plus, Volok has this creepy as fuck butler skulking around."

"Fesperman." Adrian's voice is grim. "So that sniveling fuck is still working for him, then."

I'd chuckle if my skin wasn't crawling just thinking about him. I glance around again, expecting him to be smiling at my elbow. "Is he . . .?"

"One of them?" Adrian snorts. "Oh, yeah."

"He seems the proper servile type, so I'll have to assume he'll be down there when I'm presented to Volok."

"Fucking viper in a bowtie," Adrian spits. He's on a roll.

When he's calmed down, his tone turns tentative. "What's your plan, then? If you won't be alone with Volok, how are you going to take him out?"

I say the two words carefully: "With help."

I can all but hear Adrian's eyebrows enter the stratosphere.

Another glance down the gangway before I stand under the hiss of the waterfall to whisper it. "I'm going to turn Radomir against him."

There's a long silence on the line. "I don't know if that's a good idea."

"Why not?"

"It's . . . risky."

I snort a humorless laugh. "Really? And which part of this whole thing *isn't*, exactly?" I claw a hand through my hair and shut my eyes, waiting for my exasperation to subside. "Why don't you want me to? What's the history between you two, anyway?"

Ruefulness tinges Adrian's reply. "I think you know. Back in the day, we were blood brothers. The two favored blood sons of the Commodore. Our relationship was . . . complicated. Though there was love there, for a time, we were encouraged to compete for our blood father's love. I had no interest in that. I hated what I was, tried not to engage in Volok's manipulations. Maybe it was this disinterest, the challenge of getting my love, that made me Volok's favorite. I was the prince of the fleet. They even called me the Vice Commodore."

Cold seeps into my bones.

"Radomir never forgave me for that." Adrian grunts a bitter laugh. "Now, his hate for Volok can't be untangled from his love for him. You can't trust a man who doesn't know himself. And"—he breaks off here, and this seems hard—"it'd require you to get closer to him."

So that's where all this was coming from.

I push away an unpleasant twinge of guilt and say, "I don't see any other options at the moment."

A sigh. He'd be pinching the bridge of his nose now, those gorgeous blue eyes shut.

I say it as gently as I can. "Any tips for me?"

He takes so long to answer, I begin to think the line has been disconnected. "Open up about how you were abused. That will . . . resonate with him."

A chill passes over my skin. "How do you mean?"

"You'll see." I can tell he's being very careful with how he phrases what's next. "Just . . . promise to not forget who you are, okay?"

The line goes dead before he has to hear whether or not I can.

TWENTY-ONE

I get my chance later that morning.

It's certainly not out of any generosity of spirit on Madam Bartosh's part. She gathers the stews in the cramped crew mess and looks us over with clinical precision. "As you may have heard," she clips, and there's a faint smirk here, "a guest left us last night. We must turn over her suite." She sours as she glances at me. "If I had my way, you'd tackle the mold in the head."

My stomach clenches. Madam Bartosh draws out the pause.

"However, Radomir wants you serving drinks in the beach club today." Her lips thin. "He asked for you by name."

A hum among the stews. Clearly, Madam Bartosh chose to say this in front of them to make them resent me. But I don't care. Nicole flies me a worried look, and I can't return it—a flush of anticipation is tingling across the surface of my skin.

I get there before Radomir and gape. The beach club, like the rest of the *Keep*, is stunning. It's walled with what appears to be rippling volcanic rock inlaid with slits of mood lighting, its bar looking like it's plated with superheated black metal—it glows with jagged molten slashes. And with the transom door open and the tender garage situated athwartships, the club's teak decking flows unimpeded out onto an aft deck large enough to accommodate massage tables and chaise lounges, its view the pristine white beaches of Greece.

A shadow falls on the teak before me. Tall, stooped, with pointed coattails.

The hairs on the back of my neck prick.

"I hear you will be serving drinks today," Fesperman's mellifluous voice purrs.

I turn to meet him. He looms on the stairs behind me, impeccable in his butler's livery, his spotless white gloves. They don't look innocent, those gloves. They're the gloves of a magician, a con artist. They're the hands of a murderer.

"Yes," I say, dry-mouthed.

He descends the stairs to survey me. Unhurried, comported, imbued with enigmatic purpose. I've been wondering, ever since I met this exquisitely vowelled ghoul, what the buttling duties are for vampires. But I have a feeling I'll be finding out soon enough.

Fesperman's mouth swells to nail the butler smile—friendly, hospitable, and completely inscrutable—and he glides past me for the bar. "You should know Radomir likes a good Bloody Mary," he warns over his shoulder, and one of those gloved hands racks open a backbar cooler to reveal, resting on cubes of ice, a fat bag of blood. "Heavy on the Mary."

I stand there, fighting down a hot wave of fear.

Fesperman watches me with glittering eyes. He is close. Very close. I could swear his nostrils flare as if taking my scent. He cocks his head in a curious, doglike movement, his lips curling at the corners in amusement. "Do you think your mixology skills are up to the task?"

I force myself to meet his gaze, stifling an urge to step away from him. "I should think so."

Those eyes: glittering. "Excellent." He shuts the cooler, hiding once more that sack of blood. "And how about your other skills? Any weaknesses I should know about?" He ticks them off. "Russian table service? Table setting?" He lofts a brow in a slow smile. "Trustworthiness?"

Black panic rolls through me. Does he know? Can he really know? What will I do if—

"Father's lapdog bothering you?"

I whirl. Radomir is strolling into the beach club in nothing but a pair of swim trunks, all smiles and glowing spray-tanned skin, the spitting image of a billionaire on vacation. But his voice is hard with dislike as he eyeballs Fesperman.

"No, I wouldn't say that," I reply airily, and turn back to Fesperman with a frosty smile. "He was just informing me of his views on women."

Radomir throws his head back and lets out a bark of savage delight, jerking a thumb at me. "Big balls for stewardess, no?"

Fesperman does not answer. He is still staring at me, his smile diminishing only by the faintest of degrees. It chills me to the bone.

But Radomir puts an end to this. He drops his joviality like a distasteful charade and jerks his head. "Fuck off, Fesperman."

Fesperman's eyes hood, but that butler smile remains in place. He inclines his head in a sleek bow. "Of course, Master Radomir." And with one last glance at me, he lopes away.

I watch him go. "And I thought you two were getting along so well."

Radomir snorts. "Fesperman? He is mouthpiece for Father. Because of this, he has much scorn for me." A polished sullenness enters his face and he tilts his head back, bottom lip folding up, unable to stop himself. "And why?" he breathes, placing his hands on the bartop, and shrugs his muscular shoulders. "I am asset. Volok busy with many things, so he use me as face of yachting business. It is lot of pressure. I found yacht club, shipyard, crew agency. I give them stupid names. I sit in board meetings. I strike deals. I make oodles of money." The edge of his hand chops on the bartop, accentuating his point. "And does this earn me gratitude? Respect?" His voice wavers. "Love?" He slides a hand down his face, wiping away this hurt, and my heart thuds with sympathy as I do the last thing I expect from myself—I reach out and touch his forearm.

His eyes fly at me, down at my hand as my thumb rubs the fine blonde hairs there. He swallows. My mind whirls, knowing this is it, this is my opportunity to say something. To further my agenda. I keep my voice as cool and casual as I can. "One could almost mistake you for the Commodore."

The skin tightens around Radomir's eyes. His curious, calculating look makes my pulse thump wildly at my temples. Does he know what I'm getting at? Has he considered this in dark moments? Has he felt the allure of the usurper?

Does he see an ally in me?

Then Radomir gently breaks the contact by crossing his arms and leaning on the bartop, the bulk of his biceps flashing. Back to the old, rakish Radomir. "How you finding the *Keep*?"

I retract my hand, trying not to think too much of the sudden change in topic, and glance after Fesperman again. My stomach plummets when I see he and Madam Bartosh are whispering to each other as they watch me. "Not exactly welcoming."

Radomir's eyes lower to half-mast. "Join club." He pushes away from the bartop and saunters off in search of a shaded daybed. "I take drink now."

I take my time prepping the Bloody Mary mix in a pint glass. I need time to think, to figure out how to approach this. My thoughts can't take my mind off the blood, though. As I lift the sack out of the cooler and bobble it in my hands, I wonder what the last moments were like for the woman it belonged to and remember the scream I heard last night. Chills dart like lightning down the backs of my legs.

I can do this. I *must* do this.

I hold my breath as I make the drink.

The ice clinks in the pint glass as I walk it over to Radomir. I ask before all the boldness is struck out of me, "When will the Commodore see me?"

Radomir's lips draw back into an admiring smirk. "So eager." He tips back the cocktail, strong neck muscles working as he drains it, and smacks his lips with a satisfied "Ah" as he studies the glass. "How I love taste of fear," he sighs.

I shift my weight. "Radomir—"

"Call me Rasha," he encourages, setting the glass aside.

"Rasha." The intimacy of the nickname makes me uncomfortable. I force away any thoughts of Adrian and open my mouth. "Does he know that I want—"

"And what you want, Jamie?" Radomir muses, fixing me with his light blue eyes. "Why be like me?"

My throat bobs in a swallow. He does not blink. He lies on the daybed, his fingers linked in his lap, watching me.

This is the razor's edge. I have to be honest here. If I offer him any duplicity, any hint of falsehood, he will smell it.

My legs are shaking as I choose my answer. "Because I'm done being a victim."

He cocks his head, eyes narrowing. I hold my breath.

Then he rises from his daybed and looms over me, lean and fierce and infernally handsome. It's almost dizzying. "Then you know what is like," he says, inches from me. "Manipulation. Degradation of the spirit. To be made to feel you're worthless."

My chest rises and falls, taking small shallow breaths. Yes. I know that well. We lock eyes, and I can see it—the long history of abuse, resentment, rage. Lifetimes of it.

It's like looking at myself.

The astonishment, the queasy, unsettling feeling of kinship, jolts through me like the sparking of crossed wires. It's enough to almost make me lose my way, to forget to exploit this opening and get him on my side.

Our lips drift close, almost brushing each other.

Then Radomir turns away, and I feel as if I've been snapped out of a trance. "But you must wait for turn," the party boy is saying. He is staring out to sea. "Volok has other . . . distractions."

Before I can pursue what he's referring to, there's a *kathunk* and a smooth, prolonged, hydraulic whine. The aftmost bulwarks of the *Keep* are *moving*. They're rotating outward to expand the transom, additional decking lifting up to become flush with the aft deck. It's mesmeric. It fans out like a peacock's plumage, dazzling the eye—and I can't help but feel that the *Keep* is laying a trap, hoping to entice the young and sun-loving.

Which it has.

A long black tender is approaching. A swim platform unfolds to meet it, sliding out of a cassette within the aft deck and pivoting over the water so a slender bare foot can descend upon it. A woman's foot.

The new guests are arriving.

Radomir leans toward me in a confiding whisper. "Can't fault his taste in aft sections, no?" he smirks and slinks away.

He's referring to the ass of the taller of the two guests, clad in a frilly black bikini bottom. I follow his gaze and my jaw drops. The blood drains from my brain, making the world tremble at the edges. I'd know that ass anywhere. But it can't be. I lift my eyes, praying that I'm wrong, that I'm seeing things, I've made a mistake—

But I haven't.

The ass belongs to my best friend, Cailee Summers.

TWENTY-TWO

An ice-cold poker of fear slides into my back, puncturing my lungs. Followed by an absurd urge to laugh. Of course she'd wind up here. Growing up, after that first, fusing bond of summer camp where we'd met at age nine, we'd been inseparable. We conducted sleepovers almost every night, staying up into the late hours sharing what no one else knew about us, let alone our parents: our dreams, our crushes, our mortifying humiliations. We pored over *Cosmopolitan* and *Seventeen*. We read each other romance novels I'd snuck from my mother's room, giggling at all the descriptions of heaving bosoms and glistening man-chests. And despite mercilessly mocking all the improbable happily ever afters in those books, we still promised we'd find each other a husband who'd whisk us away to a better life. When we had our first fight it felt like the world ending, and afterward we held each other and touched brows, whispering, "I'm sorry, I was stupid, you're my best friend and I'll always be there for you."

And now she *is* here. Here, of all the yachts in the world. My best friend.

Don't you see the danger you've put yourself in, Cailee?

The danger you've put me in.

I scan the stern of the *Keep*. There are two bodyguards watching up on the aft main deck. And Madam Bartosh has bustled out. I can hear her speaking to the other guest, a Latinx with a cute button nose who looks no older than eighteen. She announces herself, precociously, as Marisol Martina. A swimwear model. This cuts no ice with Madam Bartosh. The chief stewardess says something, indicating the shoe basket, and Marisol looks down at her strappy high heel sandals on the teak and blushes.

But I can't concentrate on any of this. Because my world is splitting in two. Because Cailee has turned around and lifted the long lashes of her eyes.

She's seen me.

Her brow furrows and I whirl on the spot, chest heaving, my pulse snapping in my ears. Did she recognize me? Do I walk away?

Yes. Approach her later, in private, when there's less chance of her—

"Arie? Is that you?"

Fuck.

All heads turn to me. There's nothing for it, then. I unroot myself and march forward, a wide smile plastered over my face. "Cailee!" I squeal and crush her in a hug. "What are the chances?"

Madam Bartosh looks between us, hard-faced and oozing suspicion. "What did she call you?"

The pumping of my heart slows. Above me, one of the bodyguards reaches for his two-way radio.

"My middle name," I blurt out, and the bodyguard's hand freezes. "I sometimes go by my middle name." I let out a tinkly little laugh. "I know, it's silly."

Madam Bartosh blinks like a toad, brows lifting. "And how do you know each other?"

Cailee begins to reply, but I beat her to it. "We met back in Fort Lauderdale. When we roomed in the same crew house. Isn't that right, Cailee?"

Cailee's jaw drops in a big fat *what?* but I give her a silencing look and wrap my arm around her shoulders, squeeze hard with sunny smile in place. "You know. The bond of aspiring yachties and all that."

The blood rackets through my veins as Madam Bartosh narrows her eyes. Does she buy it? Do the guards buy it? How do they not see right through me?

I don't wait to find out. Madam Bartosh opens her mouth, and I railroad right over her. "I'll show her to her cabin, shall I?" And before either Cailee or Madam Bartosh can protest, I grab Cailee by the wrist and drag her away and out of sight of those guards, all but hyperventilating.

Holy shit.

Cailee doesn't put up with it for long. As soon as the door to the cabin is shut behind us, she plants her hands on her hips. "What the hell is going on, Arie?"

I take a deep breath, glance at the door and lower my voice. "You can't call me that on this boat, okay? It's important."

Cailee's eyebrows forklift up. "What?"

"I go by 'Jamie' here."

Cailee's eyes grow so round I'm afraid they're going to pop out of her head. She shuts them and spreads her fingers in the air, her words slow and controlled. "Okay. So, explanations, please."

"Cailee—"

"Why are you here as a stew? What happened with Adrian?"

My shoulders slump. "It . . . didn't work out."

All the anger goes out of Cailee's face. "Oh, babe."

She crushes me in her arms, and I'm overwhelmed by the realization of how much I've missed her. How much I've missed my best friend. My eyes prick with tears, a vague guilt roiling in my gut. What am I going to tell her? How do I get her off this boat?

"Everything you went through," she marvels over my shoulder. "I thought you two would end up together. I didn't think anything could tear you apart."

A lump bolts into my throat. "I thought so, too." I pull away and look at her, my hands on her arms. "Why didn't you stay away like I told you?"

Cailee crosses her arms and squints. "I did stay away, thank you very much. I can't help it if I was invited here."

I get a sinking feeling in my gut. "Invited?"

Cailee huffs a breath and offers her phone with a flick of her wrist. I arch a brow but take it, glancing at the familiar sight of her Instagram account. Only her number of followers is now . . .

My jaw drops. "You're an *Influencer* now?" I gasp, scrolling through a parade of glamorous selfies and photoshoots.

Cailee shrugs, a faint smirk teasing her lips. "Apparently, you're not the only one in need of my advice. I call it 'The Cailee Method'. Who knew women needed a role model to unapologetically be themselves?"

Themselves. I stop on a photo of Cailee making out with another girl, and something in my head clicks.

A high-pitched whine fills my ears. Far away, I can hear Cailee warming up to it. "And holy guacamole, girl, does Insta' eat that shit *up*."

But I'm not listening. "Cailee," I interrupt, looking up at her. "Are you . . .?"

Our eyes meet, and she straightens her spine, a helpless, rueful, stubborn look on her face, and I know it's true. My stomach tightens with hurt. It's not only that Cailee hadn't told me something so momentous; it's as if she's crossed a threshold without me. When we were younger, we'd promised to tell each other everything. When Cailee had her first period, she'd told me before her mom. When she knew she was going to lose her virginity, she forewarned me so I could lose mine the same night and not be left behind with the little kids.

And now she *has* left me behind, become something else without me.

"When did you know?" I ask, my throat tight.

Cailee shrugs, both sheepish and defiant. "Recently. I'd suspected for a while, but . . . it's confusing."

I nod, as if I can understand any of it. "And are you—?"

"Bisexual, I think. I'm still figuring it out."

I stand there feeling like an idiot, heavy with loss. I reach for her hand. "Cailee—"

"Anyway," she announces. She plucks the phone out of my hands and turns away with a strange glassiness to her eyes, soaking in the magnificence of the cabin. "I hear the owner is some kind of Russian oligarch?"

My blood chills. "No," I say, shaking my head. "No, no, no. You need to get off this boat. *Now*."

Her eyebrows go down. "Why?"

Why, indeed.

My mouth works. My mind gropes for an answer, for something that's as close to the truth as I can get without sounding batshit crazy.

It just comes out.

"I think there's sexual trafficking on this boat."

There's a moment of stunned silence. Cailee levels a look at me. "Sexual trafficking."

God, please let this work. "I came here to get away from Adrian. That's why I changed my name. But this boat—I've *seen* things—"

"Things."

"Yes."

She lifts her brows. "Like what?"

I open my mouth, groping for words. But they won't come.

This seems to be the final nail in the coffin for Cailee's open-mindedness. She crosses her arms and squints at me, as if trying to figure me out. "Are you"—she wiggles a finger—"are you jealous?"

"*What?* No—"

"Look," Cailee says, throwing up a hand. "Just because it didn't work out for you doesn't mean it won't for me, okay?" She shrugs a coquettish shoulder. "Why not be the bombshell wife on a bombproof yacht?"

My stomach drops out of me. I don't know what's going on here. This is not like her. This is not like my best friend at all.

Is she—is she having some kind of personality change?

I drag in a big breath, try one last time. "Cailee, I'm serious—"

But she kisses my cheek and breezes past me to the door. "See you around, *Jamie.*"

TWENTY-THREE

I'm in a restless daze for the remainder of the day. I barely get through my tasks, sneaking glances as Cailee luxuriates in her new lifestyle. She struts across the foredeck like it was a runway. She orders an endless string of cocktails and regales Marisol with all-too-vivid accounts of her sexual exploits. Marisol blushes and ducks her head; she'd look like a child if not for the scarily developed body under a luscious sheer cover-up. But Cailee finds this endearing. Scarcely an hour has passed and the two are leaning their heads together and giggling like sisters. They toy with each other's hair, comparing curls, tans, breast sizes, laughing hysterically, and I feel a sick pang of jealousy before reminding myself how stupid I'm being. There can be both. She can be that and still have me as her friend. I'm not losing her.

Not losing her.

I watch my best friend's tender-looking flesh glisten in the sun and feel my stomach churn with dread.

"See you tomorrow," she singsongs when she turns in for the evening, patting my cheek. "Buckle up, buttercup! We're finally back together!"

Yes. Back together.

Isn't it grand.

When I turn back to look up at the gangway above, the slender form of Radomir stands silhouetted against the orange blaze of dusk.

True dark has fallen by the time I finish my duties. I help Nicole with the last of the dishes in the crew mess and present myself before Madam Bartosh. "Do you need anything else before I turn in?"

The chief stewardess does not look up from the tablet in her hands. She swipes at the screen, perusing inscrutable items for the *Keep*'s inventory. In its glow, her birthmark looks like the map of some demonic, malformed moon.

When I've decided she's forgotten about me, she says in the lightest of tones, "You may go."

The act of kindness is so unexpected I almost don't believe my ears at first. Nicole and I exchange an astonished look, and she flutters her drying cloth at me. *Go, before she changes her mind.*

I don't need telling twice. But when I crack a grin and open a door leading outside, Nicole's head whips. "Where are you going?"

The tension in her voice jerks me up short. "Just getting some air."

Nicole's face falls. She darts a look at Madam Bartosh and lowers her voice. "I don't think that's a—"

"Did she ask for your opinion?" Madam Bartosh inquires in a bland tone, still not looking up from her tablet, and Nicole shrinks into herself.

"I just—"

"Just what?" Nicole's lips press together, and Madam Bartosh finally lifts her glowing face so her red mouth can show me a carnivorous smile. "Enjoy your walk, Miss Harris."

Utterly bewildered, I step outside and glide the door shut behind me.

What was that about?

I don't have time to linger on that, though. I need to make a call.

I need to figure out this Cailee situation.

The night hushes against my ears as I make my way toward the stern, fingering the burner phone in my skort pocket. It's deceivingly still out here, the only perceivable movement being the *Keep* trailing its green light in the water like phosphorus. That, and the silhouettes of the bodyguards strolling the deck. I nod to them and hurry past.

High above, great patches of sailcloth hum in the wind. The uplights shining up from their placements in the deck make them glow like the sails of a haunted ship.

Only a couple flights of stairs and I'll be down on the main deck by the waterfall.

I don't get far. I'm about to descend the stairs near the aft bridge deck when there's a series of *thunk, thunk, thunks* down the length of the boat and the *Keep* plunges into darkness.

I stand rooted to the spot, my heart in my throat. There's not a single light to be seen. All the superstructures of the boat, interior and exterior, have gone dark. The only illumination comes from the full moon gleaming on the polished brightwork of the *Keep*. It's as if the ship has died at sea.

Was there a power outage? But that makes no sense. You'd think the boat would have stopped, or there'd be crew about to address it.

A wind moans, long and lonely, in the sails above.

"Hello?" I call. No answer. There's not a sign of the bodyguards anywhere. When I try the glass doors of the darkened salon, I find they're locked.

A prickling chill works its way down to the base of my spine.

Thud, thud, thud. Footsteps are approaching, growing louder and louder down the gangway. Headed straight for me.

My chest seizes. I take a step back as a shape rounds the corner, a black shape outlined against the night sky. I draw breath to scream—and the ghostly face of Marisol appears before me.

I try not to cry, to laugh. I feel a shameful wave of relief that it's not Cailee.

"What the hell is going on?" she hisses in a whisper. "Those fuckers, they said there was a surprise for me out here and locked the door behind me. If this is some kind of joke—"

"I don't think it is," I say in a dry voice.

Marisol stops. "What does that mean?"

I don't answer. Instead, I unclip the crew radio from my hip with shaking fingers and slowly lift it to my lips. "Madam Bartosh?" I venture. "It's Miss Harris. I'm locked outside with Marisol on the aft bridge deck. Could you let us in, please?"

We both stand very still, listening. But the only thing to be heard is the wind whining in our ears.

Oh, I think. *Oh, no.*

"This isn't funny," Marisol warns, a wavery note in her voice.

But I'm not looking at her. Movement above has caught my eye, and I crane my head back so far I put a crick in my neck. Some of the lights have been left on, it seems, for the sails still glow green from the uplights below them. And there's a shadow there, flung high and huge upon the canvas of the main mast. It's tall, thin, high-shouldered. Splayed-fingered hands reach, impossibly long, across the expanse of white.

The blood stops in my veins.

"What are you—" Marisol bleats, and I clap a hand over her mouth.

"Don't. Make. A. Sound," I breathe into her ear. She gapes at me, eyes scleral with terror, and I lean in again to state the fact that's set my world on fire.

"We're being hunted."

TWENTY-FOUR

Marisol stills in my hands, and I drop them. We both look up—but the shadow on the sailcloth is gone.

"What the hell do you—" she begins, but I don't have to stop her. Because she's heard the distinct, quiet *thump* above us, as of a body dropping from one deck to another.

Her face slackens. She looks at me, and I can see the little muscles jumping in her face. All her earlier bluster has evaporated, revealing the scared teenager beneath. "What was that?" she whispers.

I think I know, but I can't tell her that. I hold out a calming hand and lift a finger to my lips. "We have to go. *Now*."

"What the fuck *was* that?" she hisses, slapping my hand away and backing up in jittery petulance. "I don't know what the fuck is going on here, but—"

She cuts herself short. Because she's heard what I've heard. Footsteps, faint but definite. Someone is walking along the deck above us.

I force myself to look up, and she follows my gaze. The stern of the deck above is edged by a stainless-steel rail.

And there's movement there. It takes me a moment to realize what it is: a cold effeminate hand, its long pale fingers wrapping one by one around the rail, talon-like nails scraping against metal, and I know that whatever it belongs to is about to look over and peer down at us.

Marisol bolts. I follow her down the stairs in a mad panic, chest heaving, breath searing my throat, pulse cracking behind my ears, hurling myself down the gangway and onto the upper deck.

I whirl about. Nothing. Empty deck, empty gangways. Not a soul anywhere.

Nothing coming down the stairs after us.

A series of shivers have overtaken me. My skin tingles as if numb; I'm almost out of my body with fright. And I'm not alone. Marisol is crying now. She paces in a daze, shaking her head as she searches for escape, tears streaking her cheeks. "They kept telling me," she gibbers. "Try modeling. Become an Influencer. Live the glamorous life." She hiccups something that's halfway between a laugh and a sob. "Why didn't I just go to fucking nursing school like my abuela wanted?"

I push this away, because an awful feeling is crowding my throat. I have to check. I edge to the starboard rail and peer over. Nothing. Then I cross the deck and peer over the port rail.

There's a shadow there, clinging impossibly to the gleaming fiberglass hull. Crawling toward us.

I pull away like the rail is on fire, a scream catching in my throat. "It's coming," I manage to whisper, bumping into a deck chair as I back away. And then, under my breath, "*He's* coming . . ."

Marisol stiffens like a cornered animal. Her eyes dart about. Her fingers shake in the air. "Can we hide?" she mutters. "We have to hide!"

"Shh!" I hiss, trying to think. But I can't think of anywhere to hide. The boat is battened down. All we're left with is what's on deck—or what's accessible from the deck. The anchor chain locker? We could hide in the anchor chain locker, like . . . like that girl I'd found sucked dry on that boat Cailee nearly died on, only a few months ago. And then it occurs to me that maybe that girl wasn't bitten and dumped down there. Maybe she had hid in there, like I'm considering now, and whatever had been hunting her had found her and crawled down inside with her . . .

"This is crazy," Marisol bawls, her voice rising to a hysterical pitch close to witlessness. "They can't just leave us out here! They have to—they have to—" She starts banging on the glass doors of the upper deck salon. "*Hey! Help us!*" she shrieks. "*HELP US!*"

"Marisol, no!" I grab at her, but she shoves me back, hard enough to make me stagger, and keeps banging and screaming. I gape at her. The racket is like an assault on the night, freezing the marrow in my bones, an appalling meltdown almost too shameful to witness. It's a goddamn dinner bell drawing that thing right to us.

She's snapped.

She throws a deck chair at the glass in a wild attempt to shatter it, and it bounces off and clatters across the deck. Bulletproof. But I'm no longer watching. The fact has struck home now: I can't help her. I turn, electric with fright, and dash down the stairs, my heart cracking in my chest, a sob wanting to get out. *I'm sorry, Marisol.*

I skitter to a stop on the main deck and look about, my mind a boiling black clot of terror. Then I remember, like a jolt of lightning: the burner phone. I pull it out of my skort pocket and almost weep with relief. This is it. This is the moment Adrian warned me about. This is the moment where all seems lost and I need him to save me.

No.

A ruthless resolve hardens my jaw. I'm not giving up that easily. That moment hasn't come yet. Only if there's no other choice.

Where to hide?

The waterfall drops as neat and clean as a handkerchief before me. Beyond, the pool stretches in a long rectangle of inky blackness lined with daybeds.

The pool.

You can't even see the bottom. Wouldn't I blend away in that featureless water, with my dark hair and dark stewardess outfit? And wouldn't it hide my scent from that creature? From there, I could see anything coming. And if I did, I could duck under the surface and wait until it had gone.

Maybe, maybe, I'd stand a chance.

I chuck my crew radio over the side and clutch the burner phone. Where to stash it? I'm still hesitating when the banging above me stops and I hear the scream.

My body bursts out into goose bumps. I tuck the phone under a pillow on one of the daybeds and slip into the water as quietly as I can. The cold steals my breath away. But I ignore that, striking out into the middle so I can watch from every direction.

I bob there, shivering and treading water, and strain to listen.

The boat hums. The masts rise up and up, their sails luffing in the wind. The *Keep* is as dark and deserted as a plague ship.

Why can't I hear anything? The silence—the not knowing—is unbearable. It gnaws at my nerves like a rabid animal. Why nothing after that first scream? Is she alive? Did she get away?

My teeth have begun to chatter when I hear it.

Footsteps. Someone's running, heels thudding wildly across teak planks. A pause. Then the screams again. Clearly a woman's screams. My heart smacks against the backs of my ribs. Tears push at my eyes. There's a pattering of bare feet somewhere, breathless sobs, a forlorn offering of begging. Then the screams once more, so loud and startling I have to clamp a hand over my mouth to cut off my own. They are the chest-hitching, lung-shredding screams every living creature knows—the bottomless, bereft, inconsolable grief of knowing you are going to die and there is nothing you can do about it.

The screams die away, turn into a gurgle. There's a thump on the deck, and then all is silent.

I hang there in the water with my heart slamming against my throat, a cold sweat on my brow, locks of wet hair plastered to my face. I want to weep, to scream, but I hold on, willing my teeth not to chatter.

Is it coming for me?

A tingling paranoia creeps in. I turn about in the pool with flagging strength, twitching at every shadow, waiting for them to take form. Perhaps it's waiting for me, trying to lure me out. But I won't fall for that. I can hide here all night. I can wait here, shivering and alone, until the sun comes up. I will be smart. I will survive.

But will I? My lips are blue now from the cold, my jaws clacking together like a doll's; my whole body is shaking. Will my muscles shut down? How long before I get pneumonia? How long can I withstand this?

Will I be forced to crawl out into the open?

I feel a silkiness on my skin, a new substantiality to the water, and look down. Red hangs in a dark cloud about me in the pool, coiling and thinning as my treading hands swirl through it. Chilly premonition grips me, and the waterfall behind me takes on a heightened roar, a new prickling, defined presence. But it has not sunk in, I have not accepted it yet. So I do it—I slowly twist about in the pool to look.

The waterfall is turning red with blood.

My jaws seize. I hang frozen and mute as a stone in the water, cold certainty seeping into my gut. As I watch, the redness expands, introduced from above like some malignant dye, darkening the middle third of the fall a shocking crimson.

No, I think as my eye twitches. *Don't do it. Don't look up.*

My lips part in stupid awe when I do.

I crane my gaze up, and up, following that flowing stain to where the waterfall is sheeting off the cliff of the curving fiberglass stern of the deck above. There's a black shape up there. It's hunched over something, engaged in some act of congress, the two forming a silhouette of obscene intimacy against the wash of stars. And they are not still. They pulse together like vermin, like a werewolf at its gorging. The sight is so visceral I can't help myself—I flounder backward in the pool with a splash, unable to stop a sharp intake of breath.

A feral slobbering noise rips through the night, the sound of raw meat tearing away, and a bald head jerks up into view as if answering the moon's summons, a sudden brilliance of pale skin in the illumination of the uplights. It's like a sickening optical effect out of a nightmare: floating, disembodied, like a cut-out, a spotlight in an opera. Fine-skulled and fiendishly profiled with fluked hound's ears filled with hair. It swings toward me, and as the blood freezes in my veins I see it has a ghastly overbite, with two long forefangs crowded at the front of its mouth like the teeth of a rat, mouth open and dripping viscous blood. It blinks down at me with lambent eyes as if interrupted from a dream.

"Uh," it belches, dully, a gout of regurgitated blood dribbling down its chin.

And all the air is sucked out of my lungs.

Arie, meet Volok.

TWENTY-FIVE

I don't remember the next few moments. Near-blinding fear overtakes my animal brain. I scramble whimpering out of the pool, knocking deck pillows aside as I frantically sweep up the burner phone and huddle dripping and shivering at the foot of the glass doors leading to the atrium. The image won't leave me. I see, over and over, that white blotch of a face. The blood dribbling down its chin. Those eyes. I can feel my mind becoming uncottered, trembling at the strain. Because whatever primitive part of me that lies beneath reason knows what I have seen. I have glimpsed the face of sheerest bestiality.

Something blurs down out of the sky and splashes into the pool before the waterfall. I almost jump out of my skin and clap a hand over my mouth.

But no. It's not the creature. It's not him coming after me.

It's the body. Marisol's body, bobbing obscenely in the water. She's been discarded like a scrap of after-dinner leftovers.

I hold my silence, lungs burning, fighting to keep the screams down, until I hear the footsteps padding away on the deck above. Until I know it's gone. And still I wait, listening to the purling of the waterfall, paranoid that it's waiting, that it might come back.

It doesn't. It's gone.

Only then do I give in. My body's reaction is catastrophic: I lower my hand, sucking in a wild breath, and begin to shake with violent, almost incapacitating spasms, making wrenching noises that have too much anger in them to be sobs. What a fool I've been. I thought I knew. I thought I knew what this world was like, what these beings were. But I didn't know anything. I was an idiot. This is no suave and sophisticated billionaire with a redeeming soft side. This is something else. This is the monster they make legends from, something that's been around far longer than any of these other bloodsucking whelps, and which I haven't the faintest hope against. What was I thinking would happen here?

My hands close into fists in my hair. Still. It was right there. Volok was there. I had my chance to face the Commodore and ran like a witless animal. And because of that, Marisol . . .

I beat my hands on my thighs, the sounds real sobs now, wracking hiccups of helpless shame, my head tilted back and the tears streaming from beneath my closed lids. When the deckhands come down to drag the body out of the pool and dump it overboard, mop the blood into the drains, I look away, my mind turning dark with rage and merciless resolution.

Next time, I vow. *Next time I'll be ready.*

The first light of dawn is tingeing the sky pink when the atrium doors are unlocked and Nicole is holding me, rocking me, whispering a rush of words into my ear. "I'm sorry. I'm so sorry I didn't tell you, Jamie. I tried to. He has a female guest locked outside the yacht every night. He likes to hunt his prey."

Every night, I think, cold-eyed and stone-heavy in Nicole's arms. And I think, *Cailee*.

As soon as I get myself sorted, I go to her cabin to find her. Not there. The cabin is as empty as a crypt. Cold foreboding grips me. I hurry abovedeck in a breathless rush, rattle back a sliding door leading outside—and bump right into the domineering bulk of Madam Bartosh.

We blink at each other, stunned. The chief stew's face drains of all color.

And I remember last night.

"Surprised to see me?" I ask.

Madam Bartosh twitches her head.

"Oh. Oh, no," I exclaim in mock concern, and put a hand to my chest. "You really thought you'd gotten rid of me, didn't you?"

The woman breathes in hard through her nose.

"Well," I say in a conspiratorial tone, and show her my teeth as I breathe it into her face. "At least we finally see each other."

Her pupils dilate to enormous size.

The slap almost staggers me, leaving my left cheek stinging with numbness. She looks as astonished as I am. But I do not back down. I turn back to her with outthrust chin, brimming over with nasty triumph.

Someone joins my side: Nicole. Her entire body trembles with a cold passion. She slips her hand into mine and says, quite calmly, "Shame on you."

Madam Bartosh blinks and jerks her head back into her neck. She opens her mouth, shuts it. Then lifts her nose and pushes past us.

Nicole and I look at each other. She's glassy-eyed and out of breath, as if she's been woken from some dreadful enchantment, as if a dazzling sunbreak has poured through into her world.

I squeeze her hand and give her a look of pure pride. "Thank you, Nicole."

And looking back at me, she glows.

The stinging in my cheek has turned to a dull throb by the time I find Cailee. She's under the shaded overhang on the main deck by the waterfall, in a long cover-up dress with a plunging neckline that looks like it's about to slip off her body at any moment. And she's not alone. Radomir is with her. As he leans to whisper something into her ear, he presses a hand to the small of her back. She looks up into his eyes and smiles.

The blood pulses in my ears.

I wait for Radomir to leave before I approach. Cailee waggles her eyebrows at me. "How about that Radomir, huh?" She fans herself. "Talk about a slice of beefcake. I wouldn't mind having a little side-piece of that—"

"Cailee." My throat dries up. Even after I swallow, my voice comes out a squeak. "I have to tell you something."

"Oh, please," she says, rolling her eyes. "What now?"

"You have to leave this boat. Today."

She lets out an exasperated breath and shakes her head. "Not this again." She starts to stalk off.

Then she goes stock-still, looks down at my hand that's caught her wrist.

"Cailee, I'm serious." I glance about before I lean in. "It's not safe for you here."

She plucks her wrist free with huffy drama and backs away. "Look, this sexual trafficking thing? I don't buy it, okay? So—"

"That's not the real reason."

She crosses her arms and arches a brow.

"You want to know why I told you to leave the yachting industry?"

Her certainty slips a little. "All right."

I'd been thinking about this all morning. How to tell her? How to make her listen to me? And the answer had smacked me right in the face: with an appeal to our shared history.

"Do you remember when we were little and we promised we'd protect each other from monsters? The ones under the bed, the ones in the closet, the ones who were smelly and wanted to kiss you? Well, they're real, Cailee. The monsters are real."

Cailee snorts. "Yes, boys exist. Thanks for the update, Arie."

I give her a long look. "I'm talking about the other kind, Cailee."

The humor leaves Cailee's face. "What are you saying?"

Now for the deep plunge. "You wanted to know what Adrian's dark secret was? Why he was violent?"

Cailee cocks her head, wary.

"He needs to feed on blood, Cailee," I say, feeling an almost cathartic rush as the words come out. "All these yacht owners feed on blood. They're not like us. They've been alive for a very long time. And it's why I need you to leave. You're in danger."

A silence stretches out for nearly a full minute after this pronouncement.

Then Cailee laughs.

She throws her head back and lets it out, a pretty, cruel tumbling of sound. "*Vampires*, Arie?" she says in a disappointed voice, shaking her head and wiping tears from her eyes. "Vampires? *Really?*"

I feel the blood fill my face. "It's true," I say, so soft I'm barely audible.

"I should have known you'd do something like this."

A hard hurt forms in my throat. "What do you mean?"

Cailee waves a hand. "I'm finally able to be on my own and enjoy life without you, and you can't stand it. You're jealous. *Look* at you." She gestures up and down. "It's eating you from the inside out."

"*What?* No, that's not—"

This isn't how it was supposed to go. This is nothing like it was supposed to go. How could she ever think this of me?

"Arie," Cailee says, speaking slowly. "If you could hear yourself, you'd feel embarrassed."

"I have nothing to be embarrassed about," I reply stiffly, louder than I mean to. "I'm trying to *save* you—"

"Right. *You*. Save *me*," Cailee mutters.

I shut my eyes, willing my voice steady. "Cailee," I plead, pressing my hands together. "This is me here. I'm your best friend. We've known each other almost all our lives. I'm begging you—"

"Arie," Cailee says in a low tone.

"You don't believe me? Have you not noticed Marisol isn't around? What do you think happened to her? You think she'd really leave without telling you?"

Cailee's eyes go stony, as if I've crossed a line. She grips my arm. "Arie, I'm worried about you. I really am. You have secrets. And aliases. First, you feed me a story about sexual traffickers, and now *vampires* . . ." She throws up a hand and places it over her eyes, shakes her head. "How am I supposed to believe anything you say?" She drops her hand and settles her shoulders, looks at me intensely.

"You really need help. But I'm not the one who can be there for you anymore."

I feel something round and hard sink slowly from my chest to my gut. My voice cracks as I say it, small and alone and filled with the raw betrayal of the girl I'd once been with her. "You said we'd always be there for each other."

A sheen of tears fills Cailee's eyes and she blinks and looks away. When she looks back, that sheen—and what it means—is gone. "I'm sorry it didn't work out with Adrian," she declares in a formal tone, straightening her spine. "I really am. And I'm sorry it's taken this kind of toll on you. But this isn't fair."

"Cailee—"

"You know what the funny thing is?" she continues with a bitter laugh. "You held me back for so long, making me take care of you, I didn't even know who I was. Well, I know now. And you're not going to take that from me." Her lips thin in scorn. "I'm sorry you have a crush on Radomir and you can't stand that he's into me. I guess you'll just have to find some other rebound from Adrian."

And she brushes past me in her flowy beach dress, leaving me there with my bottom lip trembling and the tears pooling in my eyes.

TWENTY-SIX

"So you're saying we have until tonight to get Cailee off the boat," Adrian growls through the phone, "or she's next."

It's taken a long time for his venting to be over. I've told him and Ilsa everything. Last night. The *Keep* locking down. The hunt in the dark, and my informal introduction to the Commodore. And, finally, my failure to convince Cailee. To which Adrian's responses were, respectively: *Fuck, fuck me, I'll fucking kill him*, and *God-fucking-damn it*.

"Ilsa?" he prompts after a while. "Any ideas?"

The Shipwright of Transmarinia sighs over the line. "The only solution I can think of is the simplest. While the *Keep* is underway, get her to jump off the stern with a life jacket on, and we'll surface and scoop her up."

I think on it long and hard as mist from the *Keep*'s waterfall dews my cheeks, and finally nod. "Okay. That works."

"It'll have to be at sunset when no one's out on deck to witness it."

"Agreed," I mutter, watching a security guard stroll past.

"Which will make it dangerous," Adrian warns unhappily. "You might get locked out again."

I shiver; I know. "It's a chance I'll have to take."

"And you're sure you'll get Cailee to go along with it?"

Cailee's scornful face pops into my head. *(I should have known you'd do something like this.)* I clench my jaw. "I'll make it work."

"Okay." Adrian falls into an uneasy silence, and then I hear Ilsa's voice, as if reading my thoughts.

"She's lucky to have you as her friend, you know."

(If you could hear yourself, you'd feel embarrassed.)

"Yeah, well," I reply, feeling that hard hurt in my throat again. "I hope she feels that way after all this is over."

"She will," Ilsa replies without hesitation. "You'll get through this. Through all of this."

"I don't know," I say, goose bumps breaking out over my skin. "Now that I've seen the Commodore . . ." The syllables stick to my lips as I see that pale fiendish face jerk up into the moonlight once more, blood dribbling down its chin. I swallow and wet my lips. "He's not a man. He's a *beast*, Ilsa . . ."

There's a long silence broken only by the clean fall of water into the pool. "And you're a woman," the Shipwright replies at last. "I'd say that makes you evenly matched."

I hiccup a laugh and nod, sliding a hand down my face. "Thank you."

"Call when you're on the stern, okay?" Adrian says. I can always tell when he's worried.

"I will."

"I love you, Aurora," he whispers.

"I love you too, Adrian."

I end the call, a tender smile gentling my features. Even here, even now, his voice can do that to me. I feel buoyed up, lifted, puffed full of hope.

Maybe this will work.

That smile is still there when I hear the voice behind me, flat with sarcasm. "How touching."

I pivot on my heel, already knowing what I'm going to see. Madam Bartosh stands in the shadows under the overhang with a gloating look on her face, having heard every word. "Yes," she simpers with sweet venom, "I think we do finally see each other, *Aurora*." And she unclips the crew radio at her hip. "How about we let the Commodore decide what to do with you?"

TWENTY-SEVEN

My spine locks. I throw up my hands like a character in a schlocky drive-in horror movie and shout, "Wait!"

Madam Bartosh freezes, radio almost to lips. The sun hitting the waterfall refracts everywhere under the overhang, making her birthmark look as if it's writhing in the sudden shifts of light. One could even mistake her, in that light, to be smiling.

"Yes?" she prompts, tart with smugness.

"You don't have to do this," I find myself saying. It's hard to speak; I'm jittery with panic. Adrenaline spikes my brain. "I know why you hate me, but you don't have to do this."

"Do you?" she sneers, full of contempt, and her eyes rake me up and down. My legs. My breasts. My face. It's a violation.

And I know in that moment what Madam Bartosh has been twisted into.

"Yes," I whisper, and lower my hands. "I'd feel the same if I were you. I'd be enraged."

She can't hold back a guffaw. "Is that so?"

It's a risk I'm taking, I know. Madam Bartosh is a hard case. Even if I cracked her open with what I say next, there might be nothing but a seed of malice inside her, hard and petrified, like a stone.

But I don't have any other choice, do I?

So I go for it.

"I see how they treat you. Fesperman. Radomir. Even the security guards. As if you're a nuisance. As if you don't keep this boat running."

Madam Bartosh goes very, very still.

"I know what it's like to feel unseen. Unappreciated. Having to hold that in for years."

One of Madam Bartosh's eyelids flutters.

"And why? Why would they treat you like that?" I whisper, edging closer. "You're intelligent. Beautiful. Exceptional at what you do."

Madam Bartosh eyes me sidelong, her face filling—amazingly—with something approximating fear. And it hits me: She's never been told this. She doesn't know what to do with what I'm saying.

Time to go all in.

"It's almost like—it hurts to say it—but it's almost like Radomir hired you because of your birthmark."

Madam Bartosh blinks. A single, fat teardrop clings to her lashes.

"You see the women he surrounds himself with," I rush on, unstoppable now. "Young pretty things. Disposable. But not you. He doesn't want to have to replace you. So he hired a woman he wouldn't be tempted to feed on.

Which is so fucked up. Because you *are* beautiful. How would that not make you miserable?"

Madam Bartosh's lip trembles. I pout in sympathy, lowering my voice.

"Why do they deserve your loyalty? Why not help me make the Commodore go away? Why not get *fucking angry?*" I'm feet away now. My hands reach for the crew radio, gentling, pleading, as if talking someone off a ledge. "Wouldn't it be a relief? Wouldn't it be a relief to not feel this way anymore? We're on the same side, Dragica. Why not help me?"

And I see her, for a split moment, teeter on the edge, full of a youthful, trembling hope, desperate for release. A study in tragedy. For she reminds me of many women I've known before out in the country—women who have sad backgrounds and sadder prospects, but who still find a hard-faced satisfaction in bearing burdens no one else can. Those too weak to do the same are to be treated with contempt.

As is the case now.

Her eyes clear, as if waking from the cheap enticements of a scam artist, and her nostrils flare. "You filthy little bitch," she breathes.

And she lifts the crew radio to her lips.

I don't remember moving. Suddenly, my hands are wrapped around hers, wrestling the radio away from her face. We sway and bend and stagger, slamming into each other. Madam Bartosh huffs heavily, her lips lifting away from her teeth like an animal. "Fucking—bitch," she hisses, codifying it into a chant, a promise. "Fucking—kill—you."

How did I get here? I think in dull wonder. *How is this possibly going to end well?*

And with an almighty effort, Madam Bartosh wrenches the crew radio out of my hands—and overbalances.

There's a jarring, almost comical *bong* as her skull strikes the aft deck's side rail.

I stare, agape, a hand over my mouth. The chief stew lies spread out on the gangway with one of her hands flung above her head, still clutching the radio. Her eyes are unfocused, not quite shut. A trickle of pink stuff dribbles out of her open mouth into the maroon continent of her birthmark. Not blood.

At least, it doesn't look like blood. It looks, if anything, like the froth you skim off strawberries when making jam.

There's a sudden surge of bile at the back of my throat.

"Oh my God," I whisper. I suck in a sob, my hands fluttering to my hair. *What just happened? What did I just do?*

Nicole watches me beside the double doors of the atrium, her eyes huge.

My heart drops.

"It . . . it was a mistake," I hurry to explain, feeling a hot push of tears behind my eyes. "I didn't mean to . . ."

Nicole opens her mouth, then whips her head around.

Two shadows are lengthening down the far gangway.

Bodyguards. Bodyguards strolling toward us. They'll be on us in moments.

Nicole whips back to me, at a loss with terror. Then her jaw clicks up and her voice becomes flat with practicality. "We can try to save her or make this go away. I'll back whatever you decide. But it needs to happen now."

I drop my eyes to the body at my feet, thinking of the limits of mercy. Would anything change if I saved her? Would her gratitude outweigh her spite?

When I look up at Nicole, her face slackens and she nods, marches away down the gangway. "Hey there," I hear her drawl, voice deep and drawn out with flirtation. "Hard at work keeping me safe again?"

Time. She's giving me time. To do what I have to.

I stand, unsteady on my feet, and lean on the rail.

Far below, water roils past the hull of the *Keep*, white-capped and hungry.

"Fucking . . . bitch . . ."

A wet gurgle of a voice. A hand lifts, gropes at my ankle. I flinch at its touch.

"Guards'll . . . fucking . . . kill you . . ."

Don't look.

"See you later!" The shadows are rounding the corner now.

In one fluid movement, I lift my foot and push Madam Bartosh under the rail and over the side.

The splash is lost in the churning wake of the boat. It's as if, when that body rolled over the side, it dropped out of all existence.

When the bodyguards stroll past, sparing me a lazy glance, all that's to be seen is a stew taking in the view at the rail.

A stew. A stewardess. Not a murderess.

"You okay?"

Nicole studies me with wide, worried eyes. I'm still looking down at the water frothing about the *Keep*, as if expecting to see the roll of a body amongst the foam—the evidence of what I'm capable of.

But Madam Bartosh is gone. The magic trick complete.

"I don't know," I croak, gulping down my heartbeat. "I've done some things, but that . . ."

Nicole dismisses this. "I'm sure you gave her a chance, didn't you?" She shrugs, her voice taking on a hint of scornful satisfaction. "Some women forget which side they're on."

I don't know what to say to that.

Nicole stares at me with a strange caution, as if weighing up something. "I think I know what you're up to," she whispers, and before I can protest she lays her hand on mine. "Don't worry—we're behind you."

And she drifts off, leaving me with the sudden understanding that this is all bigger than I thought. That everything's changed.

TWENTY-EIGHT

I'm sick with anxiety as I wait for someone to notice Madam Bartosh's disappearance.

Maybe it's too hot to notice anything. Out here on the dazzling dance of light that is the sea, it's as if the dog days of summer have returned. The sky is a cloudless mirage, the sun a white hole in the emptiness above. It cooks the fiberglass hull of the *Keep* until it shimmers, bakes leather sunpads sticky, blazes stainless-steel rails so blindingly hot they'd take the skin off your palm. The crew, accordingly, have abandoned the outdoors, putting off all exterior work until sundown, and not even the bodyguards risk the heat to make their rounds. The boat feels as if it's being boiled in honey.

Maybe I'll get lucky. Maybe no one will say anything before tonight.

Then the boat wakes from its midafternoon doze.

Nicole and I are dusting light fixtures in the atrium, our skin goosepimpled from the AC working overtime to flood the *Keep* with freezing cold air. There's a hush of glass—the atrium's doors opening—and we share a wall-eyed look, feather dusters trembling like the plumage of hunted birds.

"Miss Harris?"

Fuck.

I lower my duster, turn to the stocky bodyguard standing in the entryway. "Yes?"

"Fesperman would like a word."

Nicole and I look at each other and swallow.

A wave of heat hits me when I walk out onto the aft deck. It's utterly still out here. The waterfall has been turned off during the heat spell, and the air is so dry it's practically scorched.

Fesperman stands at the exact spot I pushed Madam Bartosh overboard, his white-gloved hands clasped behind his back.

My mouth dries instantly.

Did he see me? Does he know?

He must be setting me up. How am I going to get out of this?

I have to play along, then. Play innocent.

Let's see what happens here.

Aloud, I say, "You asked for me, sir?"

He does not turn to look at me. He stays back from the burning hot rail, safe in the shade of the deckhead above. His voice is lazy with the mildness of a snake about to strike. "Did you like Madam Bartosh, Miss Harris?"

My hands go clammy.

I have to be careful here. He is one of those men who lays traps for you to fall into.

"Why?" I ask back, wrinkling my brow. "Did something happen to her?"

This draws a smile out of Fesperman. He half-turns his head to let me see it. "Would you care if something had?"

It comes to me very suddenly—a sense of what's needed here. I let my lips crook up, too. "Not particularly, no."

Fesperman nods, lets a gloved hand stray into the light. With great daintiness he wipes a finger along the blazing rail before him and inspects it.

There's a pink stain on the white cotton.

I shut my eyes.

"Perhaps you do have the taste for this," Fesperman muses to himself.

I don't know how to interpret this, what this means. My face is hot with wild panic when Fesperman glides past me and lays one of those white mittens on my shoulder. "I suppose I'll have to thank you," he whispers. "She was a cunt of a woman, wasn't she?" And his sharp brown teeth crowd this way and that in a crooked smile. As if we were sharing an inside joke. As if we were like, anything at all like, each other. "Just take care not to get up to any more foolishness, yes? I may change my mind yet."

Far off on the sweltering horizon, storm clouds are gathering.

My relief drains away as I watch in disbelief on the starboard gangway, the charged air damp on my cheeks.

It can't be. Where did those storm clouds come from? I pray for the weather to change, the wind to shift, but no such luck. The *Keep* heads straight for them.

Please don't, I think. *I have to rescue my best friend tonight.*

The predicted time for sunset is 7:00 p.m.

The weather only worsens as the day progresses. Dread ices my heart over as the clouds grow bruised and brooding, blundering across the sky to blot out the sun with almost suspicious swiftness. By 5:00, the impossible brilliance of the day has faded to the remoteness of a dream, and the *Keep* is heading into a gray and angry waste of churning thunderheads and waves whipped into a white chop. Far off in the distance, lightning flares out of the void and foots itself to the sea without a sound. Something oppressive and malign grips all and squeezes.

It's okay. Everything will be okay.

This won't interfere with the mission.

At 5:30 I'm on break, and I head to my cabin to take a nap before tonight. I'll need my head clear to face Cailee.

I try not to hurry, constantly checking to make sure Fesperman isn't watching me. At the head of a spiral staircase leading to the main deck, a spit of static roots me to the spot. Bodyguards are huddling in a circle by the glass doors leading to the aft deck, speaking in low voices. Beyond, black shapes pace outside, bulky shoulders hunched against the wind, machine guns held tightly against their vests as they sweep the deck and speak into their two-way radios. "Nothing here," a voice crackles.

They're searching for Madam Bartosh.

One of the bodyguards glances up at me, and I duck my head and fast-pedal down the stairs, my heart hammering in my throat. I'm going so fast I bump right into the person at the bottom.

It's Cailee.

We both stare. I open my mouth to speak, I don't know what, but she only gives her head a pitying shake and brushes past me.

My heart is still trying to unclench in hurt when I crawl into my bunk and set an alarm on my burner phone. What am I doing? Maybe I have no right to be doing this. Would she even want it? Won't she struggle and jeopardize everything? Am I being stupid?

Am I weighing Cailee's life against Adrian's right now?

I hug my pillow to my chest and squinch my eyes shut, cheeks burning in shame. The boat lurches sickeningly in the storm, rocking me in my bunk, and I'm certain I won't sleep a wink. Somehow, though, I do. And I dream. In my dream everything is back to the way it was. Cailee and I are driving out to Florida together in her rust bucket pickup, windows down, our hair blowing about our faces as Britney Spears blasts from the radio, and the air smells of palmettos and hurricanes and our limitless futures and we haven't fallen out yet, there's no aching heartbreak, no things said that can't be taken back, and as we sing along in big, happy, braying voices, out of tune and not caring at all, I look over and smile and Cailee smiles back, alive and glowing with the thrill of what we're doing, and that's when I see there's something strange on her throat, two small pinlets of blood that begin to run, and when she opens her mouth and says, "Why didn't you save me, Arie?" her neck gapes back like a filleted fish to show the wet gleam of windpipe within and I'm screaming and headlights are filling the windshield and when I open my eyes all the cabin doors are banging in the storm and the alarm on my phone is blaring over and over into the dim light of dusk.

6:30. Time to go.

"I'm going to save you, Cailee," I whisper into the dark.

TWENTY-NINE

The first raindrops are splatting against the portholes as I make my way to Cailee's cabin. The hall tilts drunkenly as a wave broadsides the *Keep* and I stagger, bracing one hand on a wall, my stomach in my throat. Bulkheads groan, wooden paneling creaks. Somewhere far away, I hear china sliding inside magnetically locked cabinets, a brittle breaking sound and a muffled curse. I glance over my shoulder.

A gloomy hallway glowing with a dim wall lamp here and there, no shape silhouetted at its end. No one following me.

I'm almost there.

I don't know how I'm going to do this. I don't know how I'm going to talk Cailee into it, or how the *Lady Revenge* is supposed to follow the *Keep* through this storm, let alone find and rescue a woman jumping overboard. A deep flush of panic floods through me. Maybe this is a disaster. I don't know anything. Can't I wait another night? Will Volok really hunt again during something like this?

And if he does? What will I tell myself then?

I rap two knuckles on Cailee's door. "Cailee?" I say in a low voice, glancing down the hall again.

When she doesn't answer, I turn the handle and open the door.

I have to strain my eyes to see; it's almost pitch-black in here. The curtains are half-drawn, and beyond the windows, giant waves heave and crash in explosions of spume. Occasionally lightning cracks, so loud it sends my heart thumping, and in those dull white flashes I can make out the cabin's bed and its rumple of sheets. The form beneath them.

Cailee moans.

She's having a dream, a nightmare. I'd heard her make many sounds in her sleep before, when we were younger, but nothing like this. She writhes and squirms and shakes her head, whimpering.

"Cailee," I whisper.

I rush forward, and for a moment—I must be seeing things—I glimpse a long-fingered shadow lift away from the bed and retreat across the wall.

"Hey," I hush, brushing Cailee's hair back from her face. It's damp with sweat, almost feverish. "Cailee, come on. We got to go."

I tug at her, but she groans, listless, unresponsive. When I try to pull her up, she scrunches up her forehead in a pouty way and whimpers.

"Cailee," I say, more firmly, and shake her. "Wake up. We have to go. Now."

She's beginning to cry in her sleep now, the whiny, performative, hiccupy crying of a little girl. She turns away, and when I touch her side she sucks in a hissing breath.

My muscles lock. My adrenal glands activate. Sweat drips down my ribs.

When I lift the duvet back, I clap a hand over my mouth.

The marks are everywhere. Dark purple wounds bracketed on either side by puncture marks. They look swollen and infected, some of them recent and still oozing blood, their edges torn and ragged. There must be dozens of them: on her neck, her breasts, her wrists, the tender-looking flesh of her belly, her inner thighs . . .

Something in my stomach rolls over.

He's been here. He's been here before, many times. He—

"My father is little rough when feeding," says a voice behind me.

I almost let out a scream as I whirl around.

A dark shape leans against the doorway, arms crossed over its chest. It chuckles, low and deep, then dislodges itself from the doorway and steps into the room. I stumble back, eyes walled, and almost bump into the wall, a pulse quivering at my throat. The shape stops. Lightning flares it white, and for a moment I can see every dimple in Radomir's cheeks, every molar glinting in his smiling mouth.

The smile widens.

"He's been looking for new concubine, after loss of his beloved Evangeline," the blood son continues, strolling toward the bed. I fight down the urge to turn and bolt, my eyes never leaving his face. Radomir smirks, then slants his gaze down to Cailee tossing on the sheets. "And he may have found her."

My insides go cold.

"Get away from her," I spit, standing between him and the bed. My voice wavers slightly. I am aware, with great humiliation, of a pang of sickly lust.

Radomir's eyes are very knowing as he rolls them up at me. "Unless you're interested?"

The room trembles.

I don't know what to say, what to do. I didn't hear right. He's not proposing this.

But he is.

"It is great honor," he says, solemn now. "Very few are offered it. Who would be fool enough to let best friend have it instead?" That knowing smile returns. "Of course, you will have to be tested for your . . . *sweetness*," he adds, his eyes moving over me, up and down. "As one making your case to Commodore, that responsibility fall on me." And as he looks at me his eyes dance with a wicked spark.

I close my eyes to let the nausea—the sickening desire—pass.

"Is up to you," Radomir says, his voice fading. "Can find me in my suite when you make decision."

THIRTY

I pace on the aft of the pitching main deck, my breathing ragged, my eyes squinted against the stinging salt wind, waiting for my call to go through to Adrian.

In preparation for the storm, the waterfall had been turned off and the pool half-emptied, and choppy waves slosh against the pool's tiled walls as I pace. I don't know what I'm going to say. I don't know if I'm calling to let him know what I'll be doing or to ask for his permission. *Am* I going to do it? If I say no, Cailee will be damned forever. If I say yes, I feel like I'll be damning myself. And that's not even getting into what it'll do to Adrian.

I glance behind me, scanning the dark interior of the atrium through rain-slicked glass doors. I'm gripped by the certainty that Fesperman is watching me. Or having me watched. I think of the look Radomir gave me before he asked me if I was interested, and the memory is tinged with both arousal and a terrible humiliation.

No. Don't go there. Don't think of that.

RRR. RRR. RRR.

The burner phone rings over and over. Will it get through? I turn about to take in the calamitous roil of the sea, the waves cannonading against the *Keep*'s hull in booms of spray, the black boil of clouds sending a horizontal blast of wind and rain across the deck in beautiful fury, soaking me to the bone. How can I get a connection through that?

"Aurora?" Adrian's voice is almost lost in a great roar of black static. "Is everything okay? Are you ready?"

My heart clenches in my chest. I can't speak.

"Arie?" Ilsa now, sounding worried. "Is Cailee there? I don't know if this can work in this weather, it came out of nowhere—"

Tell them, goddamn it.

"I don't have Cailee with me," I whisper.

The static turns into a vast gulf of darkness.

"What do you mean?" Adrian's patchy voice sounds alarmed.

"The Commodore wants her," I explain in a dull voice. "For his concubine." I put a hand over my eyes, my bottom lip beginning to tremble. "Unless I offer myself up in her stead."

There's an astonished silence on the line.

Then . . .

"*What?*" Adrian shouts.

"Mein Gott," Ilsa breathes.

"But I need to be . . . tasted first."

Adrian's voice goes dangerously low. "By whom?"

The words stick in my throat.

"*WHO IS GOING TO TASTE YOU?*" Adrian roars.

I shut my eyes against his fury all but melting the phone at my ear.

"Radomir," I whisper.

"Radomir," Adrian repeats, dazed, as if the word is beyond his understanding.

"Adrian. Baby." I brush lank threads of hair out of my face, eyes squinted against the rain. "This is what gets me to him. To the Commodore. And I won't be turned, right? I can be"—I swallow—"*fed on*, but not turned, because I won't be dying. It won't be long enough for his venom to turn me. I'll be okay."

Adrian's voice is hollow, interrupted by patchy bursts of static. "You can't actually be considering this. There has to be another way . . ."

"We don't know if there will be. And we can't count on that. I need to do this before something happens to Cailee."

"She's right, Adrian," Ilsa says in a small, faraway voice.

Adrian ignores her. "You know what feeding is like for us," he snarls, his voice swimming up out of the void with an edge of petulance. "You know what it means. How . . . *sexual* it is."

He sounds as if he can barely say the word. I can barely stand to hear it. "I know." I have to bite my lip now to keep it together, to keep from going under a black wave of misery. "I'm sorry."

"So that's it, then," Adrian snaps in a betrayed tone, ready to hurt. "You've made your decision."

"Adrian, that's not what I—"

"Is there another reason you're doing this?"

The air turns hard.

"What?" I breathe.

"Adrian, stop," Ilsa says.

"Well? Is there?" Adrian pushes on, reckless now. "Or are you going to deny it?"

A roiling of anger and guilt wells up in me. "How could you even—"

"You know what this will be like for you, right?" Adrian steamrolls over me, not caring at all now. "After what your ex did to you?"

My flesh goes cold. A sharp pain throbs once between my legs.

Adrian barks a bitter laugh. "I can't believe this . . ."

"Adrian," I plead, a sob rising in my throat. "Please don't be like this . . ."

But his response is broken up in the following crackle of static.

"Adrian?" The *Keep* plows into a wave, rattling my teeth, and I have to grab onto the corner of a fiberglass buttress to keep my footing. "Adrian, are you there?"

Only a wind moans down the phone line, spitting out words between pops of static. "Can't . . . hear . . . connection . . . Aurora . . ."

The line goes dead.

I stare at the phone in shock, my insides turning watery and sick.

No. He can't leave me like this. Not with this unresolved.

Not without his understanding.

That is what I'd been hoping for, wasn't it? Not to hear him say it was a good plan, or that it could work. But that he was okay with it. I was seeking his absolution. Would he forgive me if I went through with it now? Would I forgive myself?

And would both of us look at me differently after this? As a soiled thing, indecent, defiled?

Would that be worse than not going through with it?

I turn into the gale to take it all in. The wind howls. The rain stings. A mountain of a wave rises behind the *Keep* like a great rippling muscle, and when lightning flashes behind it, for a moment—suspended in silhouette in the glowing swell—there is the whale-sized shadow of the submarine yacht containing my love.

"I'm sorry, Adrian," I whisper and turn away.

My stomach feels empty as I return to my cabin. I strip off my clinging wet clothes and change into a black evening gown, its stretch fabric hugging my every curve, making me feel naked. Thunder rumbles. Waves crash against the hull, bumping me against the walls of the cabin head as I ready myself in the mirror. I dry my hair, comb it out and curl it at the end to give it a touch of body. Then eyeliner, mascara, blush. My hands are shaking as I gloss up my lips, thinking of sharp teeth hidden in a sly smile. My finger throbs like an accusation where my engagement ring had been.

Finally, a spritz of perfume at the neck. An invitation.

I study myself in the mirror. I do not recognize the woman before me. I do not know who she is anymore.

My veins are coursing with a depraved thrill as I pad barefoot to Radomir's suite.

It lies near the bow of the *Keep* on the main deck, as far from the elevator as possible. The door a dense slab of black oak.

Just a taste, I think. *Just a taste and it'll be done.*

I raise my hand and knock.

Radomir opens the door. He's wearing a black silk robe, cinched at the waist and open at the chest to give me a glimpse of the hard valley of his pectorals. Behind him is a black hole like the entrance to a tomb.

He steps aside and gestures.

I walk into the room and blink. A pair of bedside lamps glow on dimmers, their light glistening on the red silk sheets of a circular bed. It looks ridiculous, obscene, like an enormous loveseat in some gaudy Las Vegas hotel, an object presented in a dream. A stage.

The door shuts behind me, and I turn about so we face each other across the room.

He's staring at me, his eyes crawling over my flesh, seeing all of me with a rawness that makes me want to cover my face. My legs begin to shake. Fear dumps into my bloodstream, constricting the skin on my scalp. And all the while, all the while, my body grows warm in hidden places.

How? How can he do this to me? How can my body be responding this way?

He's before me now. I can only focus on the hollow of his throat, a blur of skin golden with spray tan; speech is beyond me in this moment. He lifts a hand and traces a burning trail along my jaw, the lightest of touches, and still—it sends a shiver down my body, dark and delicious. I suck in a breath, flushed with disgust at myself. I think of catching his hand in my teeth and biting down, hard. A terrifying lightning bolt of desire and hatred.

I swallow in a dry throat, try to hold on to a sense of transaction. This is business.

"What do you want—" I begin, but he stops me with a finger.

"Shh," he says, and steps away again, looking me up and down.

Then he says it.

"Strip."

The word is like a slap, waking me again to the reality of what is about to happen. What is happening. Before I can stop myself, I unzip my dress and shimmy it down my hips and step out of it. Hot blood drains from my brain and rushes to other parts of me, leaving me dizzy. The room spins and I think, *I might faint here*. The darkness pushes in on all sides. All has gone still and quiet. The storm is suddenly very far away.

Some terrible forfeit is at hand.

Somehow, I go on. Feverish, breath quick and shallow, I unsnap my bra and shuck it off, slip my panties down my legs onto the floor and kick my clothes to the side. The cool air of the suite bites at my hips and belly and exposed breasts, but I make no move to cover myself. I meet his eyes.

He watches me, his gaze holding mine as he undoes the sash at his waist and disrobes, the black silk puddling on the floor. He wants me to see him. To take in his broad swimmer's shoulders and the hard molding of his abs, the thick thews of his thighs and what's between them. Something terrible stirs in me, a terrible familiarity. A memory of waking in the middle of the night to see Josh panting above me whispering, "Is this what you wanted?" and being scoured with guilt for my body experiencing pleasure while he raped me. This is what I was always left with. The sort of confusion that can destroy a soul, the wondering thought: How could I be abused by a man I was attracted to?

Radomir smiles and steps forward.

A black cloud of dread smothers me. It takes all my will to remain standing there and not scream. But his mouth does not descend. No ferocious pain paralyzes my neck. He pushes me down onto the bed, and back. Then places a hand on either of my knees and spreads my legs.

Horror gapes within me.

He kneels on the floor and smiles, framed by my quivering thighs, and my skin breaks out in gooseflesh, my nipples hardening in panic and sickly lust. I am a victim on the altar.

But, for the first time in my life, I'm not.

Because I am choosing this. The crucial difference: I am using this to get what I want. I *want* this to happen.

Remember. Remember why you're here. Remember what the Shipwright said.

(You will come to the heart of it, then.)

An easiness comes into me, a dazzling, unforeseen calm. This is not victimhood; I have changed my role. I asked for this. Because I am strong enough to take it. And I am not afraid. I am not afraid.

(You will face it, or you will fall.)

This is a new Arie. In this moment, I am someone else. I am a stranger. I am aware, with a breathtaking pang of wonder, that somewhere along the way I have undergone a glistening culmination of myself. In the time it takes Radomir to cup the backs of my thighs in his big hands, fingers digging into soft flesh, I have changed. I have become the Arie I was always meant to be, and at the same time, paradoxically, I'm every woman who has ever suffered at the hands of a man, every woman who was ever raped by a man who was supposed to love her, every woman who was ever manipulated into believing she wasn't enough. I look up at the high dark ceiling with tears spilling out of my eyes and down my temples and I'm the woman in the blood-reddened waters as she swims for her life, I'm Marisol as she howls at the awful injustice of the world, I'm the Shipwright biding her time through the long centuries waiting for vengeance that may never come, almost never comes for any woman. Because that is how men win. That is how they hold sway over you. Make you feel there is something wrong with you to deserve this. But there isn't. There is nothing broken in me that attracts such men. They would do this to anyone who'd have them.

Not broken.

I look down at the face between my spread legs, and it is Josh's face, smiling wide as two fangs snick out long and sharp.

It provokes no reaction in me at all.

(Are you ready?)

(Yes.)

And I look up at the shadows of the ceiling, my breath slow and even and the tears dry on my cheeks, and then Radomir's breath tickles my sex and when his fangs slide into me I know, for the first time in my life, what power feels like.

THIRTY-ONE

Afterward, as I lie there staring unseeingly at the ceiling, Radomir wipes his mouth and averts his eyes.

"Well?" I ask in a flat voice.

He looks down at me for a long time as he shrugs his robe on again. I can't work out what's behind that look. "Meet me at elevator at dawn."

"Thank you, Rasha," I whisper, and he pauses at the door. Then I hear it click shut.

Once his footsteps have faded, I turn onto my side and hug myself over the throbbing pain that wants to split me in two, trying to make myself grow smaller and lighter, as light as air.

The first light of morning is bluing the bottom of the sky when I shuffle out onto the aft main deck. The storm has passed as if it had never happened, leaving the world utterly placid, clean and purified. Someone has turned the waterfall back on, and I hobble up behind its masking sheet of noise, my pelvis aching with every step, making my skull throb. I'm shivery with sweat.

I stare at the burner phone a long time before I call.

Adrian doesn't bother with a greeting. He gets right to it.

"Did you do it?"

I close my eyes, pinch the bridge of my nose. I'm not ready for this.

"Yes," I whisper.

I hear a harsh inhalation, then the clap of a hand over a mouth.

"It worked," I hurry to add, throat thickening with shame. "He's gonna take me to see Volok."

Adrian doesn't say anything. I look upward to keep the tears from falling, chin quivering. Waiting. But it's the Shipwright who speaks instead.

"Are you okay?"

I nod, blinking back tears, and let out a great, cleansing sigh. "Yeah. Yeah, I am."

"I'm proud of you, Arie. I know how hard that must have been for you—"

"I can't believe you." Adrian has finally found words, all but snarling with fury. "How could you—how *could* you—"

"I told you this might be necessary," I remind him, voice hardening with both irritation and disappointment. How could he not know what this means for me? How could he not know how my world's been changed? "And let's not forget, I did this for *you*—"

"For me?" Adrian says, his voice growing ragged. "I thought it was for *us*." I can all but hear his teeth chipping as they clench. "I'm worried about you, Aurora. You're *changing*. The old you would never have done what you did. What am I to do with that?"

"Love what I've become," I snap, voice wavering with a throat-tightening swell of anger. "That is what you do, Adrian. That's what love is."

Trembling silence. I wipe impatiently at my eyes and place a hand on my hip, daring him to argue. Then Adrian lets out a cross breath.

"We should just get you back on the *Lady Revenge*, torpedo Volok's boat—"

"Uh-uh," I say, shaking my head. "Nope. There's no certainty Volok would die. I have to see this through myself."

"*You* might die," Adrian spits, twisting the knife. "You know that, right? There's a very real chance that if you go down there, you're not coming back out."

"Maybe," I agree, settling my shoulders. "But this isn't just about us anymore, is it? It's bigger than that now."

"Yeah, I can see that," Adrian says, with a woundedness that wrenches at me. "Do you even—do you still love—" I can hear his breathing, loud and harsh, trying to fight down his anger. His impulse to argue. Then, "Fine," he says, and I hear the relinquishment—the new distance—in his voice. "Call when—when it's over. Okay?"

"Okay." I wait, heart in throat.

"Good luck," he finally adds, every word wrung from him. "I love you."

"I love you, too."

And there's silence on the line.

"Adrian?" I whisper.

"He's left," the Shipwright says. "I . . . I'm sorry."

Tears fill my eyes. I put a hand over them.

"He's just worried. He doesn't know what to do."

I nod, rubbing my forehead. "I know."

"You did the right thing, Arie. Remember that. I could not be prouder of you."

"Thank you," I manage.

The Shipwright sighs. "This is moving faster than we thought. Do you feel like you have Radomir on your side?"

I swallow, thinking of the look on his face as he stared down at me on the bed. Of the way he smiled at me before he lowered his mouth between my spread legs.

I shut my eyes, shivering. "I don't know," I confess. "I'll have to hope so."

"And do you know how you'll do it? Kill the Commodore?"

I look astern, to where the engine room will be. Contemplating. "I think so."

I can hear the smile in the Shipwright's voice. "I'm jealous, you know. You get to do what I've only dreamt of for years. I hope it's satisfying."

I have a grim feeling nothing about this will be.

"In case . . ." the Shipwright starts, and then stops herself. "I know you'll come back. I know that. But in case, for whatever reason, I don't see you again—I want you to know I'm never going back to Transmarinia. And that's because of you. I'm glad I met you, Arie."

I hiccup a laugh and run a hand through my hair, clamping my jaw tight to keep down a wild urge to sob. "I'm glad I met you too, Ilsa."

As the coming dawn brightens the sky, I make my preparations.

I redo my hair and makeup, change into an elegant mauve silk blouse and black ruffled skirt, stuff my bloodstained evening gown in the back of my cabin closet. Then I slip on black flats, drop the burner phone into a skirt pocket, and knock on the door of Cailee's cabin and call her name. No answer. I try the handle and find it locked, rest my brow on the door. "Please be okay," I whisper. "I'll come back for you. I promise."

I find the engine room of the *Keep* behind the lazaret: a humid, humming maze of surgically clean white surfaces. Stainless-steel diamond plates vibrate under my feet as I edge past pumps mounted over light alloy drip trays to a locker where the marine tools are kept. I glance about. No blur of the white boiler suits of engineers. No sign of this creepfest of a crew.

I swing open the locker.

Shelves of boxes filled with spare parts. A jumble of hose clamps, trim cylinder ends, gimbal bearings and fuel filters and repair tape. Beneath this is a waterproof Seastar toolbox. I unlatch it and lift the lid. Nestled inside are rows of wrenches, pliers, socket sets. And what I really want.

At the end of a row of its kind is a slot-edged screwdriver as long as an icepick.

Radomir waits before the elevator as I enter the shadowy atrium, straight-backed with one hand slipped into a trouser pocket. His blonde hair is neatly slicked back, his body fitted in a dark Tom Ford suit. No sign anywhere of the wayward prodigal son. He's dressed to impress daddy.

Behind him the elevator's uncanny light shines a radioactive shade of green.

I stop before him, and he looks me up and down with an appreciative grin on his lips, lifts a hand to graze my hair.

I can't help it—I shiver.

"Ready?" he says.

I nod, and he places a thumb on the fingerprint sensor beside the door. There's a beep as it's accepted, a light flashes green, and the glass doors of the elevator glide apart. He gestures.

It's claustrophobic inside, a glass box suffused with an emerald glow. The light is everywhere, seeming to come from within my very flesh. It's almost supernatural. The color of decay. Of death. Radomir steps in beside me and presses the down arrow button. Sheets of glass glide shut like the doors of a tomb and a numbing dread spreads through me, flattening my lungs, squeezing all the air out of me. Animal instinct kicks in and I touch the small of my back. To make sure it's still there. The long, murderously sharp screwdriver jammed into the waistband of my skirt.

Radomir looks over and smiles at me, smug and handsome and cheeks smudged with green death, and I see that his chest is puffed up with happiness, as if we were prom dates. As if he were escorting me to the altar.

Which he is.

I love you, Adrian, I think, and smile back.

With a slight, nauseating lurch, braided steel cables unreel and the elevator moves, begins its descent into the bowels of the *Keep* and the lair of the Commodore.

THIRTY-TWO

As the atrium slides away from view, I edge a look at Radomir. I have only a few more moments alone with him. What am I to do to ensure his loyalty? To suss out where he stands? *Does* he stand with me? And if he doesn't, shouldn't I use this moment to take care of him? A wild panic settles on me, and I have a crazy image of whipping out that screwdriver and burying it in his temple. My mind shrinks in on itself. I can't. I can't do that. Because he is staring ahead as the elevator glides down into darkness, feeling restlessly at a gold signet ring on his finger I haven't seen before. It looks old, worn, stamped with the letter V—V for Volok. For the one who turned him. For his father. The strong muscles of his neck work in a swallow, and the apprehension there, the nervous vulnerability of a little boy, softens my heart with unexpected tenderness.

A last doubt steals into his face. "You sure you want to do this?" He edges a look at me, not quite meeting my eyes, and I feel as if I'm never seen him so naked. He shrugs, lifting his chin in an air of cool detachment. "We could be . . . good match."

My heart hammers. The blood rushes into my ears. The delicacy, the tentative hope in that question, brings an ache of sympathy into my throat. And I know what to do.

I slip my hand into his.

He startles a look at me, and I smile. *It's okay*, my smile says. *Everything will be all right. We're in this together.*

His lips crook up in abashed gratitude.

The light changes and I look ahead. We're here. We've arrived at the innermost chamber of Dracula's castle. The shaft is opening up and a dark scene slides into view. I have a sudden feeling of being on a ride, some kind of ghastly theme park attraction. For I am no longer on a gleaming superyacht. I have traveled back in time. The elevator has descended into a crypt, a low space as bare as the den of a groundsloth. It is floored in dirt and crowded in by brick walls, a vaulted brick ceiling, and is empty but for an immense canopy bed that looks draped in bridal satin. Cailee lies naked upon that bed, her blonde hair spread out on the pillow in a golden wave, her eyes closed in sleep.

But there is something else in there, too. A closed coffin. Large and lampblacked, supported upon small stone pillars. I'd read about that somewhere. A security against the attacks of vermin.

Fesperman stands beside the coffin.

He looks like a drummer boy. A nutcracker. A devil's porter, born to buttle. He holds a branch of candles in his gloved hand, the only light in that room. And he is smiling.

The elevator slows to a halt and its doors slide back. An odor of earth and pestilence, rotting cerecloth, assaults my nostrils. A smell of putrefaction.

Radomir's hand is crushing mine as it lets go.

I don't move, though. Movement, suddenly, seems impossible. Because that coffin is filling my world, and the import of it makes every nerve in my body scream at me to run, run away from this place, run and keep running until there are no more monsters, no more men, no more horror.

But there is no place like that.

There's a touch at my back, a gentle prompt, and I chuck up my chin and step forward into that crypt.

My legs are shaking, I can barely stand, and still I am propelled forward as in a dream. As we pass the bed, I sneak a look at Cailee. Her body is drained to a milky pallor, marked everywhere with fresh and ragged bitemarks, the signs of a ravenous appetite.

But her chest rises and falls. She's breathing.

Not dead.

The gratitude that follows is dizzying, and I'm still reeling from it when Radomir stops me some ten paces from the coffin. For a moment I don't know what he's doing. He's going down on one knee and pulling me down to do the same. We're kneeling. Kneeling in the cool earth of that crypt. I glance up at Fesperman and he is pleased, as if in approval. This is expected. This is ritual.

Fesperman moves now. He bends low to the crack in the coffin lid and whispers, "They are here, Master."

The hairs on the nape of my neck rise.

I hear nothing at first. And then there's a light scrabbling, as of fingernails scraping across wood. Something ancient stirring. My heart thuds in my chest. My gorge rises in my throat. Then the coffin lid creaks up and back, pushed from within by a pale white hand, fingers splayed wide, and the thing inside the coffin begins to clamber out.

It's as sickly pale as an albino frog, spilling out of its deathbed as if darkness were birthing its opposite. I glimpse a bald misshapen skull with pointed ears fluked rearward. Scrawny shoulders. Then it's standing, impossibly tall—rising up, and up, toward the vaulted ceiling of that crypt, like some gangrel idol—ill-joined and wasted but for a pooched stomach with the skin pulled too tightly over it, as if it had once bloated and become hard. The mark of a lecher.

It is completely, hideously naked.

I cannot look. I cannot breathe. I have to try hard, very hard, to keep from vomiting.

Fesperman is kneeling, too. The branch of candles has been set down, and he has fetched a bowl of water from somewhere. He is washing this thing's feet with the care of a lover. I glimpse toes gnarled with age, knuckled with bunions and drawn into themselves in great curlings of corneous toenails.

I look away.

"There we are," Fesperman croons. "Yes. There we are."

The thing above holding itself with hands dangled at the wrist, as if it were fraught with cold.

I risk a sidelong glance at Radomir. His eyes are downcast, his face twitching, his thumb nervously feeling at his signet ring. This surrender, this humiliating obeisance, is also part of the ritual.

Now Fesperman is returning from the bed, a set of black clothes draped over one arm. He begins to clothe his master like a devoted cupbearer. Black silk underpants. Wool trousers. A watered white silk shirt. Black boots that come almost to the knees. Layer by layer, that hideous pale flesh is hidden away. Then an old tailcoat is slipped on, arms spread, and for a moment its shadow, thrown on the wall by the flickering candlelight, takes on the aspect of some winged thing changing shape.

When Fesperman steps away and takes up the branch of candles once more, I can see the tailcoat has a double line of brass buttons down its front. The sort of thing a legionnaire or naval officer might wear, a mariner in a foreign country. I cannot see this thing's face—my eyes will not go there—but I can see its hands, its nails calcified into horny claws. It folds those long thin fingers over a limp wrist. They look, against the solid black of the coat, like icicles.

It stands there, tall and narrow and hands held before it like a being laid in state, and studies me.

It hisses.

It's not a solitary hiss, but a series of them, lazy and sinewy. And I realize, with a sudden crawling of my flesh, that it's speaking.

The Commodore is speaking to me.

Fesperman smiles. "You are very lovely," he translates.

I find I'm trembling.

I wet my lips. I have to take great care to not let my voice shake. "Your lord is very kind."

More hisses, sibilant susurrations, the remnants of some Slavic language so old no one living can remember it. Fesperman nods and turns to me. "Do you know what it will entail? To enter into concubinage with me."

My throat fails me. I merely nod.

Hisses. Translation. "My blood son tells me your taste is satisfactory. But then, how can we trust my blood son's taste in women?"

Radomir's face spasms. He remains bowed, but rolls his eyes up at Fesperman, a vein throbbing on his brow. "Is *that* what his fiendship said?" he drawls with venomous sweetness.

Fesperman's smile doesn't reach his eyes. His voice has become silky. "I take great pride in translating my master's speech as accurately as possible."

Radomir's face contorts in contempt, then slackens—because that bloodlorn freak in its antique coat is moving. I do not see it walk, precisely. It *glooms* across the floor, a gliding of morbid grace. Goose bumps run up my arms. I carefully keep my head lowered as it holds the backs of its bulbed knuckles to Radomir's face in a gesture of paternal gentleness, and the blood son looks up at the blood father, caught. A fragile hope shines on his features.

Then the taloned fingers brutally flick, opening Radomir's cheek. Blood spatters the floor.

Radomir grunts and turns away, shoulders hunched with a hurt that's not altogether physical.

Fesperman looks on in gleeful satisfaction.

The Commodore glides away again, lifting his curved fingernails to his lips. I hear a rasping lapping sound. Then hissing.

Fesperman listens in reverent rapture, as if he were translating scripture. His face gleams with pride as he watches his master. He is flowing over with the gloating assuredness of the sycophant. "To make something holy is to make it bleed. Virgins, martyrs, gods." His black eyes come to rest on me. "Are you ready to be holy?"

I swallow hard in a dry throat. I can say it. "Yes," I whisper.

The Commodore has stopped. He looms before me, idly scraping his long fingernails together in a gesture of consideration. They rattle like knives.

He hisses.

"Rise," Fesperman orders, eyes glittering.

The blood booms in my ears. I dart a look at Radomir, but he will not look at me, his face is averted in shame. So I stand. My knees pop and wobble under me, and I suddenly feel light-headed. I take a deep breath, rallying myself. Then I lift my eyes and look into the face of Commodore Volok.

I'm hit with its immediate visceral ugliness. The bald, bulging skull with tufts of white hair above the ears. The pale skin creased with wrinkles like an old woman's. The sunken chin and two forefangs dipping down from beneath the top lip, giving it an almost feebleminded look. But it's the eyes that entrance. They glow like silver disks in that rat-like face, as if they were filmed over with some kind of nictitating membrane, as terrifyingly bland and pearlescent as the reflective eyes of some night-hunting animal.

I suck in a breath. To scream. To voice my horror at something so wrong in the world. But the Commodore places a finger to my lips—*shhh*—and I am too startled, too sick with revulsion at the touch, to object.

He sighs out a hiss.

"Bite your lip," Fesperman breathes. "Hard."

I do. I bite down until I taste the sweet tang of blood, and as the Commodore watches those cloudy eyes hood over and his tongue slithers out of his mouth, pasty white and glistening and obscene, and wets his dry lips.

I suddenly feel ill. I have to close my eyes to let the nausea pass, and Radomir kneeling beside me cannot watch. He is shaking with helpless anger.

Fesperman smiles.

This is it, I think. *This is the moment. If I make my move now, Radomir will be with me.*

I reach behind for the screwdriver jammed into my skirt.

But all that is forgotten as the Commodore leans forward, eyes fluttering and wet lips pursed, and that plaguey mouth descends upon me.

Black horror.

The kiss tastes of sour corruption, of sensually spoiled meat, sweetly rotting. It is a graceless, slick smearing of mouths, obliterating all self. I cannot move, cannot breathe. I am petrified. I am lost in violation, in slobbering defilement. His tongue slips inside me and waggles about.

Wrath kindles in me like a sun.

I grab the handle of the screwdriver, my heart bursting with murderous conviction. My whole life funnels down to this moment.

And it vanishes as the Commodore is suddenly gone, Fesperman gliding between us.

"Very nice," the butler purrs, and I'm overcome with a feeling of profound loss as he cocks his head to give his ear. The Commodore is in the act of turning away, lifting one taloned hand to hide a tremulous creasing up of his blood-wet lips, the gesture of a tittering flirt. And a hiss floats back.

"Let's get you changed into something more suitable," the butler says, and nods at a revoltingly lacy wedding dress laid out on the bed beside a senseless Cailee. "He would like to show you something."

THIRTY-THREE

I am in a daze as the four of us file into the elevator and it ascends, its soft fey light casting a green glow on our faces. I feel naked and devastated. I could not bring the burner phone or screwdriver with me in this dress; the best I could do was leave them hidden under my heap of clothes when I changed back in that crypt. A consuming hopelessness envelops me. I cannot escape the sense of everything unraveling, all my chances slipping away. The Commodore stands at the front—so tantalizingly close I can see the frail ossicles in those curved ears, the profusion of white hair there—with Fesperman between us; I cannot get to him. I am boxed in, suffocated, diminished. I feel like a sacrifice in this itchy, ridiculous dress. A fraud.

I am failing you, Adrian. I am failing you.

The elevator dings open on a floor I've never seen before. A long immaculate hallway now. I am marching to my doom. What's in store for me? Radomir gives me no clue, he will not look at me, his face is stiff and pained and shut off.

Then light grows ahead, brightening the world. It's full morning now. We've come to the bridge of the *Keep*, a sweep of bombproof windows tinted to keep out the summery glare of light off the ocean. It looks like the bridge of a starship. It's cavernous and bare, and a couple of crew members—the first and second officers—tap at touchscreen helm stations that are nothing more than floating sheets of glass. When they catch sight of the Commodore, the color drains from their faces and they stumble back. I don't blame them. Even if they knew the fiend was aboard, it's clear he does not belong here. He looks like a creature out of time as he glides out of the gloom into that high-tech space, stiff shoulders drawn almost up to fluked ears, hands convulsed at his sides like spiders. A thing come from transylvanic origins. A being without foreking.

This ripple of dismay does not go unnoticed by the *Keep*'s commander. A man in a white polo with the four gold stripes of a captain rises from a skipper's chair made from alligator hide and wickedly spiraling kudo horns. His grizzled hair is cropped short, highlighting a silvery scar snaking down through a cleft in his hairline. If he is as horror-struck as his crew, he does not show it.

He drops to one knee. "My lord."

"Are we ready?" Fesperman asks in an oily voice.

"All set, sir."

I feel an ill tickle of disquiet and drift toward the floor-to-ceiling windows. I have to know. To verify my suspicions. The sun flashing off the sea makes it hard to place where we've dropped anchor, but after a time it comes to me. We are, inarguably, back in the Mediterranean. We float in a grouping of jagged islets that look very familiar: Sardinia. We're off Sardinia again, in lovely turquoise water too shallow for a submarine yacht. Which is why the *Lady Revenge* has been forced to surface a half mile off our bow, looking like a superyacht above water.

My heart turns over in my chest.

He can't know, I convince myself. *Volok can't know it's the Shipwright's boat. No one does.*

Adrian is safe. He has to be.

When I turn about, there are many eyes on me. Many knowing smiles.

The Commodore, having taken the captain's place in that horned skipper's chair as if it were a throne, folds one hand over the other with icicle fingers dangling, Fesperman at his elbow.

His slithery urlanguage fills the bridge.

"Did you really think I would not know why you're here?" Fesperman translates in a sheen of gloating triumph. "I always knew the reason you were here. That you had come to assassinate me."

A sickening numbness tingles down to the tips of my fingers. I feel my legs might buckle under me, and I think of bracing myself on a helm station to keep from collapsing. But I don't.

Radomir won't look at me. His jaw muscles clench and relax.

Did he know?

The hissing continues, burrowing into my ears like cockroaches, making my skin go crawly and strange.

"And you willingly debased yourself in your pursuit. Lied. Murdered. Threw away your body. All to get to me." He lifts his upper lip and expels a disdainful breath: *tsss.* "How charming."

I feel woozy now, shivery with an ill sweat of humiliation. Tears spring to my eyes. How could I not see this coming? And was he right? Had I become an awful person to get here? The ground moves beneath me, and I do it. I hold out a hand to support myself—I am drifting apart in this moment.

Radomir's chin has begun to tremble.

The gaunt shape on that throne scrapes its long fingernails over its bald head in thought: *sssSShriiiiKKK.* That upper lip retracts again to let out its animal hissings. "Do you not see, then?" Fesperman translates. "All these things—these things you were willing to do to kill me—make you my perfect concubine."

No. No. That's not me. That's not who I am.

"Which is why I will still accept your offer." The scraping stops. An eye glows flat and reflective out of that skull at me. "If you take your phone and call Adrian Voper."

And Fesperman holds up my burner phone in two cottony white fingers.

My stomach drops out of me. Blackness closes in around my vision.

"Yes," Fesperman continues, looking down at his master with the adoring gaze of a proud father. "I know what has been following us." The Commodore makes a languid shooing motion at the *Lady Revenge*: a gesture of contempt. "I know that contraption belongs to the Shipwright, and that Adrian is aboard."

I shut my eyes to stop the tears from falling.

"I know everything that happens in my domain. I have my spies in Transmarinia. I have my spies everywhere. All seek my love. They are willing to do anything for it. As you will soon." The Commodore oozes pride as he takes in my wet eyes, staring down his aquiline nose in amusement. "Such passion. Such tenderness. It has been some time since I've been shown that. But you will share it with me, I do assure you. You will come to love me." Those taloned hands arrange themselves in effeminate stateliness. "So call him. Tell him to come in, so he can answer for his crimes." Fesperman offers me the phone with a chilling smile. "Or he can answer for them another way."

I don't understand. The skipper taps one of the helm stations, and I look out across the *Keep*. Double teak panels are sheathing back into the foredeck, revealing a hidden silo of white-capped shells as bright and shiny as candy: an array of ballistic missiles ready to launch.

I taste bile at the back of my throat.

"No," I croak. "Please." I cast a desperate look at Radomir.

The Commodore's mouth writhes in a sneer. "You think he can help you? One who was so easily smitten by you he could not perceive your true purpose here?" That sound again: *tsss*. "No. He will stay where he is. He knows his place."

Radomir shies his eyes away, shoulders slumped in defeat.

That hissing all around me. The Commodore watches me as his rat-like mouth moves. The glowing orbs of his eyes like hypnotic selenoscopes, an unblinking basilisk's gaze. Radiating malevolent pleasure.

And Fesperman is close. A hand on my shoulder, a whisper in my ear. "Just call him and be my concubine. That's all you need to do."

I look at the phone. The call is already going through. No say in the matter.

No choice.

I hold it to my ear. It rings and rings.

The crew of the *Keep* watch me. I lower my eyes, feeling like a child. A traitor.

I can warn him at least, I think. *I'm lost now, but he can still get away.*

The ringing goes on and on. Six times, seven times. He normally picks up on the first ring. What is going on?

And the truth sinks in, as undeniable as a cancer: He's not coming. He's not picking up.

I hurt him that deeply.

"Aurora?" Adrian's voice suddenly fills my ear, weary and reserved, and I gulp in air, choking back a sob.

"Baby," I whisper.

Fesperman's gloved hand tightens like a vise on my shoulder.

"Are you okay? How'd it go?"

"I . . ." The words won't come out. I don't know what to say. I feel the Commodore's gaze on the back of my neck, making me bristle with gooseflesh.

A murderer. I'm a murderer.

And Adrian senses it—how could he not?—that something's wrong. His voice drops, becomes hard. "Baby, whatever they're trying to make you do, don't you fucking do it. Do you understand?"

I hiccup a sob. I am out of my body. I am floating away. Let me float away.

Fesperman looks over my shoulder at the Commodore, shakes his head.

"Don't you fucking do it, do you hear me?" Adrian snaps. "I will not let him do that to you—"

"Baby," I gasp, the tears splashing down my cheeks. I dash them away and shake my hair out of my face, school my voice into something firmer. "Please—please listen to me—"

"I love you, baby. I will always love you—"

The Commodore's face twists in sheerest disdain—a disdain concealing a hurt that stings to the core. Then a lazy hissing. "How disappointing," Fesperman says. He nods at the skipper, and the skipper taps the helm. White smoke mushrooms as the missiles blast out of their hidden silo into the air.

"No!" I gasp, lifting my hand as at some appalling illusion. This isn't happening. This isn't real. "No—*no!*"

"I'll always be with you," Adrian promises. "My Northern Light."

The missiles arc down onto the *Lady Revenge* in a silent swoop of death, and the explosion fills my eyes with flame.

"*NOOOOOOOO!*"

My howl brings me to my knees, bent over double. Even from here, even this far away, I can feel the shockwave, and the hot air that smells like ozone, like burning flesh.

I cannot see. I am wracked with sobs. I am howling, blind with amazement, and I am scattered into a hundred different parts reliving my relationship with Adrian.

A part of me is holding his hand in a submersible at the bottom of the sea as he tries to tell me what he is.

A part of me is falling in love with him as he plays the piano for me.

A part of me is falling in love with him all over again as he proposes to me under the Northern Lights.

A part of me knows I will never fall for another man like this again.

And all of me is falling, falling, falling.

I could have stopped it. I could have let the Shipwright torpedo this boat. Adrian could still be alive.

If it wasn't for me.

The Commodore watches me with a look of distaste, wrinkles his nose and hisses air through those two snaggle fangs.

"So very disappointing," Fesperman breathes in my ear, as intimate as a lover. "I suppose I'll just have to keep your best friend as my concubine, then. And find a new yacht builder." The butler addresses the bridge now. "I'll be calling a meeting tonight at the Nosferyachtu Club. To appoint a new Shipwright."

The Commodore spares me one last disgusted look before he rises from his throne, wraps his spider hands about himself and nosferatues back into the gloom. Leaving Fesperman to consider Radomir and I as if we were two unruly children.

"You can take care of this one," he sniffs, waving a gloved hand at me in casual dismissal. "Enjoy her if you want. And meet us at the clubhouse later." And with that the butler lopes after his master waiting in the glowing elevator, as neat of foot as a wolfhound, and the only sound in that bridge is my agonized breathing.

Adrian, my Adrian, I think, watching the flaming wreckage of the *Lady Revenge* sink into the sea, and then Radomir is dragging me up with painful strength, his voice harsh in my ear. "Come," he says, marching me toward the *Keep*'s aft. "Let us take little boat ride."

And I follow Radomir, blood son of Commodore Volok, as he leads me to my death.

THIRTY-FOUR

I stumble along behind Radomir in a disbelieving daze, the blood singing in my ears. *He's gone*, is all I can think, over and over. *My Adrian is gone.*

And then: *Why can't I cry? Why can't I cry for him?*

What folly.

All along, then, all along, the Commodore had been toying with me. They'd all been toying with me. Laughing at me. Mocking me. Letting me think I was clever, that I was getting close to him. When all I was doing was playing into the Commodore's hands. Playing his game.

All to show how powerful he was.

Stupid, stupid girl.

Down long companionways to a stern locker on the lower deck. A gull wing door has gaped open in the hull, and a limo tender bobs in the shaded water there. Thirty feet long, sleek and beamy with livery as black as a hearse. A casket.

My death casket.

That's fine, I think with ferocious fatalism. *I deserve this.*

Radomir leads me onto the tender's stern, an open teak boarding platform. My eyes latch onto the *Lady Revenge* glowing inside a billowing of dull, dirty pink smoke—my heart cracks in my chest—but Radomir tugs me on, inexorable, and soon I'm ducking into the tender's enclosed cabin.

I blink. Tranquil lights on dimmers illuminate two couches installed lengthwise down the boat, a luxurious spread of handstitched white leather; the floor varnished teak, the walls and ceiling deep black lacquer. It looks like the inside of a stretch limo.

Radomir seats himself midway down one of the couches and crosses his legs, stretches an arm along the couch's back and smooths down his tie. He has apparently recovered from his humiliation. He is well-practiced in this.

As the tender's twin diesel engines thrum to life, he gestures at the couch opposite him, as if this were like any other charter jaunt. "Please."

I sink unsteadily onto cool leather and glance astern. I can see, framed by the cabin doorway, the *Keep* gliding away at full sail like some spectre-bark caught in the merciless blaze of day. Leaving us heading out to open sea.

The grim reality of my situation begins to sink in, and a chill runs down my spine. I look over at Radomir and find him feeling the cut on his cheek. He catches me looking and drops his hand into his lap, stares at me with smug, heavy-lidded eyes.

My tongue sticks in the back of my throat.

Soon we'll be out of sight of land, and the engines will cut out. Soon there'll be what comes next.

A heaviness settles over me, smothering all hope. And then I remember, like a jolt to the brainstem: *Cailee*.

The black edges of grief recede like a thinning fog. Gradually, cell by cell, my body remembers its desire to live.

Fuck this.

I look out again at the black dot of the *Keep* fading into the horizon, and my hands clench into fists at my sides. *I may have failed Adrian, but I can't fail her. I can still rescue her. I can still have my vengeance. Somehow, somehow, I will make it out of this, and get my best friend to safety. I will make the Commodore pay.*

For Adrian.

I scan the tender for something that will give me a weapon. A wet bar or concealed refrigerator stocked with chilled glassware. Fucking anything.

Radomir watches me with mocking eyes from his couch, one thumb slowly, hypnotically rotating his signet ring on his finger.

Soon, those eyes promise. *Soon*.

I want to cry, I want to scream with frustration. There's nothing of use in here. Nothing.

Radomir is studying my body, his eyes lingering on my legs, my breasts pushed up high and full in my wedding dress. He studies my throat.

A black panic begins to set in, scattering my wits. What to do? How will I get out of this?

The twin engines putter and thrum down and the tender slows. We've stopped.

My heart leaps into my throat. I fly a look at Radomir and find he's smiling.

No, I think with a sudden cramping of my lungs. *It can't be. Not yet.*

I'm not ready.

After a moment there's a splash, and then a blaze of light as a door at the front of the tender slides back. It's the pilot. He looks like a kid, freckly-faced and unsure in his tight black polo. He steps in from the open helm and shuts the door behind him, glances between Radomir and me. His smooth throat dips in a swallow.

"I've dropped anchor," he stammers. "I'll . . . be on the swim deck." And he awkwardly side-shuffles between us out onto the stern.

Leaving me alone with a smiling Radomir.

The boat bobs in the silence. A distant part of me registers the lapping of waves, the crying of gulls, but I can't hear any of it. I am blocked up with desperate thoughts fluttering through my mind like disturbed bats. *This can't be how this ends. It can't be.* A wild, jumpy despair infuses my limbs, making my hands shake, my knees clack together. And then I know. I know what to do. How to shake his comfort with this.

I squeeze my knees still and clasp my hands in my lap.

"He didn't even tell you," I remind him. "He didn't even let you in on what he was up to. He let you begin to care for me, and all the while he was planning to kill me. You were as in the dark as I was."

The self-satisfaction drains out of Radomir's face.

"Why stay with a person like that? Wouldn't you prefer being freed?"

He smirks, shakes his head. "No."

"You could be turned again," I point out. "You'd be the new Commodore, after all."

A hesitancy now, as if feeling the dark pull of that temptation. But this, too, is in turn dismissed. He snorts—a sound of amazed disgust, as if this is beneath me—and summons up a requisite grimness. "Don't worry," he gruffs. "I will make it gentle." And he scooches forward in a creaking of leather.

My skin shrinks all around my body.

"I know you resent him," I blurt, and this gets his attention. He stills all over. His pupils constrict. So I go on, panic-talking now. "I know you're terrified of him. Don't you want to be free of that? To not be his beaten dog anymore?"

Radomir's face has slackened into something ugly.

"I know," I exclaim, soft with revelation. "I know why you party, why you lose yourself in debauchery. It's to get away from it. The hatred you have for yourself. The self-hatred he's taught you."

Radomir jerks his head away, lips pressed tightly together.

"I know," I whisper, and lift a hand to touch his face, the cut on his cheek. "You know I know. But we can end it. Together."

"Stop," he chokes, his voice throaty with appeal.

"Take off that ring," I urge. "Cast off his power over you."

He shakes his head like a child, looks down at the gold band on his hand, the fingers twisting it.

"Rasha," I say, and he shuts his eyes. My throat, to my surprise—my astonishment—lumps up with tears. "He doesn't love you. He never did."

It happens faster than I can follow. There's a blur of movement and a hand is seizing my face, pinching my cheeks, pufferfishing my lips. A finger points at me, right between the eyes. "*Stop. Talking*," Radomir breathes with deadly quiet.

My blood turns cold.

Something's happening now. His pupils bleed outwards until the whole of his eyes are completely black. A pair of fangs curve down, wriggling out of his gums in unnatural birth.

"Shh," he says, holding a finger to his lips, and tilts my head to the side. "Next part hurts."

Yes, I think. *Yes, it will.*

My nails slashing across his cheek sounds like scissors shearing through paper. He roars and curses, touches his face and checks the blood shining on his fingertips. Then his lips snarl up, and in a blur of ferocity he snatches me off the couch—my heart stops—and tosses me bodily into the air.

Wind whistles past my ears. I glimpse dimmer lights overhead and gleaming black lacquer. Then I bounce off a tinted window with a hollow *thunk* and tumble into the floor in a heap, head spinning, feeling like the right side of my ribcage has been thumped with a tire iron. The tender rocks slightly from the impact, or maybe that's a concussion, and everything I see slears into quavering doubles.

There are two pilots on the stern now, tightly overlapping one another, both very carefully not paying attention to what's happening inside the tender.

I try to elbow my way up, and Radomir hammers a fist into my stomach, slamming me back down. I cough explosively and curl into a ball, hugging the pain to me as if it were a precious thing. I'm so winded I don't think I'll ever breathe again; my lungs have gone into shock. Then I drag in a big whooping gasp of air and it's as if I've been reborn.

There's a slice of light at the front of the tender. The door. The door to the helm—and daylight.

I begin to crawl on hands and knees toward it.

A low, marveling chuckle behind me. "You got heart, little rabbit. I give you that."

I push off the floor for the door in a staggering lunge and I'm never going to make it, Radomir shoves a foot in my ass and I go down on my chin mere feet before the door. My teeth bang together, and darkness startles up into my skull like a flock of birds. I reach up and my hand snags the handle, but Radomir has grabbed me by the ankle and yanked, twisting me onto my back. "No!" I cry out, a howl of pain and protest and defiant rage. "*No!*" My hands scrabble, finding purchase on a small service alcove beside the door, sending a champagne cooler clattering.

"I was nice before," Radomir grunts, giving a great tug and letting my lower body drop to the floor. "You no get nice now."

Now he's crawling over me, kneeling above me, fangtips flashing like butcher knives, and for a moment I wish I'd black out already. I don't want to be awake for this.

"Shh," he coos, brushing my hair away from my neck with seductive poise. "Don't worry, you will like it. You like it last time."

The empty champagne cooler rolls past my head, following the rocking of the boat. But it's not empty. Something is sliding inside it with a metallic scraping sound.

"You like it when daddy rough, yes?"

He rubs a thumb across my throat, across the heavy pulse of my jugular, and I feel a sudden sensation of intense violation.

"Yeah," I breathe. "I like it rough."

And I sit up and thump the steel corkscrew of a wine opener into his chest.

I hear the crunch of bone and Radomir blinks and looks down at the big gloopy runnels of blood dripping off that coiling steel, looks at me with hooded eyes and twitches a finger. "Tsk, tsk," he scolds. "Missed the heart."

And with a flick of his talons, he slashes the side of my neck open.

The pain is so sharp and lovely it's almost blissful. I unthinkingly clap a hand there, feeling the hot gush between my fingers, the mighty pumping of a severed artery. The sudden runoff of blood is so great I go light-headed and blackness rushes in. And I think, with real surprise, *I've been killed. He just killed me.*

My head thumps on the floor and I stare up at the gleaming ceiling of the tender, the lights blurring into a humming white glow as my mouth fills with blood. There's not even any pain anymore. This experience is so big it's beyond pain, beyond what's possible. And I think, with not a little wonder, *It's really happening. My life is ending. This is dying.*

Radomir leans over me.

"Oof. Ariushka, darling," he tuts and wrenches the wine opener out of his chest, tosses it aside. "Why are you lying on floor? Bit hard, no? Here." He lifts my head—the world throbs—and tucks a fluffy throw pillow under the base of my skull. "I make sure my girls comfortable."

Then he pulls my hand—gently, very gently—away from my neck.

There's a sudden, breath-stealing outrushing of pressure and my body jerks, my eyes go wide.

"Is okay," he soothes. "Is okay now."

And he dips his head to drink from my neck.

A faint horror screams inside me, making me kick weakly. It doesn't last long. A paralyzing sweetness spreads, a sort of dazed languor, and I feel no desire to fight, to scream, to cry, to worry about anything at all. All that's gone now. All of that is very far away. A tumultuous music rises in me, and I feel the rapture of my blood. This being, so close, does not seem so terrible.

The world is filling up with wonder.

Things are getting dimmer now, making my eyelids heavy. I can hear the crying of a gull. I can hear, very faint, the calming hush of the sea. It's the most beautiful sound I've ever heard.

A thump flutters my eyelids open. I have to concentrate very hard to make out the shape framed by a sparkling brilliance of light at the stern. Tall, pale, burned, dripping wet. It stands over another shape crumpled on the swim deck: the pilot. The pilot is lying there with his head wrenched around so it's facing backwards, mouth open in amazed horror.

How odd.

Radomir doesn't notice, doesn't lift his head from his ministrations. His eyelids flutter drunkenly, and I feel an appalling wave of tenderness, like a mother's love, as he suckles me.

This is not fear. The worst thing—the very worst thing—has happened, and there's no longer anything to be afraid of.

I smile with blood-stained lips. I'm free.

I wake to feel Radomir ripped from me. I whimper—a weak sound of protest—but Radomir doesn't return. Somewhere far away, there's a ferocious snarling, the mighty din of two bodies crashing about, and my head bobbles back and forth on the pillow as the tender rocks. I watch my pool of blood migrate across the varnished teak.

Everything is growing darker.

There's another blur above me now. It's speaking to me.
Is it sobbing? It's hard to hear.

Then I hear it.

"Aurora? Aurora!"

A wild, anguished sound makes my eyelids flutter. Then a familiar voice, constrained and pleading. "Baby. My Northern Light. Come back to me."

Adrian?

"I'm here, baby. I'm here. You're safe now. See?"

He's lifting my hand, and I feel a touch of coolness. My ring. My engagement ring. He's sliding it onto my finger. I can see it flashing there when I lift my hand to his face. His beautiful face.

But it can't be him. Adrian's dead. I must be dead. Dying.

My angel-Adrian chokes back a noise and holds my hand to his cheek. I can feel a wetness, the tears sliding down his cheeks. My eyes strain to stay open.

"There," he says, drawing in a great shuddering breath, as if struggling not to cry. "You can't leave now, okay?" His voice cracks. "Please don't leave me."

It's okay, I want to tell him, and smile. *We're together now. I've met you in that better place.*

And I can feel it. The new countryside. The immortal shining cities, silent and waiting.

We'll never be apart.

"AURORA!"

You always told me I was your Northern Light, baby. But you were mine. You were always mine.

My guiding star.

He's shaking me now, he's holding me to him and rocking back and forth, howling.

He must be so happy.

Adrian, my Adrian. I'm coming to you. I see you.

I'm joining you now.   *I'm dying.*

We're both stars now.

THIRTY-FIVE

The world is rocking.

It rocks me back up from a luxuriant darkness, my awareness a long, excruciating rising to the surface. At first I am bodyless, a cinder in the dark, pulsing with pain. Then, there is *more*. Legs, arms, fitting themselves back together. The parts that make up a person.

After a multitude of eons, I remember my name.

Somewhere the sea slaps, a crisp, sparkling sound, and I become aware of the thirst. I have never felt so thirsty in my life. I lick my lips and find they're dry and cracked, beginning to split. I decide it's time to move. I twitch a finger and rub at something cold and metallic, slightly spiky: my engagement ring.

My eyes snap open.

And yes, it's there, that clear diamond twinkling like a star. My mouth gapes, I can't believe it. I look up.

Adrian stares down at me.

My body jolts. His dark blue suit clings to him, wet and soot-streaked and pocked with holes, and half his face is jaggedly blackened with burn marks and spots of boiled red flesh, as if it had borne the brunt of a landmine. But it's him.

My Adrian.

"Hey you," he whispers, tears leaking out of his eyes.

I fly up into his arms, clutching him, holding him to me, fingers digging into his jacket. "Baby?" I whisper, disbelieving, and my voice flutters into a shriek. "*Baby?*" And I'm kissing him, crying, hiccupping sobs of joy, the happiness so intense I think my ribs will crack. I pull back and look at him, gripping his shoulders, feeling the solid weight of him, and he's still there. Still real.

He's come back to me.

"I thought I lost you," he whispers, touching my cheek. "I was so scared."

"I thought," I begin, and break into a long tearing sob. "I thought—"

"I'm fine," he soothes. "I got out. The Shipwright saved me. She . . ." The burnt half of his face grimaces. "She covered me with her body when it happened, so she didn't . . ."

Everything inside me goes cold. "No . . ."

He swallows hard, eyes welling again, and nods. "I owe her my life."

I glance about, and my jaw drops when I take in the limo tender. It's splattered everywhere with blood. Blood on the wholesome whiteness of its leather couches, creeping in gruesome tides on the floor. The signs of a horrific struggle.

And I remember: Radomir. My neck.

I stagger to my feet, knees wobbling, and study my reflection in a bank of tinted windows. It looks like I'm wearing a bib of blood, and my neck is still a horror show . . . but that nasty slash has ungaped in queerest styptic. A miracle.

And on the other side of my neck: a pair of fresh fang-marks.

I feel faint.

I turn to Adrian, the beginnings of an ugly rage forming. "Tell me you didn't . . ."

He swallows, touches two trembling fingertips to an eyebrow and drops them in a helpless gesture. "I didn't know what else to do . . ."

I shake my head and whirl away, making for the open door at the stern, and he trails after me, pleading. "I was losing you, Aurora. I couldn't let that happen . . ."

I'm almost to the stern now, in the shadowed doorway before the teak-finished aft deck baking in the heat. The light is blinding, scorching my eyes, filling my skull like a poisonous radiation. I whimper at the pain, but I do it—I hold my hand out into the late afternoon sunshine.

It begins to smoke.

I snatch it away and hug it to myself, dragging in great convulsing gasps, tears in my eyes. And it all rushes in at me. The new senses, the new knowledge. The exhalations of sea mist, the ghostly breaths of the moon. The heart of a bird beating its delicate rivers of blood through flesh, its raucous cries stabbing my eardrums like steel needles.

And under it all, humming away like a sinister, unifying harmonic in the universe, that maddening thirst.

I put a hand to my breast, and it's confirmed beyond all doubt: my heart, still and silent, unbeating.

"How could you?" I snarl, shoulders heaving. "How *could* you?"

"Baby . . ." He touches me, but I slap his hand away and he recoils.

"You had *no right*," I explode, whirling on him. "Do you understand? It's *my* body, *my* life. You had no right to make that decision for me."

I grip my hair, overcome with sobs, and he holds a hand to his brow, his face slack with catastrophic remorse. At last, he lowers his hand. "I'm so sorry," he gulps. "I didn't—I love you—" He turns away, holding the back of a hand to his lips, and shuts his eyes. "Oh God." He bends over, hands on knees, shivering, and lets out a great, helpless wail of anguish. Then he straightens again. "All right," he says, hard with resolution, sniffs and nods his head, talking himself through it. "I can fix this. This can be fixed. I can—I can kill myself, and you'll change back—"

"Stop," I snap.

"No," he persists, and faces me. "I deserve it. You shouldn't have to live the rest of your life like this—"

I lift a palm. "Just . . . stop."

He waits, chest heaving, and I sink down onto a couch and cup my eyes in the heels of my hands. It's happened. I've become the very thing I wanted to destroy in Adrian, the very thing that terrified me: I'm one of *them*. Now, darkness forever, filled with blood. I am cursed. I have become the abuser. Will I ever be able to forgive Adrian? What will this do to us? How can this be borne?

A crushing despair threatens to annihilate me, and it takes every last reserve of my strength to push it away. There has to be a way out of this; I've found a way out of everything else. This can't be how it ends. Not when I've gotten Adrian back. Not when we've come this far, gotten this close.

And it clicks.

"We'll just have to go back," I announce, resolve hardening my voice, "and kill the Commodore."

Adrian's head juts forward. "*What?*"

"We're going to end this once and for all."

"But how? Why would he ever give us an audience now?"

"Because we're going to beg forgiveness and offer our fealty," I say, slumping back on the couch, exhausted.

Adrian's face slackens. "You think he'll buy it?"

I nod. "He won't be able to help himself. It'll let me get close to him." I shiver. "He'll feed on me"—I turn up a pale wrist—"and that'll be my chance. We'll just have to hope that when I kill him, his death will bring not only you back to life, but me as well." I turn to Adrian. "Will that work?"

He blinks and shakes his head, jaw hanging in amazement. "I have no idea. No one's ever gone after a master maker before. I've never seen a whole lineage of our kind be reverted back at once." And a faint smile dimples his cheeks as he looks at me. "But fuck it. Let's do it."

And we grin at each other in the *Keep*'s limo tender as it bobs on the sea, blood creeping about our feet.

I spend the remainder of the day laid out on one of the couches with my head in Adrian's lap, recovering. My body feels as if it's been dropped off a cliff; everything pulsates in protest. But I can feel it healing, the long, slow work of flesh repairing itself, an uncanny writhing at my neck. From time to time I touch the wound, gingerly. It's already becoming smooth.

I sleep.

In my sleep I can feel Adrian stroking my hair, over and over, like a prayer. Just like Mrs. Colding once did. It almost makes me forget that I don't know who I am anymore. It almost makes me forget that I'm angry with him.

When I wake, I'm alone.

I sit up. We're underway: I can hear the thrum of the engines, feel the passage of water beneath me. Darkness has fallen, and my body responds to it, drawn to that velvety blackness like a moth to light, singing in relief.

It lures me out to the helm where Adrian is piloting us toward Sanguisuga and the Nosferyachtu Club.

He knows the way well: he deftly hugs the coastline of Sardinia, evading its shoals and groupings of isles. He glances at me as I join him. I grip a steel support strut, the wind in my hair, the night a symphony of noises about me, and drink in this new world.

"How do you feel?" he asks as I stand there, listening.

I slant a look at him, all of my anger and hurt and disappointment behind it, and he nods, taking that in. His eyes shine pale blue in the starlight as he stares ahead. "I want you to know," he says above the spray and wind, and swallows. "I'm sorry. I'll never do anything like that again. I'm done . . . trying to control everything."

I let the wind slip my hair out of my face and watch him. Waiting.

"The reason Volok wants me so badly is . . ." He falters, and then lifts his chin, facing it. "He has a terrible need to control things. He is my blood father, and like any father he tried to mold me in his image. But it went beyond that. You had to reflect back the version of himself he wanted to see. Anything could be perceived as a slight against him. And if he felt slighted, you can believe he got his vengeance. Everything you did, everything you said, everything you thought was used against you. Twisted. Manipulated. Turned into something irrational and selfish. Until the very air you moved through was charged with terror. Until you began to contort yourself into a different person to make him happy." His throat dips. "Until you started to believe you were as awful a person as he claimed you to be."

I can sense it now. His whole body trembling, the manifestation of internalized trauma.

I touch his arm, urging him: *Go on*.

"After a while, I took on those same controlling ways in my efforts to keep alive the memory of my wife. Volok was beyond pleased; I had become like him. My horror was complete. It was like waking from a dream. His grip on me was broken. And so when I finally turned my back on him, he couldn't stand it—the true mark of a narcissist. The greatest insult is to show you don't need them." He eases his jaw forward and lets out a slow, unburdening breath. "And ever since he's been trying to win me back."

I feel a deep tingle of revelation open within me, working on my skin like magic. *That's why I love this man*, I think. *That's why we have this connection. Only those who have lived through that can understand.* I look up at his face, clean and beautiful in the moonlight, his dark hair sucked back from his brow in the roaring wind, eyes filled with a nervous determination as they scan the night for the Nosferyachtu Club, and I think, *But he got away. I helped free him. Unlike Radomir, he didn't let that abuse consume him. And now, like me, he's facing his abuser.*

A heavy love suffuses me, a new and startling capacity for forgiveness, and I curl my fingers into his hair at the back of his head. He looks at me.

"I'm proud of you," I whisper, and his eyes glisten with tears.

Something flashes in the moonlight, and I look down to see he's pulling something out of his pocket. A gold band, stamped with the letter V. A companion to Radomir's signet ring.

The stamp of Volok, binding his blood sons to him.

I'm amazed I haven't seen it before. All this time, he must have hidden it. But still kept it on him. A reminder of what he once had been. What he overcame.

Now, he slips it on the ring finger of his right hand and stares at it, as if he has taken on an old curse. His lips twitch with bitter irony. "I never thought I'd wear it again. Least of all under these circumstances."

I watch him as he places both hands on the wheel again, gripping hard. I place my hand on his, the cold touch of the signet ring against my palm. "I'm sorry. About Radomir."

Adrian stills.

"That you had to . . ." I wave at the blood-splashed horror show of the boat behind us. "After everything, I know there was still love there. That—that must have been hard."

Adrian nods, his lips pressing together, his face screwing up as he looks away. Then, "He lost his way," he gruffs, and he lets out a breath, turns and smiles down at me. "But we're finding ours now." He laces his fingers with mine on the wheel, his signet ring flashing. His face turns grim, and he looks ahead. "Time to play the dutiful son again."

We round a bay toward a lone island, and ahead the Nosferyachtu Club looms like a slab of white in the moonlight, like a turn-of-the-century seaside house in

Cape Cod. Its white-washed trim gleams. Its befanged burgee flutters in the wind. Yachts float in rows at its dock, among them the *Keep* with its queer green lights shining like balefire in the night, shiveringly reflected in the water. And above all, bats wheel and flitter and circle the club's high turret, returning from their nocturnal hunt.

It's almost dawn.

THIRTY-SIX

As we approach, I see there are ghoulish green glows in the water along the dock, like beckoning corpse lights or patches of phosphorescence—underwater dock lights. In that eerie illumination, tall bulky shapes can be seen waiting at the end of a jetty for us. Black-suited, earpieces plugged in, leather shoulder holsters glimpsed inside their jackets. They seem impassive at our appearance out of the predawn gloom. Perhaps we've been expected.

We had to have been. Radomir never returned after all, did he?

Steady, I think as Adrian kills the engine and we coast toward the jetty. *You can do this.*

I slip my hand into Adrian's. Our eyes lock.

"I love you," he whispers.

"I love you, too," I whisper back, every part of me aching.

Adrian noses the limo tender alongside the jetty, and I toss up a line. Then those black shapes are helping us out and patting us down, frisking us with casual efficiency. All done without a word spoken. Adrian hisses when they slide their hands along my thighs, and they recoil at the pricks of white glinting in his mouth. Then one of them touches his ear and murmurs something, jerks his head and steps aside.

The jetty boards creak under our feet. Ahead of us, that clubhouse looms, its burgee snapping faintly in the wind.

My skin hums. I can hear a buoy clanging somewhere out there on the sea. I can hear bats going *shree-shree* in the dark. Black shapes swoop by in erratic dips, felty wings disturbing my hair.

I glance over my shoulder. The security team watches us from the dock, mute as statues. The yachts bob in the water, lights flashing. Beyond, a faint pink line is brightening the horizon.

All silent. All still.

Waiting.

Dread goosepimples my flesh.

Then we're before the clubhouse and looking up its steps to the wraparound porch, the slab of door flanked by two security guards, the bright white clapboards and turrets and flagpole atop it. On the lintel in huge black-letter font a motto in German, something I swear I've read somewhere: *Die Todten reiten schnell*. What was the translation? Oh, yeah: *For the Dead travel fast*. The words, for some reason, summon up a ghastly pulse of excitement, the sticky horror of an end coming, whether it be good or ill.

Then I know.

It's the thrill of finality. Of a reckoning. The momentum of hurtling toward your fate and knowing that what lies on the other side, whichever way it goes, will be deliverance.

That's something, I think. *That, surely, is worth it.*

Adrian beside me, I know, is thinking similar thoughts. He squares his shoulders, somehow still painfully handsome in his ruined suit with half his face scorched, and lets out a measured breath. "Ready?"

I nod, and he squeezes my hand.

Then he remembers something.

"I forgot." He draws out a folded note and offers it to me. "Ilsa asked me to give you this if I ever saw you again."

My fingers are shaking as I take it. It's smudged with soot, still slightly damp. I feel a sudden desire to not know this dead woman's last words.

When I read what's written there, the shock closes my ears and blocks out the world.

Then the security guards are creaking the doors wide and Adrian is leading me into the Nosferyachtu Club.

The inside of the clubhouse does not match its innocent New England façade. It *soars*, rich with darkness, an immense foyer like the dining hall of a castle with a collection of round tables no doubt used for club meetings. Exquisite candelabra pick out the gloss in dark scrolled wood, brass fixtures and walls painted a sea green. A stone fireplace presides on the far wall, carved with snarling faces with fangs and split tongues. But it's the dazzling fleet of half-hull boat models hanging on the wall that grabs attention. There must be a hundred of them, arrayed in stunning design—the vessels of the club members.

There's not a member to be seen anywhere.

Adrian's hand clutches mine with painful intensity as he leads me across the Model Room toward an adjoining hallway. I barely notice. I am in a daze as I plod through that silent space, my nostrils filled with the reek of old money, must, and time. I am thinking of that note.

Down the hallway now. Dim lamps on the walls. We pass a door opening onto a dark club room, and when I glance inside, I stop.

Adrian looks back at me. "Aurora?"

My eyeballs sweat; an eyelid twitches. I am staring into horror. I want to cry.

"Come on," Adrian says, and pulls at my hand. "You can't help them."

A dirty, wan face lifts from the floor, pale throat bruised with puncture wounds. A hand reaches out. "Please," the girl says. "Please."

Behind her, naked bodies huddled in heaps. Stirring. Moaning.

"Come on."

It dawns on me, suddenly, that I can smell their blood. I can hear the life hammering through them like a warm sea. That appalling thirst wakens in me, making my mouth fill with saliva, my new teeth ache to drop down, and when Adrian hauls me stumbling after him, I don't know if I could have done it of my own accord. A sob catches in my throat.

I'm passing portraits hung on the walls now. They're ancient, oil-brushed, some kind of history of the nightfolk. They hit me like blows to the gut.

I see a woman in a nightgown swooning in the arms of a red-fanged shadow, a window behind it open to the night.

I see a bat-shaped thing hanging by some cunning from high branches, a naked maiden wrapped in its funiculate wings as torches storm the forest.

I see a hunched figure with a woman slung over its back sneaking onto a tall-masted ship.

I'm almost whimpering now. I see all this but do not see. A part of me is back in that room with those women. A part of me is reading the Shipwright's note.

A part of me, long dormant, wakens.

At the end of the hall stands a door of glossy mahogany, the brass plate on it proclaiming what lies beyond: ANTISOLARIUM. Adrian opens it.

The Commodore waits inside.

THIRTY-SEVEN

The Antisolarium of the Nosferyachtu Club looks like the hold of a galleon. It's windowless, walled in rich hull panels and roofed with the curving beams of a sailing ship. Triangular pennants hang in dense rows from the ceiling like a colony of bats—the personal signal flags of the club members. And all along the far wall, fantastically arranged like medieval arms on display, hang dozens of racked spearguns.

Commodore Volok sits enthroned on a dais at the end of the room.

His chair is hewn of dark wood from distant forests; he's the only one seated. The club members cluster in the shadows about him like so many couriers at court, gold signet rings flashing on their pale hands, and Fesperman has taken up station at his side with one gloved hand resting on the tall chairback, all bowed in whispered consultation.

Silence falls as the door creaks open.

The temperature in the room changes; astonishment spreads like a mist as all realize it's Adrian. They take in his ragged suit, his singed hair, his burnt face, their pale features twisted in hatred and uncertainty. They have waited a long time for this day—for Adrian to make his way back here. And he has done so after all thought him dead.

Fesperman is the first to recover. He tips his head back and smiles. "Ah," he breathes in a plummy voice. "He comes."

The back of Adrian's hand brushes mine, and we start forward.

The club members draw away as we approach. I can feel many eyes crawling over my body, making it bump up with chickenflesh. I keep my head held high, gaze straight ahead. It doesn't help. The room stretches before me, impossibly long; this moment is tinged with unreality.

The Commodore's eyes wait for us like glowing moons.

As we near, I notice a shape huddled at the archfiend's feet like a whipped dog. Draped in a wisp of a white slip, shoulders hunched and head hung, straggled blonde hair covering her face: Cailee.

An icy numbness spreads in my gut.

We stop ten paces before the dais. There's a moment of silence, of hushed expectation.

Then Adrian kneels.

The Commodore's mouth writhes up on one side, those two forefangs glinting as sharp and bright as the double rows of brass buttons down the placket of his tailcoat. And when those sickly moons drop to the gold signet ring on Adrian's hand, the mouth writhes up even more.

I feel a dull twinge of disgust.

So this is his pleasure: witnessing such choreographed submission. Obedience as arousal.

I drop to one knee beside Adrian, and the Commodore slides his eyes to me, my bloody wedding dress. The ring on my finger.

He hisses.

Fesperman sneers. "Quite the bride you've found." Hungry stares from the dark. "You should feel honored, Miss Strand. You're the first woman to ever set foot in this room." The butler glances down at Cailee, shrugs. "Well. As a guest."

Titters among the shadows.

Cailee gives no indication she's heard this. She doesn't seem to be aware of her surroundings at all.

"Cailee," I whisper, faint with sympathy. But she does not lift her head.

The Commodore again speaks, lips pulling back from his overbite. The words slither around me like snakes.

"So here he is. Adrian Voper, the lost son. For so long I have waited with open arms, ready to welcome you back into the fold—yet you rebuffed me. I even reunited you with your beloved wife, and what did you do?" The Commodore spreads elegant talons. "Slay her to spite me."

The muscles at the corners of Adrian's jaw bunch, and he shakes his head, almost imperceptibly.

Don't, I think. *Don't rise to his bait.*

"And now, after you refused my gift, you evidently slay your blood brother for this whore before coming to me." There's a long, long silence. "Why?"

I glance at Adrian. Can he sell it? Pretend to do what the Commodore wants—submit to his control—when he's spent so long to break free of it?

Or will he let his anger sabotage him?

Adrian's teeth grind together, so hard his molars pop, and his hands knuckle white. He takes a breath. "I was wrong to turn from you, blood father," he grits out, every word hard as granite, his thumb twisting at his signet ring. "I see that now. I . . . humble myself before you."

He drops his head lower, eyes shut and nostrils flared.

The Commodore's bland eyes glow with pleasure.

"I want to make things right. Radomir threatened the life of my partner, so I hope you can understand what had to be done. But I have turned her and brought her here, so we can come before you"—slowly, very slowly, Adrian offers up a pale wrist with its blue tracery of veins, signet ring flashing—"and offer our fealty."

All eyes turn to the Commodore as he sits there on his throne, one hand draped over the wrist of the other, fingers dangling like the long and bulb-jointed legs of spiders.

Then he twists his bald head down into the collar of his coat and lets out a series of pants, dry and rattling, and I realize the Commodore is laughing.

The spiteful force of it slaps me, making me shrink back. The room echoes with that laughter. It bounces crazily around the room, growing stronger and stronger, a dying man's depraved wheeze. Adrian's face slackens, his teeth clenching in helpless anger. But it doesn't stop. That fiend's high stiff shoulders hitch, his rat-like overbite obscene as he hunches over in wicked delight.

I don't know what to do. I feel small and humiliated. I feel like a stupid little girl.

Finally, the wheezing stops, leaving the Commodore short of breath.

Fesperman is fighting back a smile. "Do you really think," he translates as the Commodore gasps for air, "I'm that stupid? When did your estimation of me fall so low?" The Commodore drops back in his chair and lifts a long, tapered finger, waggles it. "No, no. I haven't changed, Voper. And neither have you. You betrayed me. You sank the ships of my children. You sent this assassin"—he flicks those long nails at me—"to do a man's job. Then you killed my blood son and came here to deliver this sad story in the hopes of getting close to me . . . so you could slay your father."

I can't make my legs stop shaking. I come down onto both knees and brace myself on the floor with my hands, arms trembling, feeling ridiculous. Veins cord out on Adrian's neck as he stares at the floor.

The Commodore lets out a hiss of contempt.

"Look at you, Adrian. Look at me. Look at my happy family." And I sense them creeping in, drawing a tight circle around us. Their faces shining like enamel. Their teeth needle sharp. "You could have had all of this, but you threw it away. You thought you were better. Your entitlement amazes me, Adrian."

Adrian's face jumps, and I reach out and grab his hand, telling him with that touch, *Don't listen to him. It's all right. I'm here for you. You can do it.*

You can stand up to him.

Adrian's responding grip is strong enough to crack bone.

"Would it have mattered?" he replies, quite calmly, and lifts his head to stare straight into the Commodore's eyes. "You can never give enough love to a thing that hates itself."

The Commodore blinks. Shock rings in the air. And I think, *I don't know if I could love you more in this moment, Adrian.*

Then the Commodore twists away in that throne as if slapped by the face of the rising sun, arms held out in crooked bent at the elbows, fingers splayed wide. He sucks in a breath and holds it, sucks in another. A wrathful, snarling hissing, as if he were on the verge of sneezing.

A profound silence falls over that room. I've never heard a more terrible silence.

I know what it means.

It's over. It's all over. Our plan has failed. What do we do now?

The Commodore turns very slowly back to us, eyes slitted, shoulders almost to fluked ears. He lifts a condemning finger. Death is in his face.

But I speak before he gives the order. "Adrian may think you stupid, but I don't."

The Commodore stills, those slits sliding toward me. All stare. Adrian jerks at me, eyes round in shock.

I cannot look at him. I know if I do, I won't go through with it. So I lift my face to meet the Commodore's gaze. "I haven't come to offer you fealty. Not exactly." I tilt up my chin in a stubborn angle. "I've come to accept your offer to be your concubine."

Cailee stirs for the first time, looks up at this. Adrian flinches, gawping at me in horror. "What are you doing—"

But the Commodore is hissing, waving his long, thin fingers. Fesperman's own incredulity is relayed in the question. "And why should I trust you?"

I swallow a lump in my throat, trapped in a high, dizzy feeling. The awareness of an act that will be terrible and isolating, irrevocable and final. Will I be able to live with it?

And I make my choice.

"Because of this." I turn to Adrian staring at me in hurt and confusion and cradle his face. "I'm sorry," I whisper, tears burning my eyes, and rub his cheek with my thumb. "I'm so sorry."

And with a ferocious wrench, I snap Adrian Voper's neck.

THIRTY-EIGHT

The sound of bone breaking is unmistakable. Adrian drops instantly to the floor, jerking and twitching, walled eyes staring up at me in horror. Those eyes have no hurt, no accusation, no anger in them. They have only one question: *Why?*

But I can't look. I don't want to see this. I don't want to see what I've done. I stagger to my feet and away, blinking back tears. Stomach acid scalds my throat. I want to sob.

I force all this away and turn to my audience in grim resolve.

"I'm done," I announce, my voice flat with cold rage. "All my life, I've let men bully me. Control me. Abuse me. I've let them tell me what to wear, what to say, what to think. I've even, God help me, let them decide who I am." I shake my head, eyes tearing up in disgust. "How pathetic. I made myself small and weak so the men in my life could feel better about themselves. I waited for the violence to end, thinking they weren't showing me who they really were, that if I just hung in there long enough I'd somehow save them. But you can't. Because all along they *were* showing me who they were. That's who they are. Men destroy, and women transform. Women create life, and men create death. This is how it's always been. Well, maybe this is my final transformation, and in death I'll have no more to fear. Because no man will ever touch me again." And, trembling, I lower my voice to a whisper. "Unless it's you."

Stunned silence follows. The club members exchange looks. Cailee gapes.

Almost there. Time for the big finish.

"It's why I came back," I go on with feverish intensity. "I know now. Now that I'm . . . *this* . . . I know what I want. How would I not want all this power? How could I be such a fool to refuse your offer?" I lock my eyes on that starved skullface and make my throat go raw and husky with sexuality. "I want it. I want to be your concubine. I *deserve* to be your concubine." I sweep a hand at Adrian on the floor. "Look what I'm willing to do for you." And I lean forward, trembling with need. "Please . . . *Master*."

The club members are nodding along now, smug grins playing about their mouths. Fesperman, shining with satisfaction, glances at the Commodore.

The Commodore is smiling. It's an atrocity.

He beckons with those long talons, summoning me.

I feel every eyeball in the room follow me as I march toward the dais. The nape of my neck crawls. Expectation slams in my ears. I don't need to be told what to do—I know what's required here.

The Commodore's eyes glow with pleasure as I kneel like a demure schoolgirl on the dais before him, fresh face upturned, and offer my wrist.

I'm careful to not look away as he bends forward like a spider breaking its predatory stillness, long fingers unfurling to cradle my wrist as if it were a priceless jewel. His eyelids droop as he dips his head to take my scent, lost in sensation, a shivery sigh escaping his lips. Then he lunges to sink those two verminous fangs into my flesh.

The pain is breathtaking, the sudden, ravenous feeding twisting my arm and sending a bone-deep ache lancing up my shoulder. I bite the inside of my lip to stay silent, eyes strained and watering as he sucks and slobbers, fused to me like an engorged sack of blood.

Then it's over. He discards my wrist and lets his jaw drop in dull-eyed bliss, a glut of blood shining in his mouth. And I do it. I roll my eyes up at him in an adoring look and wipe a smear of red from his chin with a thumb.

He stills all over, ruddy lips quavering in a smile.

Then his gaze goes past me to Adrian twitching on the floor, and his face changes. He turns his head, eyes never leaving Adrian, and hisses.

"What do we do with this one?" Fesperman muses.

That feeling again. The weight of many eyes on me, charged with malicious anticipation.

I don't let them down.

"We finish it," I say, and jerk my chin at the wall of spearguns.

This sends the club members into a tizzy. Fesperman looks questioningly to the Commodore.

The Commodore, a sly, satisfied look stealing over his gaunt face, nods.

Fesperman grins and kicks Cailee. She flinches, hunching her shoulders, but dutifully rises like a sleepwalker and lifts a speargun off the wall, crosses over to me and, without meeting my gaze, holds it out. "Then finish it," Fesperman says, eyes glittering.

Cailee steps away, and I look down at the speargun in my hands. Its wood stock is polished and worn smooth, the barbed steel spear wickedly sharp, with two spares affixed to the underside of the barrel.

I look down at Adrian.

His eyes are wide, glassy, his body already trying to repair itself, the spinal column healing, the tendons and gristle trying to knit themselves back together with audible clicks. "Aurora . . ." he rasps, and a single tear streaks down a charred cheek. "Please . . ."

A sob rises in my throat. Tears well in my eyes as I lower the speargun, aim it directly at his breast.

"I love you," he says.

The speargun trembles in my hand. The Commodore's eyes gloat in hate.

"I love you, too," I whisper.

And I whirl, lifting the speargun in a blur, and pull the trigger, blasting the spear across the room in a whipping of black rubber chords, a monofilament shooting line trailing after it like a glimmering spider thread.

The spear skewers the Commodore straight through the heart.

The impact rocks him back into his throne. Bright blood spurts in an arc, drips from the steel tip punched out of his back. The Commodore gapes in astonishment at the shaft impaling him, looks up at me.

And lips curling in a smirk, I yank ferociously on the speargun.

The shooting line goes taut, and the dangling steel flopper at the spear's end catches in the Commodore's back and spills him out of his throne, tumbling him bump, bump, bump down the dais steps onto the floor like a landed swordfish. There's a collective, scandalized gasp—and the club members rush forward. Fesperman lets out an anguished shriek of horror and falls upon the Commodore, trying to stanch the blood with his hands. His white cotton gloves instantly soak red through and he sobs, a piteous wail of grief and outrage. "*Master*," he croons. "*Master!*" But the Commodore does not respond. His long thin fingers whip and slap on the floor in a rattle of fingernails. He convulses, spasmodically, mindlessly, the body entering a catastrophic entropy. With his bald skull and fluked ears, he looks like a poisoned rat in its death throes. A breathless, continuous death rattle fills the room. His mouth opens and a horrific gout of blood vomits across the floor. Then he shudders and stills, narrow head flung back, mouth foamed pink, tongue lolling, the mesmerizing orbs of his eyes staring.

The Commodore is dead.

The club members stare. Cailee covers her mouth and nose with her hands. Fesperman staggers back before he remembers me.

"*You*," he seethes. And I see, for the first time, a pair of fangs snick out from under his upper lip. "Fucking *bitch*." And he flies at me, crimson mitts dripping blood like some murderous clown.

I'm ready.

I pluck a spare spear from the speargun and jam it overhand like a javelin into Fesperman's bosom.

The blow brings the butler to his knees in a click of kneecaps. He stares at the shaft, at me, disbelieving, red blossoming across his perfectly starched waistcoat. He is, for once, at a loss for words. I don't let him find any. With a brutal wrench I snap the steel spear in two—*ting!*—and he blinks and keels over onto the floor.

Then I scan the room, daring another club member to oppose me.

All back away.

I don't waste any more time. Spear and speargun clatter at my feet and I kneel beside Adrian, my hands on his chest. "Adrian?" I croak. "Baby?" I can barely speak. Tears sting my eyes. "Come on. I came back for you. Come back for me now."

He doesn't move. His eyes are closed, he looks as if he's sleeping. But his chest is not rising. There's no color in his cheeks. I put my ear to his chest, listening. *I know he didn't die*, I tell myself. *I didn't kill him. This has to work, now that I've killed his maker. He has to come back. I haven't just made the worst mistake of my life.* I put a hand over his heart, my whole being praying. *Let me feel it. Beat for me.*

Then I feel it.

A faint, jittery thump, the kickstart of a long-disused organ. I stiffen all over. My breath catches in my throat. I wait, faint with amazement, as an enchantment lifts, death working in reverse as burn marks retreat like melting frost and color flushes Adrian Voper's cold, pale skin, rosing his cheeks, pinking his ears, smudging his eyelids. Those lids open, and Adrian Voper looks at me with the brilliant blue eyes of a living man.

"Hey, baby," he whispers.

I sob out a laugh and drag him up into my arms, babbling apologies. "I'm so sorry I had to do that to you. I couldn't think of another way." I can feel the sweet warmth of his body, the precious heat of his breath at my neck, the irrefutable proof of his mortality. I feel showered in fortune. Happiness explodes in my veins. He's alive. He's changed. It's over.

Volok's gone.

It's what he's saying into my ear, again and again, voice husky with emotion. "It's okay. It's over, Aurora. You did it." When I pull back, tears sparkle in his eyes. He touches my cheek, and my body sings. Somehow his touch, now warm and alive, makes me melt more than ever.

Then his words take on a tinge of sadness. "What *did* you do?"

Reality rushes back in, turning me solemn. Yes. I'm trapped now, forever, as one of them, without a maker. Without hope of ever being turned back.

And I say, "What I had to."

I draw the Shipwright's note out of the bodice of my dress and hand it to him, leaving him to read the one word written there as I turn to face the club members of the Nosferyachtu Club:

Mammadore.

I scan the room, speargun in hand. The club members all stare, bodies tense with uncertainty. They look at the impaled corpse of the Commodore on the floor. At me. I make sure my voice carries hard and clear through the room.

"Things will be different now," I announce. "No more preying on women. No more women banished to Transmarinia." I pluck the second spare spear free and guide it into the track of the speargun, wedge the handle of the speargun against my sternum and haul the double rubber band back into a notch on the speargun shaft. "From now on," I grunt, "we prey on criminals and abusers only. Those who deserve death. Any club member who contravenes these laws will find themselves having a, shall we say"—I drop the barrel of the loaded speargun, speartip flashing, into my other hand—"*pointed* conversation with me." I look at each club member in turn to make sure it sinks in. "You can start with releasing all the blood slaves in the clubhouse."

When no one moves, I drop my voice to a dangerous whisper. "*Now.*"

This is the moment, I know. When they'll either accept my leadership . . . or not. Which makes it the most perilous moment. I stand over Adrian like a guard dog, gripping the speargun so tightly my fingertips dimple its wood, back straight and gaze unwavering.

Then a club member drops to one knee. Another. Before long, all of them are kneeling in that room in recognition of my reign, before they rise and file past me, gazes wary.

It's done. I wear the crown now.

I'm the new Commodore.

A dizziness sweeps over me, and I think of all the women I have known. I think of Cailee and Marisol and the women fed to the sharks on that blood cruise. I think of the Shipwright and her crew. I think of young, innocent, starry-eyed girls all around the world led aboard yachts to what they think will be their glittering futures, and who are never heard from again. And I think, *I did it. It's changed. I changed it.*

I did that.

Tears dazzle my eyes. I don't know what to do with this emotion; it's too big for my body. I feel as if I might float away.

It won't be as easy as that, I know. These things—they've had this way of life for far too long to give it up that easily. There will be trouble down the road. This isn't over.

A touch at my elbow, and I turn. It's Cailee. She looks as if she's been snapped out of a trance. Her lip trembles. She shakes her head. "I'm sorry," she hiccups. "I'm so sorry I didn't believe you—"

"No," I say, cutting her off. "You don't have to apologize for anything."

Her face crumples and she clutches me fiercely, her thin body trembling against mine. "Thank you."

We pull back and grin at each other, cheeks shining with tears. I laugh and wipe at hers. "You know," I say, "it's gonna be a shit ton of work, running an empire and all. I could use another female entrepreneur around."

A sly grin teases my best friend's mouth, that old Cailee returning. "I thought you'd never ask."

When I look over at Adrian, he's standing over the Commodore's body, his signet ring in his palm. Something moves through his face—satisfaction, perhaps, or pity, the relinquishment of some longstanding hold over him—and he tilts his palm, lets the ring bounce off the floor and come to a wobbly, humming stop beside the Commodore. Then he lets out a wavering breath, squares his shoulders and turns away. When he sees me watching him, his face changes and he strides toward me, beaming with pride. For me. For us. For all of it.

He holds out a hand, and I take it.

The three of us drift down the hall in a daze. It's crowded with women emerging from club rooms blinking like atomic fallout survivors. They wear wrinkled club dresses, clutching handbags and sparkly phone cases to their chests, huddling in wary groups. But the light from the Model Room draws them. The front door is flung open to the glare of full morning, and they drift through it out into the sunshine flashing off the sea and the polished exteriors of the yachts at anchor. Some of them are too dazed to do anything but blink at the outside world again. Others begin to laugh, to hug each other, crying with happiness, and I feel a lump rise in my throat.

Adrian beside me stops, a strange stillness coming over him as he sees all that light. I study his face, that face I know so well, and am hit with a bittersweet ache. I squeeze his hand. "Go on," I whisper.

He looks at me, as if for permission, and I nod. "*Go.*"

The corner of his mouth dimples. Then he faces the door, packed with nerves and a sort of heartbreaking, boyish excitement, and steps out of the shadows of the Nosferyachtu Club into the day.

He flinches, bracing for it, but there is no hiss of crisping flesh, no vaporous haze of smoke silvering the air—only a warmth that soaks down to the bone. He lets out a huff of wonder, taking it in, and lifts his face to the sun. I have to put a hand to my mouth, witnessing this. When he turns about to look at me, to include me in this revelation, tears are standing in his eyes. "It's gone," he laughs, a cracked and disbelieving sound, full of joy. "It's all gone."

I nod, my lips quivering with happiness for him. I know.

Then his face slackens as he registers me lurking in the gloom of the doorway. He's remembered.

We stand there looking at each other, feet away but worlds apart: me in shadow, he in the sun. Our positions reversed from when we first met.

"It's up to you," I tell him. "I can turn you back, if that's what you want, or you can remain a man. I would never ask you to go through that again. The choice is yours."

Adrian nods, squints once more at that sun-drenched world with its water and fiberglass and shrieking seagulls, shuts his eyes and feels it in the pores of his skin.

Then he turns back to me with a dazzling smile.

"How about I decide after the wedding?"

I can't help it—a laugh tumbles out of me, loud and pure, and I beam back at him. "Deal." I don't know how to process everything I'm feeling right now. Standing in the doorway of the Nosferyachtu Club, free at last and humming with a feeling of boundless power as the man I love promises me a lifetime of happiness with his eyes, I feel—maybe for the first time ever—as if nothing is lacking in my life. As if everything is complete.

Almost.

My gaze strays to the glistening expanse of sea, and the lands beyond. My voice sobers. "But I have something to take care of first."

The night is a quiet one in Oregon. For the farm, it is indeed already late. The cattle have been bedded down hours ago, the horses brushed, their stalls mucked out (or, as the case may be, not so much). Bowser lies with snout on paws in the yard, chain coiled before him. Behind him, there is a flickering pale blue glow in the windows of the farmhouse. Perhaps the farmer has fallen asleep in front of the TV with a six-pack of beer crushed into foil at his feet. Or perhaps he is using his belt on the latest woman unfortunate enough to stray into his life, the TV turned up to cover the sounds.

Either way, that is interrupted when the night sky explodes.

It is a chopping roar that stitches a caesura in the darkness. The horses whicker and rear in their stalls. Bowser shoots to his feet in a fit of barking, does not stop even when the treetops sway and the grass flattens, leaves and dust billowing up to haze the air. The door to the farmhouse bangs open and the farmer staggers out, plaid shirt blotchy with brown beer stains, lank hair whipped back from his brow and one hand held up to his red-rimmed eyes as he squints in the hurricane gust. "*The fuck?*" he mouths as the gleaming helicopter alights in his front yard, an alien object in that countryside. Its passenger is equally out of place: a woman blinged out like a goddess in a golden silk plunge dress, gem drop earrings winking out of her sleek black hair, gold-dusted nails sparkling.

As the helicopter rotors wind down and she saunters up to the farmer in tasseled platform heels, Bowser backs away with a whine.

But the farmer is oblivious to what his dog senses.

"The fuck you doing on my property?" he demands, his face turning beet red as he jabs a finger at the chopper. "Who the fuck do you think you are?"

He gets his answer when the woman snicks away her glittery Gucci shades, and all the color drains out of his face.

"You remember me," the woman purrs.

And that's when I show him my new teeth in a sharp smile.

"Don't you, Josh?"

EPILOGUE

"Thank you so much," I say for the dozenth time in the past hour. "I don't know what I would've done without you."

Mrs. Colding's reflection appears in the vanity mirror beside me. "Nonsense," she snaps, and gives me a close-lipped smile as she fusses with my veil. "I wouldn't have missed it for the world."

When I'd called to ask her to be my wedding planner, she'd flown in the next day. I didn't know how much I'd missed her until I saw her walking up the passerelle with her immaculate bun gleaming like architecture. It instantly felt as if the *Lair* were home again, and Mrs. Colding had never seemed happier, though there was a new poignant layer of reserve and experience underneath her prim exterior now, as if she'd undergone a harrowing ordeal and come out the other side with a greater appreciation for all things. The pair of silvery fang-puncture scars on her neck only served as a physical reminder of this.

She steps back in the master suite of the *Lair* and appraises her work. "All right. Let's see you."

I turn to face her, spreading my train out behind me, and Mrs. Colding circles, taking in the boho wedding dress with its ivory lace, daring low back and luscious, bottom-hugging gathering. She lifts a brow. "Adrian's gonna like *that*."

I snort a laugh, and her seamed eyes turn tender. I self-consciously touch the white lilies in my hair.

"What did you think of my decision?"

She knows I'm not asking about my pick of wedding dress. We both look at my reflection in the mirror, the hint of sharpness in my mouth.

"You made the decision you can live with. The decision that makes you feel safe. That's all that matters." She lays a hand on my shoulder. "But I thought it was a noble thing you did, making that sacrifice, whatever the consequences."

I reach up and grip her hand, gratitude burning behind my eyes. "Thanks for saying that."

She smiles back. "Anytime, dear."

"I can't decide which of you ladies is more beautiful," says a deep voice behind us.

Mrs. Colding blushes like a schoolgirl, and I whirl to see Captain Redfearn standing in the doorway to the master suite, looking uncomfortable but ruggedly handsome in a black tux. He's even shaved the scruff from his cheeks, combed his silver mane of hair back into a sweeping wave.

My heart leaps before I do. I lift my train, running, and Mrs. Colding blurts a warning about tearing the dress before I've launched myself into the captain's arms, wrapping my own around him, burying my face in his collarbone and inhaling his familiar musk of woodsy aftershave and yacht cleaning supplies.

"You came," I whisper.

"Of course I came," he responds in an overly gruff voice, and when I pull back, his eyes are red and glassed up. He wipes at them, harrumphing deep in his throat. "I promised to walk you down the aisle, didn't I?" Then he chucks my chin, laughing back a sob. "You're so beautiful, sweetheart."

Mrs. Colding watches the two of us with moist eyes. I tilt my head back to stop my makeup from streaking, wipe carefully beneath my bottom eyelids. "Jesus, you're gonna make me cry."

Captain Redfearn chuckles, a deep baritone of amusement, and offers his arm. "Ready?"

I nod, sniffing, and look back at Mrs. Colding.

She nods. "See you out there, darling."

The captain and I walk in silence at first as we head out through the interior and onto the port gangway. It's hard not to marvel at the *Lair* restored to her former glory. Her floor-to-ceiling windows immaculate, her salons and furniture pristine, her hull redone and buffed to a high finish, as sleek and gleaming as a bride herself. I know it means as much to me as it does to the captain. I let him take it in.

Then I ask him.

"So, you gonna tell me if you found your daughter or not? It's like Mrs. Colding is in witness protection or something. She won't say a peep."

The captain's eyes turn strange, unreadable. The corner of his mouth tugs. "I'll tell you all about that," he promises, patting my hand. "But not now. That's a story for another time." And he leads me up a short flight of teak stairs to the bow. "Today is about you and Adrian."

I have to stop to take it all in, my stomach fluttering.

Mrs. Colding has outdone herself: the foredeck area of the *Lair* is a fantasia. Bouquets of white lilies festoon the deck, and floral garlands and fairy lights wind about the handrails. An arch exploding with greenery and white flowers leads down a guest-lined aisle to Adrian at the bow, looking magnificent in a dark blue tux with hands clasped nervously before him. Beyond, a breathtaking backdrop of polar seas, icebergs floating like wedding cakes in the night. And above all, the Northern Lights shifting and shimmering as if in celebration.

Orchestral music swells, cueing the bride, and all heads turn toward me, including Adrian's. All muscle tone goes out of his face when he sees me. He looks as if he's been gut-punched. Tears spring to his eyes, and he puts a hand over his mouth.

I hiccup a laugh, humbled and thrilled and thinking I've never felt more radiantly beautiful than I do in this moment. Captain Redfearn lays his hand on mine, gives me a wink, and begins to walk me down the aisle.

My legs tremble; my ankles wobble. I feel as if I might faint, that I'm gliding through this moment, that my feet aren't even touching the ground and I'm buoyed aloft by the music and the lights and this feeling inside me. This moment I never thought would come is here. It's happening. And Captain Redfearn is guiding me through it. I snug closer to him, sneaking a look at his face, and see that he's staring straight ahead with cheeks shining with tears, chin quivering, square-shouldered and determined as if this is the most important duty of his life. The sight almost makes me sob aloud. I look about and see that the seated guests flanking the aisle on either side—the crew of the *Lair*, the residents of Transmarinia—watch with softened faces as we march by. I look up at the bow and the bridesmaids there, the freezing wind whipping at their hair and the fur of their glamorous parkas over their crimson silk bridesmaid dresses. Mrs. Colding can't stop dabbing at her eyes with a handkerchief. Cailee and Nicole keep whispering into each other's ears and linking fingers, blushing, and I grin, thinking, *Good for you, Cailee.*

Then we've stopped, and I'm looking up at the man I'm going to marry.

We lock eyes.

He's somehow even more impossibly handsome with a tan. Since his change, he's spent every moment he can get in the sun, and I've had to keep slathering sunscreen on him like a forgetful child. I can't help grinning at the memory, and marvel at the ease of that happiness.

I've never felt that before, that ease with a man. And I feel it even here, despite everything having changed. I've done things I never thought I would. Friends of mine have died. Cailee has gone through something I'm not sure she'll ever fully recover from. I've had some kind of communion with a man who wasn't my fiancé, and then was killed by him. But I was dead long before that, wasn't I? Because my fear of men didn't just take away who I was. Being either stuck in the past or always worrying about the future took away my ability to live in the present. It took away my life.

But that was gone now. That fear was gone. Forever.

Captain Redfearn hands me off with a smile, and I step up to the bow beside Adrian. He takes my hands, almost shy, the lights of the north shining in his eyes, casting a magic spell on our skin. "You ready to become Mrs. Voper?" he asks, both delicious suggestion and earnest promise, and I smile at him, glowing, composed of light.

Yes, I tell Adrian Voper with my eyes. *I'm ready now. I'm finally ready.*

I'm ready to live.

ONE

CAPTAIN REDFEARN

Back in the day, those old sea tars always had a patron saint. You know, some heavenly advocate believed to grant protection and good luck.

I'm starting to think she's mine.

Maybe it's coincidental, but she always happens to be on the aft main deck when I return. Her white yachtie shirt flashes like a beacon, as perfectly smooth and blinding as the hull of my *Lair*. She has her hands clasped before her, her hooded eyes imperious, her tight bun of silky Asian hair as polished as anchor housing in the sunshine of Monaco. Something inside me eases at the sight of her, and I can't help but grin.

Damn, she's a beautiful woman.

"Well?" she calls as the tender floats up to the superyacht's swim deck.

I wipe my face smooth and hop out, let the deckhands take over berthing the tender. "You were right as always," I admit with a grunt, and make for the stairs leading up to the main deck. I have to force myself not to bound up them like a giddy schoolboy. "Mr. Voper went for it. Didn't even hesitate when he saw her picture. We've officially hired our fourth stew."

Mrs. Colding nods, her lips creasing in the slightest suggestion of satisfaction. I don't mind that she's distracted. I'm too busy breathing in through my nose to savor what I've been waiting for the entire trip back—that scent with its hints of sandalwood and Asian blossoms, delicate and sophisticated.

I have to stop myself from closing my eyes.

"We should have bet on it," she muses.

I take my time responding. I'm enjoying the thought of undoing that fucking bun of hers so I can run my rough hands through her hair.

"You know I don't bet," I say when I'm ready. "Not anymore."

She turns to me, her fine lashes lifting to show deep brown eyes solemn with sympathy. "I know."

I know she does; nothing escapes her attention. She files everything away—every fact, every preference, every quirk of someone's personality—as a chief stew needs to know everything to deliver perfect service. But it's more than that—she cares more about the needs of others than her own. Because she's loyal. Over the years, I've done my own filing away of facts: the storing up of every detail I can get on Mrs. Colding. How she dismisses coffee as a crutch for weaklings, but has a weakness for Coca-Cola when she needs a boost. How fingerprints on reflective surfaces make her skin crawl. How she probably struggles with a major case of OCD, which I find adorable. But most of all, I love that her icy exterior hides the biggest, warmest heart I have ever known.

She's still looking at me. Those eyes curve in what could almost be mistaken for humor. "But a more devious woman would have taken advantage of the opportunity."

I love it when she teases me. It's often so subtle, most men wouldn't pick up on it. It's taken *me* years to pick up on it. But that's what I admire about her. Her subtlety. Her class.

At least, I *hope* she was teasing me.

Because I'd know what that would mean.

I've had my doubts, for sure. Working with someone for this long without knowing if your feelings are reciprocated, it's hard not to. But I didn't want to spoil it. It was enough to just be around her. To be in her presence. That was what living taught you. That sometimes not risking a thing is better. Better to keep it alive as a sweet drip of hurt, safe and dependable. A love that knows its place. These are the things that, though they never risk the trials of high romance, sustain you through the dark patches of life.

No. I didn't want to ruin that.

But what if there could be more?

"You think it'll work?" I ask, pushing away my thoughts.

"The plan? To shake that old grump out of his grief?" She turns to study the tinted glass doors of the *Lair*. "I think everyone deserves a second chance."

I lift a brow. "Everyone?"

She frowns at me. "Are you inferring something, Captain Redfearn?"

I shrug. "I'm inferring you deserve it too, even though you never consider it."

The frown deepens. "You've lost me."

Christ, I hope not.

This is ridiculous. I've been in the Navy. I've dealt with Adrian's kind. I've crawled my way out of the darkest places a man can fall into. And somehow saying what I'm about to say to this woman makes me more terrified than I've ever been in my life.

I square my shoulders and face her.

"We've known each other for some time now."

She faces me, that quizzical furrow still between her brows. "We have."

"I'd like to think we know each other well."

She is very, very still. "We do."

"And I don't, I mean . . ." My hands are shaking, and I wipe one rough palm against the other to try to still them.

She watches all this, alarmed. "Redfearn? What is it?"

Just get it out already.

"We've both been through enough to know what we want. And I know because of your past you've had no interest in . . . and Lord knows I've had my own reasons for not . . ."

She blinks at me, waiting.

"I mean to say, maybe both of us thought we were done with romance. But I've lived enough to recognize something special when I see it. And I've never met a more incredible woman than you." I let out a big, wavering breath. I can't look at her. I know if I do, if I see how she's responding to this, I might stop. "So if you think you'd ever be open to that, just let me know. There's no rush. I—I'll wait for you."

And I do. I've never heard a more awful silence. All I can hear is the raucous screech of gulls, my own unsteady breathing.

When I can't stand it any longer, I look at her.

I've never seen that expression on her face before. I have no reference for it. She looks as if she's been winded, as if she's just witnessed some terrible accident. Her shoulders rise and fall. She presses a hand to her stomach and lets out a shivery breath between her lips, looks at me and shakes her head. "Captain Redfearn," she whispers.

My heart drops.

"*Fuck*," I hiss, running a hand through my hair. "I'm sorry, I shouldn't have said anything—"

"No!" she says hastily. "I don't mind that you said that—"

"Yeah," I grunt, rolling my eyes and turning away. *Great, she didn't mind.* "Yeah, all right—"

"No," she says again, and I look down to find she's gripping my arm. A shy, disbelieving smile plays about her lips. "I meant, I *really* didn't mind."

I feel my soul fall back into my body. "Oh. You—you didn't?"

She shakes her head, lips curved.

The blood drains from my brain. I feel light-headed, breathless, struck silly. A goofy grin splashes across my face.

I'm not the only one.

"Actually," she says, and heat pinks her pale skin. "I think there's a part of me that's been waiting for you to say that ever since . . ."

But I don't hear the rest of her words. Because blood is booming in my ears like the beat of doom. Because the impossible is happening. Something has unfolded itself from the deckhead above Mrs. Colding in eerie silence: Evangeline Voper, in a lacy choir girl's dress. Hanging upside down like some batlike creature so she can craft her fangs into Mrs. Colding's neck in a heavy unrivering of blood.

All the air leaves my lungs.

"Redfearn," Mrs. Colding chokes, her eyes wide.

And my howl of anguish fills the world.

I jerk awake with my heart wanting to pound out of my chest and look about. Rain lashes the porthole. Lightning flares, illuminating a dark, industrial-looking cabin in stark white flashes. For a panic-stricken moment, I don't remember where or when I am, have to claw my way out of that dream and remind myself that it's okay. Mrs. Colding is alive. That bloodsucking bitch didn't kill her. She asked me to give her time.

The ship groans like a dying whale, pipes clanking. Definitely not the *Lair*. Definitely not a superyacht. When I glance at the cot opposite mine, a face jumps out at me in one of those bursts of white—my bunkmate eyeing me warily, one arm folded under his head, his body as wiry and tatted as a convict's. And I remember what vessel I'm on.

On an old rusting freighter in the storm-tossed Atlantic, bound for Fort Lauderdale, Florida. On my way home.

On my way to find my missing daughter.

**DON'T MISS ANY OF THIS EPIC SERIES
FROM D.V. SULLIVAN**

WWW.DVSULLIVAN.COM

ABOUT THE AUTHOR

D.V. Sullivan has been a deckhand in the Mediterranean, a bartender in New York and an English teacher in China. Now that he's no longer hosing salt off yachts during high-wind gales, he writes from his lair in the Pacific Northwest.

DVSullivan.com
Facebook.com/AuthorDVSullivan
TikTok @dvsullivanauthor
Instagram @dvsullivanauthor
X/Twitter @bydvsullivan

www.ingramcontent.com/pod-product-compliance
Lightning Source LLC
Chambersburg PA
CBHW022102310726
48972CB00007B/1846